ELVIS AND THE APOCALYPSE

ELVIS AND THE APOCALYPSE

The awful disclosures of Marie, Matron of the Motel Dew beanery

Steve Werner

Copyright © 2000 by Steve Werner.

Library of Congress Number:		00-193046
ISBN #:	Hardcover	0-7388-5256-2
	Softcover	0-7388-5257-0

All rights reserved. No part of this book may be reproduced or transmitted in any form or by any means, electronic or mechanical, including photocopying, recording, or by any information storage and retrieval system, without permission in writing from the copyright owner.

This is a work of fiction. Names, characters, places and incidents either are the product of the author's imagination or are used fictitiously, and any resemblance to any actual persons, living or dead, events, or locales is entirely coincidental.

This book was printed in the United States of America.

To order additional copies of this book, contact:
Xlibris Corporation
1-888-7-XLIBRIS
www.Xlibris.com
Orders@Xlibris.com

CONTENTS

Chapter 1: GENESIS
    THE BEGINNING 11
Chapter 2: ELVIS
    THE WANDERING MISSISSIPPIAN 23
Chapter 3: ELVIS
    A PROPHET IN THE PROMISED LAND 34
Chapter 4: ELVIS
    THE CONQUEST OF CANAAN 43
Chapter 5: ELVIS
    ON MOUNT ZION 52
Chapter 6: ELVIS
    ENSLAVED IN EGYPT 59
Chapter 7: ELVIS
    THE KING 74
Chapter 8: ELVIS
    THE BABYLONIAN CAPTIVITY 84
Chapter 9: ELVIS
    THE ACTS OF ELVIS 90
Chapter 10: ELVIS
    A WEDDING OUTSIDE OF CANA 111
Chapter 11: ELVIS
    THE SONS OF ELI 124
Chapter 12: ELVIS AND THE APOCALYPSE 135
Chapter 13: ELVIS
    THE SUFFERING ONE 145
Chapter 14: ELVIS
    THE MESSIANIC LIFE 153

Chapter 15: ELVIS
LIGHT TO ALL NATIONS 163
Chapter 16: ELVIS
DEATH OF THE KING 174
Chapter 17: ELVIS
POST MORTEM
APOLOGIA PRO VITA SUA 186
Chapter 18: ELVIS
THE STORY ENDS 199

EPILOGUE 203
POST EPILOGUE 215

ELVIS

AND THE

APOCALYPSE

THE AWFUL* DISCLOSURES OF MARIE,

MATRON OF THE MOTEL DEW BEANERY

AS REVEALED TO
STEVE WERNER
AUGUST 17, 62 ANNO ELVI (1997)

*INSPIRING AWE

Though he was almost divine,
He did not deem himself to be divine,
Rather he emptied himself,
Became like us in all things, including our obesity,
That at the name of Elvis, every knee must bow,
Every tongue proclaim:
Elvis is the King!

CHAPTER 1

GENESIS

THE BEGINNING

This story begins in August 1997. I vividly recall that sultry, overcast day when the small UPS package arrived wrapped in cut-up Piggly Wiggly grocery bags. Humidity hung like hot wet clothes on a line and my lungs labored to make use of the pasty laundromat-like air. Midwesterners know well these hated days of summer to which one never gets accustomed. I remember that day clearly—I had just been fired. Again.

Months before I had come to Chicago following a promising job lead. The work was interesting but the boss an ass—an overbearing jerk. His every word grated along my spine like a stick dragged across a chain-link fence. One day I blew up at him. After all, you can only take so much.

But my honest appraisal of the boss—to his face—earned me another pink slip. Pink has never been my color. Two days later, in my apartment—furnished with the finest second-hand furniture the curb provides on bulk trash day, I sat pondering my future, or lack thereof. As I raised a condensation-covered glass of ice water—a futile antidote to the heat—the apartment doorbell rang. I went outside the apartment, into the hall, down the steps, and opened the door of the tiny, penitentiary cell-sized lobby with its mosaic floor of small, at one time white, hexagonal tiles.

There stood a slightly sweaty, but well-tanned, attractive blond young woman in a brown shirt and shorts, white socks, and light tan work boots. A UPS uniform had never looked and fit so well. I signed for the package and with remorse watched her fit form enter the van and drive out of my life.

The package, addressed to me, had no return address. What was it? Had the Unabomber found me? By that time Ted Kaczynski lived in a bright orange jumpsuit in a federal prison. But had he mailed this package years ago? Had this package been lost in the mail since the time the Unabomber lurked as an uncaptured danger, hidden in a run-down Montana cabin, known only from the police drawing of a troubled man in a dark stocking cap?

Curiosity overruled caution. I tore open the package and pulled out a dozen photographs and a note from my cousin John in New Orleans. I was grateful the package wasn't another credit card promotion. In the photos John stood next to Andean villagers and llamas with mountains peaks in the background.

> Steve,
> I just returned from Peru where I made numerous discoveries regarding ancient manuscripts of the Incas. These Aramaic writings predict massive transformations in human society: a spiritual renaissance in human consciousness. These might be the final Insights!
> Aside from that, nothing else is happening. How are you? If you ever get a chance, look me up in New Orleans.
>
> Your cousin, John

Now seemed the chance. What did I have to lose? I had no future in Chicago, only a one year apartment lease with six months left and no way to pay. Why not skip town, visit John in New Orleans, then go home to Kansas City and live with my folks?

On the third day after receiving the package, I went to my bank, **QUASI-FIDELITY TRUST,** took out my life savings of a few hundred dollars, and returned to my apartment. It took all of an hour to pack what I wanted to keep. As for the furniture, I had gotten it for free, probably paying too much, so I left it.

I said good-bye to nobody and drove off. My car was an old 1971 Volkswagen Beetle—dark blue and rusting badly. The VW had over 185,000 miles but ran well, so I figured I would have no trouble driving it to New Orleans. But I had figured wrong. The VW started as reliably as ever, but when I turned on the ventilation fan, billows of caustic white smoke poured out the vents. As I would learn later that day my fuel lines had been leaking. Gasoline found its way into the rusted heater boxes. This gas caught fire and filled the car with smoke. I coughed and gagged my way for five blocks until I found a garage.

I pulled up to the tiny dark garage office and walked in. Two mechanics, in blue filthy coveralls, stood arguing in a room covered with wood paneling that looked just as ugly as when it had been glued to the cinder blocks with Liquid Nails thirty years earlier. As to the subject of the argument, I had no clue. It was not in English. But there they stood under dirty yellow neon lights, in front of the bikinied girl on the auto parts calendar, cursing, cussing, and gesturing in at least two languages.

In frustration I broke in, "Listen I need my car fixed. Can you help me?"

They stopped long enough to snarl, "Too busy! Today, too busy!" and resumed their fury of red faces, and accented invectives. I guessed they were immigrants from what used to be Yugoslavia, but from which part I did not know. Thus I could not determine who hated them and whom they hated.

Normally arguments frighten me and I move away quickly. But here in this adrenaline-filled room, the kinetics of confrontation drew me in.

I yelled, "Listen, I need my car fixed now!" Perhaps it was the heat. Silence hit the two mechanics like the last-place finish of a sure-bet horse. They stared at me.

"Wait here for minute. We talk," they snapped and disappeared into the back room where another brief, intense debate took place. They needed arguing the way I need coffee.

They returned. "We checked schedule, we fix car right away. What's is problem?"

Flushed with victory—I had stood my ground in a verbal exchange with two sons of the Balkans—I explained the problem. They took a quick look at the car and returned.

"We fix car now."

"Wait a minute. How much will this cost me?" I could feel the lump of savings in the bank withdrawal envelope in my back pocket. A strange fear shot through me that these two had a sixth sense telling them exactly how much money I had. I flinched, preparing myself for a price of $532.

They stopped and looked at one another.

"Forty dollars. We give you deal!" and quickly walked out to move the car into their garage. Dumbfounded, I slumped down into the stainless steel and vinyl chairs sitting next to a coffee maker with day-old—if not week-old—coffee. They went quickly to work. They were the fastest and most efficient mechanics I had ever seen as they made a quick trip to the junkyard and worked with pieces of sheet metal and duct tape.

"We fixed it good, no more smoke."

I gratefully handed them forty dollars, got into the car, and pulled away. Ten minutes of city streets later I found the entrance ramp to the interstate and fought the traffic and toll booths to make for New Orleans and put distance between Chicago and myself. I spent that afternoon heading south. Although I feel it is nice to go traveling, this trip would prove an agony beyond the nightmares of my restless nights.

The route from Chicago to Memphis, Tennessee is Interstate 57 down through the southern tip of Illinois at Cairo. There it crosses the Mississippi River and thirty miles later ends at Interstate 55. Route 55 runs south into the bootheel of Missouri, crosses the northeast corner of Arkansas, then crosses the Mississippi into

Memphis. From there I 55 runs through Jackson, Mississippi, finally ending at New Orleans.

With such a late start I became a night rider, reaching the vicinity of Memphis at about two o'clock in the morning. Hours earlier I had driven into a cold front—the temperature had dropped twenty degrees. Having finished the microwave burritos and Cokes I picked up at a Citgo station before midnight, I looked for a twenty-four hour cafe for my aching hunger and coffee for my overwhelming drowsiness. On the outskirts of Memphis a heavy fog had arisen. It was difficult to see exit signs, road signs, and semis in the distance. But through the mist a bright yellow diamond Denny's sign glared. Within two hundred feet an exit appeared and I took it. At the end of the exit ramp I turned right at an abandoned Stuckey's restaurant and headed up the service road for the Denny's. I drove almost two miles—but found only the end of the road. I turned around in a gravel driveway to get back to the interstate.

Before reaching the exit I discovered a side road on the right with a lighted parking lot about three hundred yards away. Assuming this to be the Denny's, I turned down the road and sought the light. Desperately hungry and half-awake, I pulled into the gravel lot and crunched to a stop. Not a Denny's at all, my car—idling that Volkswagen idle—had stopped before an early American truck stop diner.

Behind the diner stood an old roadside motel, completely dark. Overhead a neon sign fizzed: MOTEL DEW. Two letters, E and Y, had shorted out long ago. Generations of sparrows had crammed their nests behind the neon tubes that originally welcomed travelers to MOTEL DEWEY. A green neon coffeepot poured pulsating orange neon coffee into a rose neon cup.

In the years after the Depression, workers labored here to build this motel of individual glazed-yellow-brick units now facing a courtyard of disarray. The art deco style had curved walls, glass block windows, and garages for each unit. Now weeds grew everywhere. An old rusted Thunderbird and a '56 Chevy sat among uncontrollable spreading yews. Some garage doors hung half open, jammed, and crooked. Hardly a pane of glass remained unbroken. Had I more energy I would have pondered the memories of these empty rooms: vacationing families of exhausted, whining children; lonely, empty-order-book salesmen; teens deceived that their passion be so real that the machines in gas station restrooms were unnecessary. An active mind could imagine all kinds of famous and ordinary humans conceived at this long gone relic of the family-run-business age. But my rationed energy could not waste itself on such imaginings.

On this old two lane highway made obsolete by the interstate sat this open diner in front of an abandoned motel. It made no sense. But I could smell the coffee—even in my car—so I stepped out into the silent night and walked toward the brightly-lit diner. Paint peeled from every board. It had been years since anyone had been working on the building. Walking past a rusted Cadillac, made pink by the glowing neon OPEN sign, I opened the screen door with its bulge from hand presses and pushed back the wood-framed glass door with the "It's Kool Inside" decal. The diner, although old, looked clean. I crossed the black and white checkerboard floor and sat on a revolving stool covered with torn imitation red-marble vinyl.

I reached for the menu stuck in the rack behind the ketchup and napkins. As I scanned the menu, a figure moved behind the counter and stood in front of me.

"Coffee please," I stated, "for with long travel I am stiff and weary."

The figure found a cup and a pot, filled the cup, and pushed the cream and sugar within my reach. It said not a word as I read the stained menu—typed by hand, using carbon paper in an old clogged-vowel manual typewriter. Fatigue blurred my mind to the ridiculous prices: twenty-five cents for a hamburger and fries, twenty cents for a milkshake. Not even a complete breakfast for sixty-five cents could stun my exhausted brain.

I looked up to order eggs, bacon, sausage, and toast from the presumed waitress in front of me. A fifty-plus-year-old woman bearing a beehive tower of hair crowned with a white paper tiara stood before me. She wore a clean and neatly pressed, but old, pale blue uniform with white lapels. The nametag read "Marie." "Marie's the name," I thought. Somehow she looked as I expected her to look—like several cleaning women that worked my childhood home—except those zombie eyes staring into the distance. She noticed me looking at her.

"You don't know me," she stated in a rural, less-than-high school-educated, southern voice. She sounded like one who would regularly call a gospel radio talk show. I stated my order. "Any way you want me to fry those eggs?" she asked. "Sunnyside up," I proposed in defiance of the darkness surrounding the diner. She wrote the order and turned to the refrigerator and stove behind the counter. Eggs were broken, bacon and sausage laid on the grill, and toast—to my surprise—sliced from a full loaf and dropped into the toaster. She returned and leaned on an empty pie case while I drank my coffee. I could hear the bacon frying. In a moment the order was complete, the plate filled and placed in front of me.

"More coffee, please," I asked and she dutifully brought the Cory pot and filled my heavy white, diner mug. Some subconscious sense of duty urged me to attempt conversation, so I asked, "It is a foggy night out. Is this unusual for this part of Tennessee?" But my question seemed to invade her thoughts. Perhaps compelled by a similar duty she answered, "What's that?"

"Is this fog unusual?" I repeated.

"Oh dear no, sir," she said. "This is a Memphis peculiar. It ain't like no Kentucky Rain." Satisfied she had given the minimal necessary response, she returned to her preoccupation. She stared at the ceiling, out the window. Then she stared at her order pad, made a calculation, tore the slip, and set it next to my plate. She stepped back from the counter. I turned over the ticket and searched for the total. She had written the date of August 16, 1997, in large red letters on the bill, but no total and since it was past midnight, she should have written August 17. Confused as to what I owed, I looked at Marie, but her eyes ignored mine.

"Yesterday was the day," she said. "Yesterday was the day! And nothin' happened! Nothin' happened!" An awkward pause followed. "How much do I owe?" I asked. She repeated, "Yesterday was the day and nothin' happened. We musta' read the signs wrong."

Hoping that if we discussed her agenda for a moment she would give me the total so I could eat quickly, pay, and escape, I foolishly asked, "What was supposed to happen yesterday?" Marie turned at me in utter amazement, "Is you only a stranger in Memphis, and ain't known the things that came to pass there in these days? Don't you know that yesterday marked the twentieth anniversary a' the death of Elvis?" "Oh yes, Memphis—the home of Elvis. I had forgotten. But what was supposed to happen?" I asked.

"I don't know 'xactly, . . . but somethin', somethin' was s'pposed to happen. But nothin' did 'cause I got a feelin' in my body; we read the signs wrong again. We read the signs wrong!" With that her eyes left me and resumed their far-off stare. Yet she grabbed the coffeepot and filled a cup for herself. Why I asked the next question I will never know, but it led to the most revealing earful of my entire life: "What signs?"

"Signs a' the life of Elvis the King. Elvis lived a life chock full a' signs," she answered. "This ain't no hugger-mugger witchcraft. No ordinary man, Elvis hisself was a sign given from above: a revelation, a messenger to us lowly ones on this earth."

A terrifying shiver climbed my spine—the shiver a wild animal feels at the moment it hears the terrible rumble of the closing trap door, knowing it will never be free again. Marie launched into a wild discourse:

"His very name was a sign. Ya see if ya take 'Elvis' and drop the first and last letters you have 'l, v, i'. Now they say that's the number fifty-six in Roman numbers. Elvis died at forty-two. If ya take forty-two from fifty-six ya get fourteen: the first sign. Six years ago we waited on the fourteenth anniversary a' the death of Elvis: all day and all night, a candlelight vergil. For we trusted that it'd been he which should've redeemed us from our loneliness. But what great sorrow and agony—nothin' happened.

"So we figgered we'd read the signs wrong. We mulled it for days and decided that since Elvis ranked number one in our hearts we had to add a 'one' to the 'fourteen. This left no doubt that somethin' would surely happen on the fifteenth anniversary of his death. We passed a year in waitin', preparin', fastin', and prayin' in our hope that on the fifteenth anniversary of his death the heavens would be rent asunder and Elvis the King would descend on a cloud to reign once more over us."

Her devout eyes seemed to find the clouds of heaven through the ceiling of broken, one-foot-square acoustical tiles. Her pious pose held for minutes, then, as if she aged ten years in an instant, her countenance fell, her gaze dropped, and she switched the positions of the salt and pepper shakers in the rack. "But as ya might a' guessed, on the fifteenth anniversary of the death of Elvis nothin' happened. So we went back to figurin'."

"We next reckoned if ya started with fifty-six and then took away thirty-five, for the year Elvis was born, you'd get twenty-one. And since Elvis remains number one in our hearts, we had to adjust our figurin' by one. But rather than addin' one, we had to subtract it, 'cause Elvis, our numero uno, was gone. Thus we came up with twenty. And we was so certain on the twentieth anniversary of his death somethin' great was gonna happen. But a' course nothin', nada, zip."

Since I liked reading I had found little interest in popular music. Not raised on rock, I preferred an unusual range of classical music: Gustav Mahler, Franz Berwald, and Aran Kachaturian. Through my peripheral vision of world affairs I had seen the Elvis mania with a tolerant pity to those of such low musical tastes: noblès oblige. And so it came as a terrifying shock when a thunderbolt shot through my mind and I blurted, "Use the age of the mother of Elvis!"

My outburst stunned us both. It had been thirty-seven years since such an idea had rose up from some hidden subconscious well within me and erupted forth like a volcano—not since my grade school confirmation. At Roman Catholic School in my day, the bishop came to confirm the second and third graders. The nuns coached us that if the bishop asked a question we were to answer "Yes, your Excellency." At some point during the ceremony the bishop told a stupid joke. He slapped his rotund stomach, rocked back on his heels, and chuckled, "My aren't we funny tonight?" I shot up in my pew, "Yes, your Excellency."

After the severe punishment for that outburst, I never misbehaved again. I became a diligent student, abandoned my career dreams of becoming a nightclub comedian, threw down the torch of Henny Youngman, and went to graduate school to become an anthropologist. But I dropped out after the first semester, and somewhere in that transition, I drifted away from membership in any religious denomination.

The wheels in Marie's mind turned furiously. She speculated, "Well Gladys died at age forty-two. Now if ya subtract that from the fifty-six in the name of Elvis ya still get fourteen. But that cain't be right. We had fourteen years ago and that clearly weren't it." Her brain searched itself. "But wait, Gladys didn't die at forty-two. She lied about her age when she married the young Vernon Presley. She took four years off her age. She really died at age forty-six. If ya take forty-six from fifty-six ya get ten. But how could ten be the right number? We mourned the tenth anniversary ten years ago! Now how can that fit?"

Hour long minutes passed as Marie twisted her face in puzzlement. She mumbled many combinations of ten, fifty-six, forty-two, and forty-six. She tried to add then multiply them all together on her order book, but when the math became complex she threw down her pad in frustration and stammered, "Elvis came for us common folk. It cain't be that complicated." When she gave herself permission to find a simple answer it came, as if Occam's razor had crossed the faint whiskers on her upper lip. "Three! Three, that's it!" Her face beamed in the afterglow of insight. "The key lies in the number a' letters used to get the fifty-six and that's three: a '1,' a 'v,' and a 'i.' Now ya could take three times ten and get thirty. That'd mean a miracle'd come thirty years after his death, which'd be the year 2007. But thirty don't seem right; it's too loosey-goosey. It don't feel right. Now I's sure ya don't multiply ten by three but what if I take ten three times. What I mean is: I take ten times ten times ten and get the answer."

"You mean ten cubed," I suggested.

The irrelevance of my incomprehensible language took her back, but she continued, "Ten time ten times ten is . . .

"A thousand," I answered.

"A thousand! A thousand, that's it! The key number! One thousand! It has to be. For it says in the book a' Revelations, 'But the rest of the dead lived not again until the thousand years were finished. This is the first resurrection!' (20:5). If I can dream it! Elvis will rise again in a thousand years!"

Shocked by the insanity of this woman, I jumped from my stool and pleaded desperately, "How much do I owe?" A quick exit became essential. Ignoring my plea, her cobra arm struck and grabbed my hand with a wrestler's strength. Fang-like nails dug into my skin. I later learned this was the grab most feared by on-stage Elvis when he spasmed his way to the edge of the stage, teetering on the precipice over the clawing mob of hysteria. My mind tried to force my mouth to order her, "keep those cold icy fingers off of me!" but my tongue cleaved to my jaw.

Staring into my eyes—into my very heart—she commanded, "Sit and listen, stay you must! For you've ciphered the sign a' the number a' the name of Elvis. Don't ask me why, but surely there's a reason you're here—Fate! All I really want to do is tell ya all the signs of Elvis. Don't forbid me!"

Paralyzed, a ditty arose from the back of my brain:

>She holds him with her glittering eye—
>The Diner Guest stood still,
>And listens like a three years' child:
>The Marie has her will.

Her grip strong, her eyes intense, with a shudder I sat back down in utter disbelief.

"Listen hun'—my little friend," said she. "There's other signs beside the number 1000!"

Full of vexation sat I, with stifled complaint. Thus began the incredible night when I learned the awful disclosures of Marie, the matron of the Motel Dew beanery.

CHAPTER 2

ELVIS

THE WANDERING MISSISSIPPIAN

In the distant night a semi trucker pulled hard on his air horns and dopplered off into silence. Two nighthawks in screeching dives strafed the parking lot lights. In this museum piece of a diner the refrigerator hummed and fresh coffee drained into the pot. As I bit into my toast, Marie resumed her disclosures:

"Darlin', I's a sober woman. Yet I will a square unshellacked tale deliver a' the whole course of Elvis; what love, what drugs, what charms, what conjurin' and what mighty magic he brung to our lives. Many signs and portents foretole the life a' Elvis. These signs explain a deeper meanin'. For a great importance attached to the man. In truth, the entire life of Elvis can be augured out a' the Bible."

"What are you talking about? Are you sincere? The Bible? You can find Elvis Presley in the Bible? The Bible?" My voice rose on a crescendo of incredulity.

"Oh ye of little faith, the Good Book points to the life of Elvis time and time again," Marie snapped. "And t'all starts with the woman whose breasts gave suck to the infant she brought forth after nine months pregnant with expectation: Gladys Presley, Elvotokos!" In my disbelief I sucked toast crumbs down my windpipe. Choking and coughing, I struggled to maintain a dignified composure.

"Come on boy, cough it up!" Marie yelled. She reached across the counter and brought her hand down sharply between my shoulder blades, driving my face to within inches of my eggs. She urged, "Cough it up! What we've here is a failure to regurgitate." My spasmed throat calmed. I took a drink of water with a distant taste of the Mississippi.

Seeing I would survive, Marie carried on, "I repeat; it all begins with the mother of Elvis: Gladys—a weighty name a' great consequence. The Bible's peppered with the word 'glad.' Gladys betokes the whole purpose a' the Bible and religion and faith—to be glad." From her apron pocket she pulled an old diner Guest Check book bound with a red rubber band. Pulling out loose checks she read the scribblings on them: "In I Chronicles 16: 'Let the heavens be glad, and let the earth rejoice.' Ya see gladness is the reaction of all folk in the presence of Elvis. All people should gaze on him and proclaim, 'I will be glad and rejoice in thee,' from Psalm 9 and from Psalm 35, 'Let them shout for joy, and be glad.' 'Let all those that seek thee rejoice and be glad in thee,' Psalm 40. 'Thee' is a' course Elvis. Psalm 118: 'We will rejoice and be glad in it, for this is the day made for him.' Psalm one hundred..."

I cut her off, "I get the point! I really do not want to know all this." I had little doubt she could tick off another dozen psalm quotes. "You are right." I tried to ebb this glad tide, "there seems to be lots of happiness in the Bible despite all those wars, famines, and plagues."

"Maybe my enthusiasm carried me away just a little bit and let me run on like that." She gathered herself. "Well I searched the Bible for every use a' the word 'glad' and 'gladly' and I found ninety-seven places—took months, almost. Only later I come to find out there's this book called a Concord-dance, where I could a' looked it up in minutes."

I tried to correct her, but suspected it was in vain: "I think they call that book a 'Concordance.'"

"Thank ya for fixin' my speakin', hun'," she answered, to my surprise. "All these mentions a' the word 'glad' shows that the whole raisin to eat, the whole goal a' the Bible is to be glad. The name 'Gladys' shows and 'lucidates how Elvis brings fulfillment and gladness as we step into this earthly pail of tears. Elvis certainly brought gladness to me." I nodded to concede her point. It only fueled her eagerness to lay out more arguments.

"The parents of Elvis, Gladys and Vernon Presley, lived in Tupelo, Mississippi in a tiny shotgun house: no lights, no phone, no motorcar; not a single luxury. One day an angel swooped down to warn the barren Gladys that, 'she may not eat of any thing that cometh of the vine, neither let her drink wine or strong drink, nor eat any unclean thing.' That's in Judges chapter 13, verse 14." Marie quoted short Bible passages written on the old Guest Checks and explained, "But we knows in her declinin' years Gladys drank and took diet pills. By not heedin' the angel's warnin', she condemned Elvis to a life a' pill poppin'.

"The angel gave another warnin' in verse 5. This one they followed: 'no razor shall come on his head: for the child shall be a Nazarite.' That's why Elvis wore his hair that way: the pompadour of Elvis—a divine command!

"Now the conception of Elvis proved an event most wondrous; that's why people worshipped him. More than human, Elvis had a streak a' divinity. Ya look at me as if I's crazy. But darlin', I'm not touched, nor have I let my mind feed on fantasy. What I say to you is true and my authority's the Bible!"

From a deep pocket in her apron, Marie pulled a well-worn, pocket Bible, held together by another red rubber band. "Listen now. Be not like those who have ears but cain't hear, who have eyes but cain't see. It says, right here in the sixth chapter a' Genesis:

> And it came to pass, when men began to multiply on the face of the earth, and daughters were born unto them. That the sons of God saw the daughters of men that they were fair; and they took them wives of all which they chose.
>
> There were giants in the earth in those days; and also after that, when the sons of God came in unto the daughters of

men, and they bare children to them, the same became mighty men which were of old, men of renown. (6:1-4)

"There ya have it." She set the Bible on the counter. "Elvis came forth as the offspring of an encounter between the divine and a human bein'. Ya see these heavenly bein's, angels sorta', lusted for earthly babes and took them as wives. Well they didn't marry 'em, just shacked up with 'em. When the earthly women got knocked up, the heavenly bein's went into hidin'.

"Now the fathers of the earthly women went after 'em. But ya cain't force no heavenly bein' to get hitched by puttin' a 12 gauge to his back. The earthly women gave birth to giants who became the men a' renown. So too Elvis—a giant—one a' the mighty men of old, the men a' renown."

"There were other men of renown?" I asked with great trepidation.

"Bill Haley and Buddy Holly!" She snapped back.

"Do you mean to say angels conceived Elvis Presley, Bill Haley, and Buddy Holly?"

"Well angels of a sort, but yes, that's how they came to be. Cross my heart, lift and separate, and hope to die! Do you doubt the Good Book? Do you doubt the other signs?"

She glared.

Oscillating between dismay and intrigue, I gulped, "Other signs?"

"Signs?" she inhaled deeply. "My Lord, signs fill the life a' Elvis. But first, more about the conception of Elvis. Vernon Presley claimed he passed out at the moment a' conception. Well that's when the heavenly bein' snuck in there. Gladys—probably enraptured—didn't notice it neither. But I knows an angel musta' been there. 'Cause 'fore the births of all great heroes—Samson, Samuel, John the Baptist—angels had been 'round.

"Right away Gladys knew twins filled her womb. How? They jostled each other like Jacob and Esau. Gladys moaned, 'If it be so, why am I thus?' She treasured in her heart how they wrassled and grappled inside her.

"All through her barefoot and pregnant days Gladys pondered away. She awed how she, a hand seamstress of sharecropper estate, should be so chosen. She knew one son would 'Cast down the mighty from their thrones.' Elvis'd throw down the big bands from their music stand chairs—like old Lawrence Welk. No more let the welkin roar! This son would 'Lift up the lowly.' Elvis lifted us—the low folk of society—from our emptiness. He offered hisself and promised his love. 'He shall fill the hungry with good things.' He filled the hungry masses with excitement and life. 'All generations shall call him blessed,' (Luke 1:48-53)." Marie quoted from the Guest Checks.

She explained further, "But we now know what transpired in that womb: Elvis the Fetus was a bumpin' and a grindin' just like his early days on stage. He twitched and snapped those legs. Well no one could survive nine months a' that! What great sadness filled the Tupelo night when Elvis come forth. Tragedy marred that moment a' glory: the twin brother of Elvis—a stillborn. A Gladys woman of two goodly sons; and which was strange, the one so like the other, as could not be distinguished but by names. A woman of poor means was delivered of such a burden male twins, both alike. Both alike 'cept one was dead.

"But all this has deeper meanin'. They named the dead boy child Jesse. The Bible says clearly the King will come from the root a' Jesse. Now Elvis and Jesse had the same root, the same parents. Also, 'Jesse' is the closest English name to Jesus. Some have likened Elvis to the brother of Jesus.

"Old women of Tupelo tole stories of visitors comin' to Elvis at his birth: 'bout men who stopped to see the infant on their way to deliver wool to the garment factory in Tupelo. Men who saw the infant and exclaimed, 'A terrible beauty is born!'

"Poor black men from the other side a' Tupelo, Shakerag, came and offered gifts of three songs: 'Frankie and Johnny,' 'Oh Them Golden Slippers,' and 'Myrna, My Love.' One gazed upon the child and exclaimed, 'What is this that rises like the issue of a king, and wears upon his baby-brow the Roundtop of sovereignty?' Roundtop's an old mountain that looks like a king's crown.

"Tain't possible to check these stories. Those old women long since died. But I pass along to you what they had delivered unto me, those who was from the beginnin' eye witnesses.

"Gladys birthed Elvis in East Tupelo, a very important sign. The sun rises in the east. The three Wise Men followed a star in the east. I ain't sayin' no bright star hovered over the Presley home that night, but Vernon did claim he saw the heavens ringed with blue light. Remember this was before Wal-Marts with parkin' lots glowin' all night so no one gets mugged there.

"Elvis entered this world a' strife as a poor boy on January 8, 1935. Many Christians celebrate January 6 as Epiphany, the manifestation, when Three Wise Kings came to Bethlehem. If ya count January 6 as one, January 7 as two, ya get January 8 as the third day. In the Bible 'on the third day' means a special day a' completion. Elvis completes what the Three Kings begun. And Elvis's most important song, 'Can't Help Falling in Love,' starts with what Wise Men say.

"Elvis arrived durin' the Depression: hard luck years. It was the worst a' times, it was the best a' times, it was the age a' damn fools, it was the age a' wise guys, it was the winter of hope, it was the summer of despair, we had everythin' puked up before us, we had everythin' go down the sewer, there was a president with a fair face and his wife with a large jaw, we were all prayin' for heaven, we watched everythin' goin' to hell. This was a long time ago, back when people used Absorbine Senior.

"1935, the year Elvis came and the year Huey Long left: assassinated in Louisiana—yet another sign. For Huey Long preached, 'Every man a King.' But that proved impossible 'cause the Kingfish, Huey Long, hogged everythin' for hisself. He took all the power, the control, the limelight, and the money he could get. Huey wanted the rich to share wealth while he held on tightfisted to everythin' he'd get his hands on. By the time he died, everyone knew it foolish to claim 'Every man a king.' But Huey Long had proved 'Every land a king', meanin' that even a democracy needed a king. Elvis became the king that took the throne a' the dead and stinkin' Kingfish. But Elvis ruled no kingdom a' this world of corrupt and incompetent politics, promisin' new roads to the poor. No, Elvis came to reign in his kingdom of heavenly music to lift the spirits of the downtrodden.

"Now many have labored to trace the family tree of Elvis, but I cain't figger the point. For all ya get is one long line a' nobodies who get ya to one somebody—Elvis, but then everyone else in the family stays as nobodies. They's only near-somebodies, cause their bloodline is near the one somebody.

"Anyways, I must explain more signs, hun'. Now take the father of Elvis: Vernon. What means his name? Well ya don't need no college Ph.D. to know Spring starts at the Vernal Equinox. Vernon represents Spring: new life and a new age."

Figuring to join in this wild imagining I suggested, "Could the name of Vernon also refer to the word 'vernacular' which means 'of the common people.'"

"Say on, say on," she interjected.

"Just as the common people speak the vernacular language so Vernon came from the common people and gave his son for the common people," I explained. Marie looked surprised, "Well I'll be. You're catchin' on fast. You is thinkin' 'bout all this and decipherin' the signs, now that ya let yourself go. And if that's what that word 'ventricular' means, then I guess you is right."

I corrected, "The word is 'vernacular'."

"Oh . . . . Another woman from Tupelo who called the Presleys, 'My friends who were poor but near honest,' told me of the goin's on of the Presleys, and thereby hangs a tale. Elvis grew up a barefoot boy with cheek untanned, with his turned-up overalls. One day this woman saw Elvis a wadin' in a crick bed, whistlin' a whistling tune, hummin' a barefoot ballad, chasin' a butterfly and huntin' crawfish, when he found some clay. He molded the clay into the shape of a guitar. Elvis clapped his hands and beautiful music came from the clay guitar. That's the story she told. I know it seems too incredible to believe."

Spying an opening for a sane perspective, I leaped. "I do not believe for a moment that the boy Elvis could clap his hands and cause a clay guitar to play music miraculously."

I hit a raw nerve. Marie sneered, "You intellectual skeptic, you! Remember, blessed is they that have not seen and yet believe! Of course the boy Elvis could make a clay guitar play. The only unbelievable part in that story's that Gladys—a protective mother hen—would let Elvis out a' her sight long 'nough for him to play in a crick!"

The whine of a housefly caught my attention. My eyes were able to follow it and legitimately turn from Marie's stare without my seeming to back down in cowardice. I waved at the fly as it encircled my ear and then headed down the counter to where a mucilage-colored curled strip of flypaper hung. With near suicidal intent the fly drove its head into the paper. In the anguish of regret at its own stupidity, it buzzed its wing in a desperate but futile attempt to free itself.

The struggle for life escaped Marie. "Turn around, look at me!" she snapped as she continued to weave her oracle. "There's important symbols in the birthplace a' Elvis. Tupelo, a small town, down in the boondocks, represents Nazareth. Memphis, the center of American music, represents Jerusalem, the religious center of Israel. Elvis grew up in Nazareth of the South: Tupelo. And there he waxed strong in spirit, filled with wisdom, waitin' for his time to come in Memphis.

"The Tupelo women claimed young Elvis had none a' the beauty of his adult years, as in scripture." Marie found the right passage in her Bible, "'For he shall grow up before us as a tender plant, and as a root out of a dry ground: he hath no form nor comeliness; and when we shall see him, there is no beauty that we should desire him.' (Isaiah 54:2) A rather unauspicious beginnin' for the face that launched a thousand hips.

"I've more to tell if you'll put aside your book-learned philosophy and vain deceit, the wisdom a' men, and become like a child eager to learn." Marie found a passage from Genesis. "One day a voice from above spoke to Elvis and his parents: 'Get thee out of thy country, and from thy kindred, and from thy father's house, unto a land that I will shew thee: And I will make of thee a great nation, and I will bless thee, and make thy name great; and thou shalt be a blessin'. (12:1-2) Abraham and family left Haran to settle the Promised Land, so the Presleys left Mississippi and moved to Memphis. Vernon packed his family like Noah packed up the ark and headed for Memphis, the land promised, a land flowin' with milk and honey—a land flowin' with rhythm and blues.

"Two promises was made to Abraham and two was made to Elvis: each would have his own land and a multitude a' descendants. Now Elvis conquered the land, Memphis, where he became King."

"But what about descendants?" I asked. "Elvis did not have any male descendants. He only had a daughter, Lisa . . ."

"Marie! Lisa Marie! How could you forget that name? Lisa and I share the same name. I've always wondered if I influenced Elvis on pickin' that name."

"How could you have influenced Elvis?" I asked with a skeptical crooked mouth.

"Well it ain't no big thing, hun', but it's a bit personal," Marie said as her mind drifted into memories.

"But let's get back to the promises of Abraham. Elvis had only one child, Lisa Marie," I argued. "In the ancient world the line of descent followed male children. So technically Elvis did not have descendants according to the biblical view."

Marie sighed with relief, "Well at least you're mullin' over these signs. I've got confidence in you. Did Elvis have male descendants in fulfillment of the promise? Well there's three parts to the answer. First, I's not sure all the offspring of Elvis has ever been counted or accounted for. Who knows what to make of those paternity suits 'gainst Elvis? Second, Elvis knew he had to have a male offspring. That's why he slept with so many a woman. Now ya read in the Bible 'bout Sarah. When Sarah couldn't give birth she handed over her maidservant Hagar so that Abraham would have a male child with Hagar—a sort a' ancient Bedouin soap opera. Likewise, all the women of Elvis represent a 'group' Hagar. He may have set a record by sleeping with more women than any other man. Certainly he's at the top a' the "Fornicatin' Top Forty". Elvis outdid Don Juan, and didn't need no servant keepin' records to prove it. Now how could Elvis find that many women attractive? Well from a certain lust perspective, I reckon everyone looks good.

"Now thirdly and lastly, Elvis left a multitude of male offspring: the Elvis imitators. Elvis lives on in them. They's the descendants of Elvis. And let me tell you, there's Chinese imitators, Spanish imitators, and probably a Russian one. There's Elvis imitators fallin' out a' the skies. I don't know if these men decided on their own to be Elvis imitators or whether they was called. But they come from all walks a' life: pro bass fishermen, IRS men, one's even a zealous commie revolutionary. As one Elvis Xerox said, 'We have forsaken all, and followed Elvis, what shall we have therefore? For we have decided to follow Elvis—no turnin' back, no turnin' back.'

"These imitators—who have taken up their microphones to follow Elvis—represent the King on earth 'til Elvis returns to once again take up his microphone. When the trumpet sounds we'll hear the glorious voice a' Elvis. All the imitators will join the King in singin', 'I Did it My Way.'"

I choked on my coffee and struggled to keep from spewing it across the counter. Marie grabbed a dishtowel and shoved it at me so I could wipe the coffee dribbles from my shirt. Fearing her discourse would not miss a stride, I stood up to clean my shirt and stepped backwards to get beyond her reach.

Hysterical, she screamed, "What a minute, wait a minute, you ain't heard nothin' yet. I tell ya, wait a minute. You ain't heard nothin' yet! You think my stories is never-endin', that I'm the devil in disguise. But please do not go gently into that good night. Come on and stay, just a little bit longer. Don't leave me now, for there ain't none so blind as those that will not see, and none so deaf as those who won't listen."

Her words cut at my Achilles heel. I had always prided myself on being open-minded, and here this woman chided me. She dared me in a game of ideological chicken.

Like a losing fool at the dice table (as I would later learn, just like Colonel Parker), I sat down. Without delay she found her heading and resumed her course: "The family of Elvis left Tupelo—just like Abraham left Haran. Some say Vernon had to leave—that he got in trouble with revenuers—that he feared being collared for the moonshine's wat'ry beams. Whatever the reason, Vernon said 'we're gonna move, anyplace is paradise—'cept Tupelo. We gotta follow that dream.' The Presleys left Tupelo, Mississippi: the bosom a' Abraham—course I don't really think Abraham had much in the way of bosoms. The Presleys sojourned in stages—actually an old car—all the way up to Memphis. They arrived in the Promised Land."

Marie noticed my unfinished plate: "Be sure and eat all your breakfast. I've lots to say—you'll need the nourishment. It's good wholesome, healthy, food: bacon, sausage, and eggs fried in lard. I don't give a shit what Wilford Brimley says."

CHAPTER 3

ELVIS

A PROPHET IN THE PROMISED LAND

"The Presleys entered the Promised Land a' Memphis," Marie's pace quickened, "drivin' a beat-up green Plymouth, with Elvis on the floorboards workin' the broken gas pedal: the Joads of Tupelo, with Vernon hollerin', 'We're comin' in loaded.' But it weren't all milkshakes and Bit-a-Honey bars.

"Things started out rough. The dirt-poor Presleys had trouble findin' work. But trained in the school a' hard knocks, they survived. They figgered home is where the heart is—the cardiac domicile theory. Elvis, he attended L. C. Humes High School on North Manasas Street and that's a symbol for Manasseh, a tribe of ancient Israel." Her index finger in my face emphasized the point. She leaned at me over the counter and her lapelled uniform separated from her chest. My eyes could not but catch sight of what at present lay on the verge of wrinkles and age spots; but what must have been, at one time, an enticing cleavage now in the custody of an eighteen-hour bra. Before my confused hormones could resolve the debate of a broad definition of lustability versus the fear of Freudian guilt, she straightened up. Her words of a few moments earlier ran through my mind, "From a certain lust perspective everyone looks good." Then she resumed her line of argument:

"Elvis graduated and hired on at Crown Electric on Poplar Avenue drivin' trucks. He started fixin' his hair with Royal Crown Pomade. Ain't that fittin' for the future and once King? He sang to hisself, listened to radio, and sweated many evenin's at hot gospel music shows enraptured in harmonies a' sweet sorrow. Elvis simmered inside—like a pressure cooker with a bad gasket—all set to blow and spew pot roast all over the stove.

"Many people talk of Elvis bein' discovered. No one discovered Elvis. The higher power chose Elvis as the prophet a' Rock and Roll! A shy and reluctant boy, when he first heard the call he pined, 'I cannot sing; for I is a child.' A heavenly voice thundered back, 'Say not, "I is a child": for thou shalt go to all that I shall send thee, and whatsoever I command thee, thou shalt sing.' An angelic hand reached from above and touched his mouth. The voice bellered out, 'Behold, I have put my words in thy mouth. See, I have this day set thee over the nations and over the kingdoms, to root up, and to pull down, and to destroy, and to throw down, to build, and to plant.' (Jeremiah 1:7-10)

"Now the angel also rammed lots of 'Yes, sirs' and 'Yes, ma'ams' down the throat a' Elvis. He never stinjed on his 'Thank You's'. Lucky parents, like the Presleys, have such polite children, for as they say, 'How sharper than a cottonmouth's fang it is to have a thankless child.' 'Course if ya asks me who the they is, I must admit, I don't know. Although I've heard tell they have an office in Paris. But accordin' to my friend Bernie it would say on the door '*Ills.* '

"These events terrified Elvis. Near breathless, he moaned louder, 'Woe is me! for I is undone; because I am a man of unclean lips, and I dwell in the midst of a people of unclean lips.' 'Parently Elvis thought he couldn't sing 'cause a' his thick southern accent. Eloquence rarely visited his speech. But, below and hold, another angel, a seraphim, swooped down with a pair a' barbecue tongs squeezin' a hunk-a-burnin' coal, glowin' fresh-butchered-hog-blood red. And with a right-hand lunge faster than a desperate woman at a slot machine, shoved that coal into the face of Elvis, declarin', 'Lo, this hath touched thy lips; thine iniquity is taken away, and thy sin is purged.' (Isaiah 6:5-6) Now 'iniquity', that's the guilt of inferiority that haunted this southern boy causin' him to feel bare-ass naked whenever he spoke. But after that angel came, the iniquity, the guilt, the inferiority left forever.

"One last thing 'bout the call of Elvis. Havin' that coal sear his lips hurt like hell—Elvis flinched. That painful memory followed him the rest a' his life. That's why Elvis wore that sneer on his lips. Tell me if he don't look like someone catchin' sight of an angel totin' a hot coal aimin' to fry his lips." Marie produced a thirty-year-old black and white teen magazine picture of Elvis to prove her point.

Not ready to get back in my car for more tortuous hours of driving, I prolonged the only slightly less tortuous oration. "Someone had to record Elvis for first time. Did not that person choose Elvis?"

"You speak of Sam Phillips, hun'."

"Let me guess," regretting I had not dashed for my car. "Sam is also a sign."

"Damn right! In the Bible Samuel chose the great kings a' Saul and David. At Sun Records in Memphis, Samuel Phillips first recorded Elvis and 'inaugurated' the kingship of Elvis. Sam Phillips selected Elvis as 'head and shoulders' above all others—that's Bible talk for an outstandin' person. The King did not have dandruff! We can never talk too greatly of Sam Phillips, for the hand that cradles rock is the hand that rolls the world.

"How'd Sam Phillips learn of Elvis? Well Phillips had a business a' makin' single records for anyone what walked in. You'd go there and sing a birthday greetin' for a friend, or do prize winnin' hog callin', and they'd record it. I went with my two sisters. Singin' just like the Andrew Sisters, we recorded, 'Apple Blossom Time.' Then we did our version of Spike Jones' 'Cocktails for Two.' Well, we got into it, doin' all those hiccups, and throat chugs; but they stops us 'cause we spat all over the recordin' booth. Luckily, I still got that old record of 'Apple Blossom Time' from forty years ago. It's in back. I could get it if ya'd like to hear it, darlin'."

Fearing horrible imaginings less than present fears, I chose the known danger, "Ah, you were telling me about Elvis? It is a matter of time before I leave. Suppose you stay with Elvis," I detangentialized.

"Yes. I do tend to wander about. That's the stuff you gotta watch for. Elvis went into Sun Records to make a record for his Ma. At the tape recorder sat Marion Keisker. She symbolizes Miriam—the sister a' Moses—in the book a' Numbers chapter 12, who broke out in leprosy for speakin' 'gainst Moses. Fearin' this herself, the Marion of Memphis spoke highly of Elvis. Spared of leprosy, Marion's complexion remained Cover-Girl-model smooth.

"Marion, a prophetess, went to Sam with the record, playing along, ready to shake that tambourine—actually a timbrel—singing praises of Elvis: 'I will sing of Elvis Presley, he will triumph gloriously, a white boy singin' colored R and B.' Elvis the long-sought white boy with a colored sound. 'The people who dwelt in darkness have seen a great light.' (Isaiah 9:2)

"Months passed 'fore Phillips called Elvis. With no phone, the Presleys took calls at the apartment of their neighbor, Rabbi Goldman—another sign. Rabbis do the preachin' for Jews. And 'fore Jews had rabbis, they had temple priests who descended from Aaron, the brother a' Miriam and Moses. Marion saw Elvis as the new Moses. Ya see, signs of Elvis pop out all over the Bible."

That seemed the most twisted bit of logic I had ever encountered. She could even out logic-twist Rush Limbaugh. For the sake of adventure I let Marie continue, wondering if she might outdo even this statement. An eager Marie continued:

"When Elvis reentered Sun Records studio he filled instantly with the spirit a' Rock and Roll. He joined in a singin' with the musicians: like old Saul fallin' in among the guild prophets." Finding another Guest Check she quoted, "'And when they came thither to the hill, behold, a company of prophets met him; and the spirit came upon him, and he prophesied among them.' (I Samuel 10:10) Elvis didn't 'xactly prophesize, he harmonized as they made his first record.

"They needed to test that record to discern the will of the

almighty public. Gideon in the book of Judges heaved a fleece, a lambskin, out his barn window and he looked for a sign: that the fleece'd be wet with dew and the ground around it dry. Next day Gideon looked for a second sign: a dry fleece surrounded by wet ground. It all depended on the dew. To test the Elvis record they went to Memphis disk jockey Dewey Phillips, a man without guile. Dewey balked, 'Can there any good come out of Tupelo?' But he played the record on the radio; he made the test. And a' course the rest is histrionics. With the right 'Dew,' the prophet had been chosen. Oh, happy day! They released 'That's All Right Mama.' Everybody loved it. Elvis started to tour and make money. He began his exodus from rags to riches. Elvis dreamed the impossible dream, and it came true.

"I heard Elvis on the radio the very first night they played his song. In the bathroom fixin' my face, I beheld beautiful sounds from the parlor radio, the likes of which I'd never known. Full a' Noxema came I with compact, from the bathroom to the parlor where I sat in awed silence as with cunnin' he filched my dauntless heart." Marie stared at the ceiling with a fulfilled look.

"I am a bit confused. Do you not consider Sam Phillips a prophet for first recording Elvis?" I asked.

"It's like this: Sam Phillips came before and prefiggered the true and great prophet: Elvis; just like Elijah and Elisha in the first book a' Kings."

The thought of yet another Bible story brought a Darth Vadar constriction to my neck. Why had she not missed Sunday school as a child? My gasping for air caught her attention.

"Ya seem unwillin' to hear more Bible. Damn! How impatience lowers your face, like an outhouse droppin' fallin' into darkness. I've more Bible passages to tell and you will listen," she ordered. "I have not yet begun to cite!

"Now Elisha was a plowin' with twelve yoke of oxen. Elijah came 'long side and put his mantle—a cloak or windbreaker—over the shoulders of Elisha. Elijah did this to call Elisha to follow him and be the next prophet—new and improved. Well Elisha ran up to Elijah and said, 'Let me say good-bye to my folks.' That's not what Elijah wanted to hear so Elijah said, 'Go back again: for what have I done to thee?'. Ya see Elisha had to leave home to be a prophet and turn his back on kin. Elisha, to prove hisself prophet-ready, slaughtered all those expensive oxen, burnt up his plows as cordwood, and barbecued the meat. He destroyed his livelihood. 'Once the hand is laid to the plow there ain't no turnin' back.' Which means once ya chop up your plow, there's no more bustin' sod. Course it could also mean once ya start plowin' behind twelve pair of oxen ya'd best not turn 'round to see into what you've been steppin'.

"This all explains Elvis. 'Elisha' and 'Elvis' sound similar. Now Elijah represents colored music. No, we're not 'sposed to say 'colored' anymore, we are 'sposed to 'black.' But that ain't right. It's supposed to be 'Afro-American.' But wait even that ain't right. No, accordin' to that Jesse Jackson, it's 'sposed to be African-American—seven whole syllables. Don't know why they make it so difficult. It was hard enough learnin' to stop sayin' 'nigger.' But we'll adjust. It's the right thing to do. But where will it all end? Does this mean they'll change the old Bogart movie so that its Sam Shovel instead of Sam Spade? Does this mean we cain't say 'colored paper' anymore? Do we have to say 'chalk of color' now?

"But I ain't sure rhythm and blues is 'African-American' music. I still think it's black music or race music. Anyways Elijah represents African-American music, and the mantle represents the soul of African-American music. Also a mantel sets above the fireplace—the place where the fire burns.

"The soul of African-American music was give to Elvis. But when Elvis learned it meant sayin' good-bye to his kin, he couldn't do it. So he took them along! That's why his parents always stayed with him. Elvis owned no oxen but he had a job. Which he quit. That burned his boss. About the twelve yoke of oxen. Yoked in pairs that would mean twenty-four oxes. Twenty-four can be divided by eight and six. Elvis drove six and eight cylinder trucks for the electric company. All the signs fit.

"Oh, one last thing. Elvis couldn't barbecue and eat the pick-up trucks, but throughout his life he followed the example of Elisha cookin' them oxen. Elvis ate all that well-done bacon and those extra-well-done cheeseburgers.

"Other prophets in the Bible is also signs for Elvis." She reopened her Bible. Its binding had failed hundreds of openings earlier. Pages lay piled within the textured black paper cover. A dry, musty smell found my nostrils as Marie grabbed a loose page with a bright red square drawn on it. "In Ezekiel it says:

> The hand of the divine was upon me, and carried me out in the spirit, and set me down in the midst of the valley which was full a' bones. And it said unto me, son of man, can these bones lives?
>
> Again it said unto me, Prophesy upon these bones, and say unto them, O ye dry bones, hear the word of the divine. So I prophesied as I was commanded: and as I prophesied, there was a noise, and behold a shakin', and the bones came together, bone to his bone. (37:1, 4, 7)

"Now the dead bones represent rhythm and blues, which though alive to African-Americans, lay dead to whites—Lilian-Americans. Elvis brought these bones to life for whites. The bones, they shook. That's why Elvis started to shake, to twitch, bringin' his legs together, 'bone to his bone.' That's how Elvis moved—some say he did it to excite women—but it just ain't so. He did it cause he had a command from above: 'there was a noise, and behold a shakin'.' Elvis jerked and twitched like a four-foot catfish landed into a johnboat, about to get clobbered with a oar.

"I got to talk about another prophet: Amos, but to do so I got to explain Bible history. I compared Memphis to Jerusalem. In the Bible, after the reign a' Solomon the kingdom of Israel split. The southern part became the kingdom of Judah with Jerusalem as its capital. The northern part became the kingdom of Israel—they hogged the name 'Israel' for theirselves. Well this too is a symbol. For the state of Tennessee can be divided with a southern Kingdom of Judah with the capital of Memphis and a Northern Kingdom of Israel with a capital of Nashville. One more thing proves this. Remember how Danny, Danny Thomas kept pitchin' for his hospital in Memphis—St. Jude. That proves that Memphis represents the capital of Judah. And once Elvis donated a boat to the hospital for old Danny boy.

"This all ties in with Humes High School on North Manasas Street. Not only representin' a tribe of Israel, Manassas was the first battle of the Civil War—also called Bull Run. Now a' course the Civil War split the U.S. just like Israel split."

I began to tire of her arguments. How much longer would this bull run?

Marie continued, "In the Bible the Northern Kingdom set up an altar of idolatry at Bethel and worshipped a golden calf. In Nashville they worshipped a calf by singin' farm and cowboy songs. In the Bible the priests of Bethel rejected the true prophet, Amos. Just so, the priests of the false shrine of music at Nashville, the Grand Ole Opry, rejected Elvis. "The priest Amaziah hollered at Amos," she quoted, "'O thou seer, go, flee thee away into the land of Judah, and there eat bread, and prophesy there: but prophesy not again any more at Bethel.' (Amos 7:12-13) At the Opry they told Elvis to flee and go back to drivin' his truck, tellin' him, 'This ain't the king's chapel, and it ain't the king's court.' But, just as fate punished the Northern Kingdom with invadin' hordes a' murderous Assyrians, so fate punished the record industry of Nashville with invadin' hordes a' Rock and Roll Britains."

By now the fly had exhausted itself on the curling flypaper streamer. I surmised it had gone through five stages of dying and had accepted its fate for it seemed to wait patiently though death might be days away. For a brief moment I considered walking over and putting the fly out of its misery, but I could not figure out how to do it without becoming glued to the fly paper. I had seen too many old comedy sketches and cartoons to not be wary of the stuff. I could easily imagine myself staring at the flypaper asking, "Why am I stuck on you?". Perhaps though, in pondering mercy killing, I projected my own desire for deliverance from this late night oratory. But I could not screw up my courage to the sticking place. And so I sat.

CHAPTER 4

ELVIS

THE CONQUEST OF CANAAN

Marie grabbed the coffeepot and refilled my cup. I ached to ask, "Woman, where do you come from?". But timidity held my tongue. Only a half-inch remained in the glass coffeepot but she set it on the hot burner as she returned to her hotter discourse:

"Some is born great, some earn greatness, some have greatness dumped upon 'em like bales fallin' from the hayloft. And so with Elvis. Greatness picked up his scent, dogged him, chased him, and finally treed him.

"I have shown many Bible signs for Elvis. The book a' Joshua, where Israel conquers the Promised Land, foretells the next part: how Elvis became number one in Rock and Roll in Memphis and then across the country. Vidi, vino, da-vinci! He came, he sang, he conquered! But there's one weighty difference. The Israelites conquered Canaan—the Promised Land—after they got out of Egypt. It happened in reverse for Elvis: he conquered Memphis 'fore the Egyptians enslaved him."

"Enslaved in Egypt? Elvis Presley?" I had never known such levels of bewilderment.

"Now just hold on. You's gettin' ahead a' the story, hun'. As I said, it's backwards. First Elvis had to conquer Canaan."

Resigned to my fate I nodded for Marie to continue.

"1956 marked the turnin' point. Like a angry junkyard dog pullin' 'gainst his chain, Elvis tore free and broke loose. A' course

'56 is prefiggered in the middle letters of the name of Elvis, l, v, i—fifty-six in Latin.

"In '56 one overweight, cigar-smokin', con man and bullshit artist, one big boss man—Colonel Tom Parker, took control of Elvis. Parker, a man choked with ambition; a knave, a rascal, a browbeater of brokered feats. How like a fawnin' Republican he looked. Parker once tried to sell Kaopectate to the Harlem Globetrotters. He learned his art in the carny towns and knew how to promote 'his boy,' Elvis, with billboards, radio, posters, midgets, elephants—anythin' he could find to sing the praises of Elvis. For sweet's the uses of advertisin'.

"The Presley family had a husband, wife, and son; movin' from one place to another, like the Bible holy family. The Presleys found rejection just like the innkeeper rejected the holy family. That's why in '56 Elvis recorded 'Heartbreak Hotel' for RCA: a hit, a very palpable hit. Many rejected his music. A Herodian music critic attacked 'Heartbreak Hotel,' 'It is a tale told by an idiot, full a' sound and fury, signifyin' nothin'.'

"With 'Heartbreak Hotel' all hell broke loose. The Hillbilly Cat metamorphasized into the Memphis Flash. Events moved faster than hogs at feedin' time. Elvis made more records. Then who'd believe it: Elvis on national television—a lean, raw-boned rascal a' courage and audacity! Elvis played the Dorsey Brothers' **Stage Show**—right after two dozen, scant'ly-clad woman xylophone players—then **The Milton Berle Show** with old Uncle Miltie, then **The Steve Allen Show**. We all knows the shameful events that transpired on Stevereno's show.

"The Bible book of Acts tells of the first Christian martyr, Stephen. Well Stephen Allen martyred Elvis. On the show Elvis played a country bumpkin, Tumbleweed. It's amazin' city folk still believe those rural stereotypes. Then Steve made Elvis wear a tuxedo and sing to a hound dog. Allen blasphemed the innocent Elvis. I wrote a nasty letter to Allen. It looked like death for Elvis but as the first martyr, Stephen, rose in heaven, Elvis rose like the Flagstaff from the ashes."

Had Marie taken a breath I would have corrected her, but either she breathed so quickly between sentences that one hardly noticed, or she had mastered the embryonic breathing of Chinese Daoists and took oxygen directly through her skin. On she went:

"It became obvious that the biggest show on TV—Ed Sullivan—had to have Elvis, though Ed said he wouldn't touch Elvis with a ten-foot pole. One a' my girlfriends, Bernice—we called her Bernie, called that statement a . . . How'd she put it? . . . oh yea, 'gross metaphor of latent homo-eroticism.' Now what the hell's that mean?

"On the third Ed Sullivan show, to clean up the image of Elvis, they had him sing 'Peace in the Valley,' a religious song. But if ya asks me, Elvis had in mind a diff'rent kind a' peace in a diff'rent kind a' valley, if ya knows what I mean."

Actually I did not know what she meant, but I nodded so she would move on. Which she of course did:

"Well on that third show old Ed told the cameramen to only shoot Elvis from the waist up. But that only made Elvis do his bumpin' and a grindin' with a tad bit more intensity.

"All these events had been foretold. Stunned music critics pondered, 'Upon what beat doth this our Elvis feed, that he is grown so great.' Beatniks in smoke-filled coffeehouses chanted to bongo music." She slapped out a rhythm on the counter. "'If like man, he don't keep, step with his comrades, likely it be, it's be-cause, man he hears, a different drummer. Let him step, the cool beat he hears, however measured, or far out.'

"'Bout this time Elvis started buyin' Cadillacs, figurin' 'This is livin'.' He took great care in keeping them cars polished and shinin' brightly; Elvis waxed greater and greater.

"A' course there's much symbolism in the early career of Elvis. The gospels start with John the Baptist—J the B—at the river Jordan. When Elvis started his career—got baptized into stardom—who stood alongside? The Jordanaires, singin' backup. It's all signs. Although if ya look at the Jordanaires in the old TV shows and newsreels, why they's the most uncool lookin' men ya ever did see, in those loud plaid jackets. Each one could pass for the first Darrin on Bewitched.

"Bernie once explained the importance of 1956 for Elvis. She wrote this," Marie read from the back of an old "I Like Ike" handbill with "Like" crossed out and "Hate" written in: "'When in the course a' human events it becomes necessary for one people to dissolve the big bands which have connected them with another era, and to assume among the electrical powers of earth, separate and equal radio stations, to which the laws of broadcast and broadcast listeners entitle them, a decent respect for the opinions of womankind require that they should declare the causes which impel them to Elvis.' Well we teenage girls couldn't rightly 'xplain the causes, so we screamed at the top of our lungs." She placed the handbill in her Bible on top of an EISENHOWER and NIXON handbill with EISENHOWER crossed through and NIXON's name ferociously scratched out. She continued:

"In 1956 Elvis went to Hollywood to make his first movie, **Love Me Tender**. He befriended a handsome young actor, Nick Adams—another symbol a' course. Many saw Elvis as like a brother of Jesus, meaning Elvis must a' been the new Adam as Paul says in his letters. Who then represents the old Adam, who died and passed away? Nick Adams a' course, who played Johnny Yuma on the TV series **The Rebel**. Adams died in 1968—they said from a drug overdose. The perishable Adam gave way to the new Adam: Elvis. Sadly, Adams' death prefiggered Elvis' death. Tragic destiny killed the first Adam, evil fate haunted the second.

"Ya see Elvis came as the Messiah: the promised one to save our nation. Born a' the root of Jesse—I already 'xplained that. But Elvis must a' been preceded by a John the Baptist, a 'voice cryin' out in the wilderness.' First I thought Vernon Presley represented John the Baptist 'cause both went to prison." Marie explained. "But then it came clear, not Vernon Presley but Jerry Lee Lewis baptized a generation to Rock and Roll. And no baptism of water, Lewis baptized with fire: Great Balls a' Fire. Lewis came forth like the fiery chariot of Elijah with the fiery wheels of Ezekiel. This all shows Elvis as the Messiah."

Trying to make sense of her wild imaginings, I asked, "Did not Herod behead John the Baptist? Jerry Lee Lewis lives."

"Yes John the Baptist died," she explained methodically. "Although he started it all, he stepped aside to let the greater take the lead. But Jerry Lee Lewis did not lose his head; they crucified him. The English press killed his career when they learned of his thirteen-year-old wife. Lewis stepped aside—forced aside—and the greater one took his place. One to whom Lewis was unworthy even to untie his guitar string."

Deciding to attempt control of this conversation I asked, "How did you learn all of this?"

"I read the Bible, I read the papers, and livin' in Memphis I knows what goes on. But mostly I figger it out myself."

"How many times have you seen Elvis in person?" I asked.

"About forty different times."

"Did you ever meet Elvis?" I asked.

"Yes several times. My mother, Sylvia, ran a beauty salon. One day in '54 while I was a sweepin', Elvis come in. Mama told me later she couldn't believe the way he wore his hair all slicked back. She feared that pomade goo might jam her scissors and gunk up her comb. But she held her tongue, she needed money bad ever since my father run off leavin' her to raise four kids alone: one boy, two little girls, and me. I still recall with the vividness a' seein' my first chicken butcherin', how Elvis looked at me. Somethin' burned in his steely eyes. I, I cain't describe it. I saw a mystery wantin' to be explained. He looked strong and powerful, yet a helpless child— at the same time! His eyes looked right through me. Then he reached out and he touched me. A touch, a touch; I do confess it. He put his hand in mine.

"That was the first I saw him. In the next months I spied him walkin' the streets and drivin' his truck. I remember this time well 'cause in October of '54 we got word that Pa had died. He'd left us long before and I hadn't seen him in years. We got a telegram that he'd plowed his old Plymouth into a Sycamore tree after gettin' tanked up on Vitameatavegamin.

"At this time Elvis started doin' concerts and shows. I went to see him anytime I could. With my older girlfriends we'd drive to see Elvis at the 'Louisiana Hayride.'"

By this point I had tired of all the detail this woman could recall about the young Elvis. I longed for a break, for a few moments at least. To my horror the conversation took an even more bizarre turn: Marie made a confession.

"You've been patient listenin' to this, hun'. And I know you is a bit skeptical, but no accident brought ya here. It is your destiny! Despite your disbelief, I is sure ya hear my words and they sink deep within. I trust ya. So I can tell the secret that's been locked within my bosoms for two score and one years. In 1956 I had sexual relations with Elvis Presley."

"What?" I sat stunned.

"Yes I had sex with Elvis. A Tuesday in the month a' . . . . It's too personal to give the exact date. In the fifties Elvis did some furious tourin' in the South. Me and my friends followed his tours and hung 'round the motels where Elvis stayed. We knew there was the chance, not real big for any one particular girl, but a chance nonetheless, that Elvis would send one a' his men to fetch a girl or two to be with him. Well one night in Charlotte, North Carolina, I found myself first in line outside the motel door—beginner's luck. Someone comes out, tells me to come along. I was chose for Elvis. I got lucky—I got fetched."

"You slept with Elvis?" The stun had not worn off.

"Don't get all upcited, don't get all shook up, and don't look at me that way," Marie growled back. "I's a good girl, I is. I ain't no strumpet; but of life as honest as you. And it is crude, false, and common to say I 'slept' with Elvis. No, in truth, I became one with the King.

"The beauty of Elvis whelmed over me: a beauty described by the Bible in trout-stream clarity:

> My beloved is white and ruddy, the chiefest among ten
> thousand.
> His name spoken is a spreadin' perfume.
> His head is as the most fine gold, his locks are bushy, and
> black as a raven.
> His eyes are as the eyes of doves by the rivers of waters,
> washed with milk, and fitly set.
> His cheeks are as a bed a' spices, as sweet flowers:
> His lips like lilies, droppin' sweet smellin' myrrh.
> His hands are as gold rings set with beryl: his belly is as
> bright ivory overlaid with sapphires.
> His legs are as pillars a' marble, set upon sockets of fine gold:
> his countenance is as Lebanon, excellent as cedars.
> His mouth is most sweet: yea, he is altogether lovely.
> This is my beloved, and this is my friend, O daughters of
> Jerusalem.
> (Song of Solomon 5:10-16)

No torn Bible page did Marie need, only the memory of well-rehearsed words repeated countless times in lonely moments. Her eyes drifted heavenward. After a long pause she brought them down to my plane of purgatory and asked, "Now darlin', don't that describe Elvis exactly? Look at Elvis' sneerin' lip curled up, ready to drool forth sweet smellin' myrrh. Jerusalem means City of Peace. Daughters of Jerusalem could mean fans like me who wanted to give all to the King—'daughters of piece.' Elvis wore gold rings and his belly shined bright as ivory overlaid with sapphires. That's Elvis in his white Las Vegas rhinestone-studded jumpsuits. 'Course the name of Elvis spreads like fragrant perfume. I own 56 bottles of Elvis perfume. Here, smell!" She thrust her forearm into my nose. I detected a faint sweetness buried under layered odors of onion, mustard, fried fish, and perspiration. She withdrew her arm but not her voice.

"I had my pungent moment of ecstasy. Oh, Elvis! Oh, suave new world that has such people in it! I thought he was playin' for keeps. I kept thinkin', 'please don't stop lovin' me.' He had tasted my fruits, had drunk full measure, and when he consummated his gruntin' and gaspin', he told me to get my things and get out. Pretty rude, but he was King, and I had serviced him as a loyal subject. What a world a' hambone and spinach it is, though, ain't it!

"'Course my Ma never found out 'bout this, 'cause she'd a killed me. Very strict, my Ma considered a two-piece bathin' suit immoral. So concerned 'bout modesty, she used to mail sewin' kits a' thread, needles, and buttons to Harry Bellafonte so he could fix his shirts."

"Did you see Elvis again?" I asked. I do not know why.

"Well not in that manner, and I missed my period the next month. I felt both the terror and excitement of hell as I wondered whether one so lowly as I might bear the fruit a' the loins of Elvis within my very womb. I went to see Dr. Roland V. Wade. But alas, 'ol Dr. Roe told me I carried no child. Had it been so, I'd 'a written a book by now. Ah, Elvis!"

She began to sing a soft mournful blues:

> When woman stoops around to fool,
> And finds too late that men betray.
> What charm can soothe her melancool?
> What art can wash her blues away?

I drained the last drops of my coffee. My brain spun dizzily as this absurd woman poured out intimate details of her life faster than she poured out coffee. I couldn't believe what I heard. What is more, I thought, "She thinks I still care." I blurted out, "No more! I do not believe a word of this!"

"Blasphemy!" she screamed in anguish and grabbed her uniform lapels to rent her garments. Scarlet shot up from her neck, covering her face. "Search your truth, ya know it to be feelin's!" she snarled as fire seemed to flash from her eyes.

Terror surged within me. I stammered, "All right . . . all

right . . . I do not mean I do not believe . . . I just need more time . . . to think about all this . . . to let it sink in."

My desperate lie worked. Marie calmed down. She released her lapels. My life stopped flashing before me.

CHAPTER 5

ELVIS

ON MOUNT ZION

As the criminal returns to the crime scene, so Marie returned to spinout her discourse: "I knows you is anxious to go. But I've much of importance to say. Really, you overestimate your distraction. After all Memphis weren't built in no day. When I'm over, you can leave, hun'. Fate carried ya to my door—remain you must. 'Cause as the great guru Maharishi Yogi Berra used to say, 'Karma ain't over 'til it's over.'

"I've deciphered the year 1956, now I must 'xplain 1957. Elvis lived in a ranch home on Audubon Avenue. They called 'em ranch houses, but weren't no livestock for miles. Every Elvis fan knew the house. The street name itself symbolized all the girls, girls, girls that went there on Elvis reconnaissance and to find out what's happenin'. For we learned from the Beatles' movies a few years later the British slang word for girl: bird.

"I made frequent excursions to the home. There I'd linger and yearn to talk to or even see the great and noble Elvis. One evenin', it gets late—it's midnight, or there 'bouts—me and some friends dawdlin' for hours, and me more bored than a sore-necked chicken that cain't peck a lick. Well, my friends dared me to go sneak 'round back a' the house. They knew I weren't no angel but too big for my britches. And I must admit I was three sheets to the wind . . . no, better make that four sheets.

"I tore off up the driveway, through the carport, past the

Cadillac that Elvis gave his mother—which sat idle, it rarely idled—past the Harley-Davidson, back 'round to the patio—black as roof pitch, 'cept for the still glowin' barbecue coals. I stood among the aluminum patio furniture, not knowin' what to do. So I dove into the pool for a midnight swim. I swam across fast, like ya would in a icy spring-fed crick, and climbed out the other side, thinkin', 'Marie, you better run.' I dashed through the carport. Shoutin' broke out inside the house, 'Who's out there?' and 'Vernon, get your gun!' I ran even faster. Meanwhile my friends had gotten into the car and were arguin' over leavin' me there as a practical joke. Luckily they was still arguin' when I dove in the back window yellin', 'Get the hell out a' here,' shakin' like a leaf on a cottonwood tree. We squealed off into the distance like a speedway racecar as the disturbed house woke from its fitful sleep.

"Well 'cause a' stuff like that, Elvis had to move. He needed privacy and his neighbors wanted quiet—they didn't give a damn for Elvis, his Ma and his Pa. It don't take much figurin' to know the problems a' three country folk don't 'mount to a hill a' beans and hominy in this crazy world. Elvis went a house huntin' again. Not wanting no little cabin on a hill he found a mansion over the hill: the land of Grace. Elvis laid eyes on the house and said, 'I think I'm gonna like it here; this is my heaven.' Elvis bought Graceland and Memphis became the best of all possible worlds. 'Course Graceland needed fixin'. They had to patch it up in places. But it became a home of memories.

"Now how does one explain grace? Well grace's the favor shown by the divine to us earthly ones. The divine gave Elvis as a gift from heaven to this poor lonely world. Graceland became a sign a' this gift of amazin' grace and the center of the Promised Land, the Mount Zion a' Memphis: a house that has everythin'.

"A' course ya knows 'bout Mount Zion in the Bible. On that knob those Israelites raised up a glorious temple in the holy city of Jerusalem. Elvis dedicated Graceland as his holy temple. The Bible temple had courtyards fenced off 'round it. Foreigners could only loiter in the farthest out courtyard. Jewish womenfolk could go in the next closest courtyard. Only Jewish men could go into the next. Priests, they alone could go into the temple buildin'. Into the center a' the temple building, the Holy a' Holies, only the High Priest could go.

"Well they corduroyed off Graceland like that. Before Elvis died, we commoners could only go to the sidewalk where stood the music gates like a giant 'Do Not Disturb' sign. Members of the Elvis clan could go into Graceland. Among these, only certain people could go to the upper room, the cenacle, where Elvis the High Priest lived. The Holy a' Holies in the temple had no windows, it was completely dark. Elvis' bedroom had heavy drapes and tinfoiled windows to keep out sunlight. Near the end Elvis figgered, 'Graceland is all that I am.'

"Some say, that on the day Elvis died, those window curtains tore from top to bottom and sunlight streamed in. Uncertainty exists regardin' this account 'cause of the chaos of the scene: people runnin' all over; the hunkered-up, blue Elvis; paramedics walin' away at his chest; Lisa Marie runnin' 'round. I believe it. Some use Bible language to say those curtains was rent from top to bottom. I think that confuses folk who then think Elvis was cheap and had rent-to-own curtains.

"The torn curtains meant that the spirit of Elvis could no longer be confined to earthly flesh, livin' in that inner sanctum bedroom; but would rise, go forth, and fill the entire universe. Some even heard a celestial voice when the curtains tore: 'Elvis has left the body.' The sunlight symbolizes the multitude a' fans streamin' in mighty torrents into Graceland to walk the very halls where the King once strode in regal magnificence.

"But I've jumped ahead a' the story. I went from talkin' 'bout Elvis buyin' Graceland to the death of Elvis. In the late 50s we'd stand for hours at the Graceland fence. On several most sublime occasions he came and spoke to us. When I didn't see him I'd pull up handfuls a' grass—sentimental me. But I figgered, 'anythin' that's part a' you, Elvis, is part a' me.' Now this could be stealin'. And I wondered if it were a sin to take Elvis' grass. But I finally figgered that if ya only took one small handful each Saturday, enough to feed a kid goat, that'd be OK. I had two bushels of the green, green grass of homesite Graceland in my closet at home. My Ma, not knowin' 'bout my collection, thought she smelled a compost heap in my bedroom and complained: 'Shall I be flouted by dunghill rooms?'

"In later years Elvis had horses. In majestic splendor, seated atop a blazin' saddled Palomino named Rising Sun, Elvis came forth as the great Sun King to bend down and speak to us, his lowly and unworthy subjects who waited at the gates in anxious expectation of his audience. Some think that horse was a gelding. I do not for a moment believe Elvis rode a horse without balls! Then Elvis'd put his horse in the barn, the house a' the Risin' Sun.

"We didn't just see Elvis from the gates a' Graceland. We saw him in town too. A friend a' mine, Marcie, saw Elvis in a auto showroom. She went in, 'Aren't you Elvis?' But Elvis said 'no,' so my friend apologized and left, but Elvis chased her out to the sidewalk and said, 'Hey, little girl, whom seek ye? I am he.' Much as Elvis wanted to be hid, he wanted to be revealed.

"Despite such sightin's, we made regular evenin' novenas—Marcie called 'em—to Graceland." Marie pulled out an old hand held fan of white cardboard stapled to a flat wooden handle. Across one side it read "Most Reliable Funeral Home—Leave Your Kin in Our Hands." However, during printing the fan had shifted slightly resulting in letters with a double, ghostlike image. Marie turned the fan over to read penciled words. She explained, "As we walked up to Graceland we used to sing:

> I was glad when they said unto me, Let us go up to the house of Elvis.
> Our feet shall stand within thy gates of music notes, O, Graceland.
> Graceland is builded as a city, high on a hill.
> There the people go up, the people of Elvis, to give thanks for the songs of Elvis.

> For there are set up the gold records of judgment, the gold records of Elvis.
> Pray for the peace of Graceland, they shall prosper that love thee.
> Peace be within thy walls, and prosperity within thy palace.
> For my brethren and companions' sakes, I will now say, Peace be within thee.
> Because of the house of Elvis I will seek thy good.

"My friend Bernie put it best one day in 1973 as we wiled and sat at the Graceland gates, playin' stud poker. She looked at the mansion pencilly and then with great eloquence spoke forth, 'In a jumbo-sized sense, we can not dedicate, we can not consecrate, we can not halo this ground. A brave man, livin', struggles here to consecrate it, far above our dirt poor power to add or subtract.' I think that sums it all up."

Had she finished her discourse? Had this agony ended? I jumped up, grabbed my wallet to pay and exit. I thanked her as quickly as possible, "This was . . . impressive, yes . . . you have impressive words and . . . ideas . . . . And if we never meet again well, it's been nice." But I had not stepped far enough away from the counter. Riveted by Marie's eyes, I froze.

Marie snarled, "Your time hasn't come yet baby, you can make the mornin'." Then with Ninja-like dexterity she reached back over her shoulder and blindly grabbed a potato masher, circled it twice around her elbow, arm, and shoulder, then thrust it forward at my sternum, down my shirt, shattering each button until the masher lodged behind my belt buckle. With an upward jerk she lifted me off my feet and back onto the revolving stool. A downward wrist twist freed the masher, which she flipped skyward, snarling, "To thine own shelf be threw." It twirled twice before landing behind her back in position on the utensil rack. I rubbed my whiplashed neck; grateful she did at least twist me loose and grateful she hadn't gone for my groin.

Marie wiped her hands, "I used to work in one a' those Japanese, 'chop it up in front a' the customers' restaurants named 'Semper Fugu'—back in my salad bar days, when I was green in judgment—until one evenin' my knife lost the handle rivet durin' a' high speed airborne onion chop. The rivet shot out, blinding the right eye a' one customer, the blade flipped loose and lopped the ear off another. The ear landed smack dab 'mongst the shrimp fryin' on the table griddle. A lady sittin' at the table absorbed the whole scene and passed out, droppin' her two-week-old, $5,000 lifted face right unto the griddle where it browned with amazin' speed to the song of the sizzlin' shrimp. Her diamond necklace did a flip, flop, and fry down the griddle.

"So I gave up foreign food for this place. Although I could a' been a bartender. Ya see, ya can learn more 'bout folks in a place where people can talk instead a' strugglin' to use chopsticks. I've listened so much I could be a shrink. I ain't got no degree to prove it. But this greasy spoon is my Yale College and my Harvard. This is my purgatory, even though it might seem nothin'ville."

I dared not move an inch or say a thing. Confident she possessed my undivided attention, she resumed, "Now there is many Bible references to the Mount Zion of Elvis." She quoted from memory, "In Psalm 102 it says:

> I am like an owl of the desert;
> I am a barn owl among the ruins.
> I am without sleep and I moan.
> Like a starlin', alone I sit on the tin rooftop.

"That's Elvis in detail. He slept durin' the day and lived durin' the night: a night owl. 'Cause Elvis figgered, 'What hath night to do with sleep? Night hath better sweets to prove.' An 'owl among the ruins', that's Elvis at Graceland with its ancient Greek-like pillars. Elvis wanted a home with character and not some modern prairie house built by Frank Lloyd Weber.

"Sir, ya seem educated. Why'd those ancient Greeks build those ruins? Seems a damn waste of effort. Anyways the passage says, 'I am without sleep and I moan.' I'm not sure 'moan' describes the singin' of Elvis, . . . then again, maybe it does.

"Many biblical passages symbolize Graceland. The Bible always talks 'bout the wilderness. And so Elvis built his jungle room. The Israelites wandered in the wilderness before enterin' the Promised Land and we all know 'bout a forty-day wilderness temptation. The book of Hosea talks 'bout bein' 'led into the wilderness where the heart will be spoken to.' Elvis took his girlfriend into the jungle room as the Bible says, 'Therefore, behold, I will allure her, and bring her into the wilderness, and speak comfortably unto her.' (Hosea, 2:14)

"Another biblical symbol for Graceland is the destruction of Jericho. Elvis had a little house at Graceland, way in back. Elvis set it on fire and like Joshua fittin' the battle of Jericho, Elvis circled the house six times on a bulldozer. On the seventh time he blasted the horn and rammed the house right after someone had run in and grabbed the plumbin' fixtures. For the Good Book describes: 'They burnt the city with fire, all that was therein: only the silver, and the gold, and the vessels of brass and of iron, they put into his treasury.'" (Joshua, 6:24)

I shifted my position on the revolving stool. The torn red-marble vinyl cover caused some pain. The stool to the right looked in better condition. I pondered sliding over to it, then thought better of it.

Marie continued, "With Elvis dead the meanin' a' Graceland becomes clear. Elvis has gone before us to the eternal Land of Grace to prepare rooms in that mansion. He did this first in his Graceland mansion. He opened it up to his friends: the chosen ones. Many of his friends was sinners, but that's the key. Sinners will be welcome in the mansion Elvis prepares for us in the sky. Elvis sang 'bout all this in 'Return to Sender.' On the deepest level the song's about the journey of the immortal soul, returnin' to the heavenly mansion from whence it came.

"Back to the live Elvis! What a great piece of iron—just as he moved to Graceland, tragedy struck: Elvis got drafted!"

CHAPTER 6

ELVIS

ENSLAVED IN EGYPT

The corner of my eye caught the orange glow of a neon light outside the window. With a fizzle it blinked out. Since repair seemed to never frequent this place I surmised it would remain forever in darkness, unless fortune would rescue it for a yuppie rathskeller wet bar. I pondered the neon's dim future.

Marie noticed my gaze, "Alas, how is't with you, that you do bend your eye to the Vacancy sign? We got more important things to consider, hun'. I've detailed how Elvis consecrated Graceland as Mount Zion in the Promised Land of Memphis. But many heroes of old left their Promised Land. When famine came, Abraham left for Egypt. The family a' Jacob went to Egypt, also 'cause of famine. Matthew's gospel tells of another family that packed off to Egypt. It's obvious as a footprint in a cow pie that Elvis would leave Graceland for Egypt," Marie explained.

"Oh, the Egyptian slavery you mentioned earlier. I did not know Elvis went to Egypt," I said.

"No, ya fool, Elvis didn't go to Egypt," Marie snapped again. "Egypt symbolizes the slavery of Elvis. The United States Army enslaved Elvis! They drafted him, locked him up, banished him to a distant land, and silenced the Florence Nightingale that brightened our days." Recalling these events brought pain to Marie's face. But she did not stop, "Now if ya recall in the Bible . . . ya read your Bible daily, don't ya?"

I stumbled to respond. Assuming I would answer "no," Marie did not wait:

"As I said, the Bible tells how the kin a' Jacob—the nation of Israel—sojourned to Egypt 'cause a' this famine and the evil, power-mad, pyramid-fetished Egyptians enslaved them. They enslaved our dear Elvis not 'cause of famine but 'cause of a draft. Closely examine and the connection 'comes clear: in the ancient world strong desert winds—drafts—caused famines.

"They sent the bound Elvis to Germany, another sign. Two parts made up ancient Egypt, a upper kingdom and a lower kingdom; so Germany had been divided into East and West parts.

"But one close to Elvis—at his right hand—should 'a kept Elvis free. That man did nothin'. Just like Judah sellin' his brother into slavery, it appears the Colonel maneuvered Elvis into the army to clean up, or should I say 'sabotage' the Elvis of real Rock and Roll. Once in the army, Parker should 'a got Elvis into Special Services."

"Special Services? The Green Berets?" I asked.

"No, that's Special Forces. Entertainers go into Special Services. Instead a' drivin' tanks, shootin' bazookas, bivouacin', sloppin' chow, or marchin' over chip and dale; they goes 'round entertainin' and foolin' people into thinkin' it's right fun to be in the army. Its a kind a' propaganda. Parker should 'a got Elvis into Special Services and out a' that jeep. But that fox, the Colonel, kept Elvis out 'cause he didn't want Elvis singin' without him gettin' his manager's cut."

Needing a break, I asked, "Listen, would you mind if I taped this? I have a cassette recorder in the car."

"Well, I don't know." She thought for a moment. "Aw go ahead, this is the world's only chance to know the truth. I may never again speak these words. Get your recorder. Make it so! You goes out to your car, but ya better come back!" I got up from the stool and headed for the door, but without turning my back on her. I kept my eyes on her eyes. As I walked backwards through the door she added from a distance, "'Twere well it were done quickly. If you don't come back, I'll..."

"I'll be back," I muttered. Fear of her would have kept me there, but now intrigue and curiosity held me. I stepped into the cool night and walked to my car past the old Cadillac desperately yearning for Earl Scheib. Fumbling for the ceiling light and rooting through the boxes in my back seat, I found the recorder and a new tape of Kachaturian's Sabre Dance. "Oh what the hell," I murmured. I stuffed a scrap of paper into the hole in the cassette so I could record over Kachaturian. I headed back into the restaurant. My eyes required readjustment. Marie stood refilling the Cory machine and ignoring the empty pot boiling itself dry. Even before I got settled, Marie continued:

"They inducted Elvis on August 24, 1958—Black Monday we called it—cryin' time for Elvis fans. Parker, that old carnival-man manager, turned it into a circus. As Elvis got his medical check and haircut, Parker had photographer to the right of him, photographer to the left of him. It must a' been humiliatin' for Elvis who sat silent as a lamb before its shearers.

"It amazed me how that old carny man, Parker, used the Army to promote his boy. I suppose a man's gotta scheme; it comes with the territory. Course Nostradamus predicted..."

"Nostradamus?!" I cut her off. "He predicted Elvis?"

Marie looked shocked. "For an educated man I's surprised ya don't know the prophecies of Nostradamus."

"Wait a minute," I defended myself. "I know about Nostradamus. He lived in the 1500s and wrote hundreds of passages which people claim have predicted the future."

Marie looked pleased. "Well, I'll be, you do know. Nostradamus prophesied Elvis exactly." I glanced at her Bible. Had she written Nostradamus quotes into the Pentateuch? No, she bent over and rooted under that mysterious counter. A certain curiosity urged me to lean over and look. But my wild imagination conjured up black and white horror movie images of a bony hand reaching for my throat and dragging me into a dark abyss. I tried to force my brain to shift to the buxom horror movie heroines that were to be rescued, but to no avail. I shuddered. Marie, having found what she sought, stood up. She laid on the counter no object of terror but rather the very symbol of American cultural achievement: a green-stamp booklet. For years American families saved green-stamps from department stores, pasting them in these booklets which were traded for blenders and mixers. Marie's tattered book held few stamps, but numerous penciled-in Nostradamus quotes.

"Nostradamus predicted Colonel Parker using the army to promote Elvis:

> An ambitious colonel plots,
> To seize the great army,
> Against his royal Monarch false invention,
> He will be uncovered under the arbor. (IV, 62)

By now Marie's revelations had almost lost their power to shock. She continued, "During all their years together the Colonel never told his plans to Elvis, his Monarch. That's what 'false invention' means. After Elvis died, his estate sued Parker 'cause they discovered Parker used Elvis as a money tree, without regard for Elvis. Ya see, 'arbor' means 'tree.'

"Parker set up that photo-op haircut when they inducted Elvis. There's deeper meanin' to that clip job that made front-page news from the story of Ezekiel. Ezekiel cut off his hair and divided it in three portions. The army barber said he let the hair of Elvis mix in with the hair on the floor so no one could sell it. But t'ain't so. No, Elvis took his shaved-off hair—just like Ezekiel—and divided it into three parts. One part he burned, t'other part he cut up with his pocketknife, and the third he threw to the wind. This symbolized the fans of Elvis. One third a' his fans burned for Elvis. Another third cut up their record buyin' between Elvis and other singers. Wind blew away the last third. Elvis never regained the fans who left Rock and Roll for folk music, blown to the Weavers; Peter, Paul, and Mary; and the one blowin' in the wind: Bob Dylan.

"The haircut of Elvis also ties in with that manipulative bitch, Delilah, who wiled Samson into tellin' the source of his strength. She cut Samson's hair and he became weak and powerless. The Philistines bound him and threw him into a dungeon. So with Elvis, all that raw horniness, all that defiance—like he was flippin' the bird at middle-class American society; scornin' our parents' world as horse manure—all that disappeared as they shaved the head of Elvis like a captive goin' into exile. Oh, his hair grew back. Elvis did more singin'. But somethin' was gone forever. Elvis never was the same.

"They say a reporter asked Elvis if he felt sad and mournful goin' into the army. Elvis answered, 'No, no, no, no! Come, let's away to prison. I will sing like a bird in the cage.' If Elvis sang in the army we fans didn't hear a lick. We only got previously made recordin's: released, re-released, packaged, and repackaged—warmed over hash.

"In Genesis the family of Joseph sold him into slavery. The family of Elvis—this country—sent Elvis into slavery in Germany. The Midianites got Joseph; the Mediumites Tank Battalion got Elvis. The army tamed the wild Elvis. Joseph had his cloak a' many colors. Elvis wore bright colors. But when Elvis returned from the army to do movies, no more bright-stand-out clothes did we see, but rather blend-into-the-crowd clothes."

Marie grabbed my toast plate containing a few crust pieces. She looked pensively at the fragments, turned to the toaster and half-mumbled to me, "Tis a wonder, by your leavin's, Elvis was tamed so." She put two fresh pieces of toast on a clean plate and set them in front of me, then continued:

"In dull-green clothes, his voice silent, toutin' an Egyptian-slave haircut, our soldier boy, Elvis, stood before the meanest drill sergeant the army could muster who screamed: 'I am he, born to tame you Presley, and bring you from a wild Elvis to an Elvis conformable as other household idols—like Ricky Nelson.' But just as Joseph prospered in Egypt and got hisself a chariot; slowly but surely Elvis prospered, got hisself a jeep, and got to be sergeant. Meanwhile back at the ranch, in America, each fan cried out, 'Let my Elvis go!' But old Pharaoh hardened his heart—probably his arteries too—and wouldn't let Elvis go. Ya know who I mean by Pharaoh don't ya?"

"Pardon my ignorance, but I do not."

"Ike!"

"Ike?" Unbelievable! She had set her mouth for stun.

"Yes Ike! Eisenhower! He had a near-bald head and was elected twice, in '52 and '56. Each time he ran against and defeated Adlai Stevenson. Whether you voted Republican or Democrat you got a baldie. We'll never see that again. 'Cause after 1956 J. Edgar Hoover ordered that if anyone without a full head of hair tried to be President the FBI would make sure some accident happened. That's what they say.

"Look at those Pharaoh statues in history. Most a' them's bald too. Eisenhower looked like a Pharaoh, old Ramada hisself."

"Ramada? A hotel chain? Do you mean Ramses?" I questioned emphatically.

"Oh yea, that's right: Ramses," answered Marie. "Anyways, Ike looked just like Ramses." With that she pulled from her apron a torn **National Geographic** page picturing the statue of an ancient Egyptian figure. Then she placed an Eisenhower silver dollar next to it. The resemblance was striking.

"Now," she continued, "Ramses, they named those condoms after him. Now what gives people the fool idea that those ancients were better at sex? I simply do not know. I seen a picture a' Ramses. They got his embalmed body layin' in his pried-open coffin under glass. That dried-up-shriveled old man couldn't a' been much fun. I don't think old Egyptians were anything to brag about in bed. The same goes for the Trojans.

"If ya don't believe this 'bout Elvis and Ramses, go to downtown Memphis and look at the statue a' Ramses sittin' in front a' the pyramid. Now the Bible Pharaoh had dreams of seven fat cows and seven skinny cows. The skinny one is seven years a' famine. In the army Elvis did no recordin'. The fat cows represent the abundant recordin's before they drafted Elvis."

"But did not draftees in the 50s serve a two-year hitch?"

She clarified, "You're right, it weren't no seven years. Just seemed so."

As I finally finished my eggs, Marie went to a large pot on the stove. She stirred it and mumbled something like, "double, double, toil and trouble; fire burn and cauldron bubble." Perhaps I misunderstood her. She grabbed a ladle, filled a bowl with white mush, set the bowl in front of me. I looked confused.

"Grits," said Marie. "They come with breakfast."

I still looked confused for she explained, "Oh, you're a Yankee. Put butter, salt and pepper on them. You'll like 'em. One man who used to come here liked grits with ketchup. He said it made the charm a' the grits firm and good. We all thought him strange and foolish. We waitresses used to joke 'bout him in the back room: how he'd cool his grits with baboon's blood.

"They shipped Elvis off to Europe on the USS General Randall. Thanks to the rollin' sea, Elvis had trouble keepin' his lunch down. He was leavin' and heavin'. In Germany Elvis lived in the town of Bad Nauheim. I looked up that at the liberry. To my surprise they had a German dictionary right here in Tennessee. The word 'Bad' in Kraut means spa or bath. Must a' been bathhouses there. Anyways, near as I could reckon, Elvis hated the place 'cause the rest a' his life he never took a bath."

"What do you mean? Elvis must have taken baths or showers," I asked, vainly hoping that at least one of my questions would reduce my confusion.

"No, the King did not take baths," Marie explained. "He just wiped hisself down with a washcloth. A tabloid once called Elvis 'insecure,' sayin' that he doubted he existed—that Elvis didn't take baths so he could prove he existed just by takin' a whiff and sayin', 'I stink, therefore I is,' or 'foeto ergo sum.' The tabloid called this belief of Elvis . . . how'd they put it? . . . Oh yea . . . an 'ontology of odor.' But those tabloid writers shall suffer damnation for such blasphemy!

"Elvis lived off the army base with Vernon at number 14 Goethestrasse. The Kraut dictionary said 'strasse' means street, so 'Goethestrasse' means 'Goethe Street.' Goethe wrote a book **The Sorrows of Young Werther** 'bout a brokenhearted man. That's Elvis: brokenhearted after the recent death a' his mother."

Marie's argument baffled me until I deciphered that the word she pronounced as "go-the" was in actuality the name of the German writer Goethe, pronounced "gu-ta". Ignoring the puzzled look on my face Marie vectored off in yet another direction:

"Heaven inflicted ten awful plagues on the Egyptians for holdin' Israel captive. Moses called down plagues startin' with rivers turnin' to blood. Then frogs, lice, flies, pestilence, boils, hail, . . . let's see here, . . . one, two, three, four, five," she counted on her fingers. "Boils would be six, hail seven, . . . what was eight? Oh yea, locusts, then darkness, nine. Then the last plague: death a' the Egyptian first born. These plagues symbolized what happened when the army held Elvis captive: ten plagues struck the world a' Rock and Roll.

"For Elvis the first plague happened backwards: blood turned to a river. His beloved mother passed away. Gladys died! Ya see, when they drafted Elvis, tore her baby from her lovin' arms, it broke her heart. A' course the Bible predicted this. Simeon prophesied, 'Yea, a sword shall pierce through thy own soul.' (Luke 2:35) When Elvis went to boot camp Gladys moped 'round, drank more, and started quaffin' diet pills. Her body went to hell. She worried that Elvis'd be in danger from lightnin' and tempest; from earthquake, fire, and flood; from battle and murder, from sudden death. She worried herself to death. The army killed her just as if they'd clobbered her with a Screamin' Mimi. The army ripped the Presley family asunder, crushing the sickly-poor Gladys. Elvis lost his beloved Sattnin'."

"Sattnin?" The strange word confused me.

"Yes, Sattnin, the nickname Elvis used for his Ma. Elvis got army leave when Gladys lay dyin', but it came too late. Elvis couldn't get there in time, so he couldn't save her. For if he'd been there, she would had lived. As it was, she left this world a' agony and ecstasy 'fore her time was up.

"A crushed Elvis staggered through the funeral cryin' furiously. Some found it a scandal that Elvis wanted to see the feet of his Ma, Gladys, as she lay in the casket. But what's more natural? Did not the Master wash his followers' feet? Elvis called his mother's feet 'sooties'. Soot's a word for dirt. Well he couldn't really wash her feet, then and there, so he lamented over her sooties. His tears fell on them, such cryin' in the funeral chapel! Elvis wanted to shake the soot from his Ma's feet as she left the world that rejected her. Babylike, he cried and wailed seeing the beautiful flowers 'round the casket, cause he knew his Mama liked the roses.

"The blood that raised Elvis became a river a' tears: the first plague. Elvis went out and wept bitterly." Marie turned a page in her green-stamp booklet. "Nostradamus predicted this:

> Grieving his sad mother will die, skin and bones,
> He will die where flabby flesh sags. (IV, 7)

Nostradamus predicted Elvis hisself would die in obesity.

"Another Bible passage relates to Elvis and Gladys. In Genesis 32 Jacob wrestled with a angel. Now what does this mean? Clearly the angel represents Gladys. All his life, Elvis struggled with her. He wanted on the one hand to please her, yet on t'other to free hisself from her. He took away her poverty, but he could never make her truly happy, 'cause she couldn't stop worryin'. So ya see, Elvis's one-track heart had to wrestle with his Ma's influence. In the Bible wrestling story Jacob claims he saw God. Gladys was God to Elvis."

"Did not Jacob limp after his angel wrestling?" I asked.

"Precisely, ya see hun, after Gladys died, the heart and soul of Elvis limped ever after," she answered.

"If Jacob wrestling with an angel is an allegory for Elvis and his mother, are you suggesting Oedipal imagery?" I queried.

Marie's lips tensed, her face flashed scarlet. "Mister, I ain't sure I understands that question, and I ain't sure I want to understand! I just hope you ain't askin' what I think you is askin'. Please pose fewer questions! Absent thee from solicity awhile!"

Seeking escape from the minefield I had entered, I begged, "Please explain the second plague."

Peace and moderate pink returned to her face as she resumed, "For the second plague Moses sent frogs, and I's pretty sure this is when Elvis had an army pass to visit Paris. Ya know what they call those Frenchies. 'Parently Elvis spent a good part a' his visit with chorus girls, in amongst the frog legs. They might've been can-can dancers in a seedy part a' Paris in which case it'd been Elvis in the Underworld. Elvis only got to France, he ain't never been to Spain.

"Moses flicted off the Egyptians with the third plague: gnats, a calamity for Elvis and all a' Rock and Roll. Now gnats, some Bibles say 'lice,' cain't hurt ya directly, they drives ya insane. This plague refers to reporters—gnats—driving Jerry Lee Lewis crazy in England and ruining his career. And the whole beef was 'cause Lewis married his thirteen-year-old cousin. That is gall! Them hypocritical, snooty-assed Brits! What the hell they got to complain 'bout? They had all kinds of royalty marryin' underaged relatives. How many rules did Henry VIII break? Near as I figger, they ruined Jerry Lee Lewis to get back at us for winnin' the Revolutionary War.

"Next on Moses's smitin' list came flies. Fear of flyin' plagued Elvis. When he got back from Germany he left New York on the night train to Memphis. This plague struck Little Richard, whose bright white-toothed grin and big piercing white eyes look like a African Wadabe dancer. Years ago, he looked out his airplane window and saw the engine burnin'. Figurin' it a message from God, he quit music and studied for the ministry. Little Richard pulled out a' Rock and Roll. He later came back, but wound up makin' taco commercials, singin' 'Run for the Border.' That's what Chuck Berry did with a fourteen-year-old girl. He got arrested for breakin' the Mann Act 'gainst transportin' minors—I don't mean U.M.W.

members. Why don't they call that law the Personn Act now? Little Richard did his share a' runnin'—from the IRS! These problems foreshadowed the fifth plague: a pestilence that fell on Rock and Roll. You'd think the plagues would fall on them who enslaved Elvis. It weren't so.

"This fifth plague of pestilence swept through Rock and Roll. Carl Perkins nearly died in a car wreck. In England the rock stars Eddie Cochran and Gene Vincent wrecked their car. Cochran died, Vincent almost died. This terrible plague continued for years: Sam Cooke, Bobby Darin, Jimi Hendrix, Mama Cass, Jim Croce, Ricky Nelson, and John Lennon. Lordy, where did they go? These musicians died 'cause the U.S. Army ignored the divine command, 'Let Elvis go.' A' course one Rocker didn't die tragically: Fats Domino. If he'd a' died in a car wreck or chokin' on a ham sandwich we'd 'a called it the Domino Theory.

"Moses called forth the sixth plague: boils. Sad to say Elvis still had acne problems. They used to say once ya had sex, acne would go away. Didn't work for Elvis. Didn't work for me, Lord knows I tried. They also used to say chocolate caused acne, bit no more. Know what I think causes acne?"

"I am afraid to ask," I demurred.

"Sunspots!"

"Sunspots? That is crazy."

"It ain't crazy," Marie explained. "Sunspots: that's the sun's acne. When the sun gets acne, young people out in the sun get it too. Elvis lived at a time of lots of sunspots. It'll get worse in future years what with us trashin' the ozone.

"Back to the plagues. Moses next inflicted fallin' hail. This symbolized the fall of Haley: Bill Haley. Haley's fame fell like a comet just 'bout the time they enslaved Elvis.

"Moses sent locusts: the eighth plague. And you know what this symbolizes!"

"I am afraid I do not know."

"Listen hun', ain't no point in addin' cowardice to ignorance. No reason to fear if ya don't know. Heebie-jeebies and willies ain't no cause for shame. I'll willin'ly explain. Locusts is bugs. While Elvis drove an army jeep, in England the Beatles got set to swarm out like locusts from a Liverpool cavern. Then they came, with horrific, loud, buzzin' sounds, 'Yea, Yea, Yea,' consuming every Rock and Roll fan in sight.

"In the ninth plague a' Moses darkness crept over the land. At first I thought this referred to Elvis not making movies in the army—the dark movie screens. Then I realized that as Elvis languished in the army a darkness crept over American Rock and Roll: Motown. Yes, Motown records began in 1960, the last year of Elvis in the army. Black . . . er rather African-American music provided tough competition for Elvis.

"Even after nine terrible plagues the Pharaoh wouldn't let Israel go. 'Course I mean ancient Pharaohs and not Sam the Sham's band. Nine terrible plagues hit Rock and Roll, yet Elvis remained a prisoner. Old Ike's heart hardened. 'I'll never let you go Elvis,' said he.

"Moses called down the last and most horrible plague—death of the Egyptian first-born. In the age of Elvis the tenth plague struck, the death of the first-born of Rock and Roll: Buddy Holly, Richie Valens, and the Big Bopper. Their plane fell from the sky—a flamin' chariot consumed in great balls a' fire.

"These plagues befell Rock and Roll 'cause the King stayed a slave. Eisenhower could harden his heart no longer. He let Elvis go to free the people and restore Rock and Roll. Ike did right, saying, 'I'll never stand in your way, Elvis.'"

"But," I asked, "If Elvis symbolizes the nation of Israel in Egypt, who symbolizes the Moses that delivered him?"

"I 'spose it's Parker—one thing he did right. When Israel got enslaved it looked like curtains, but Moses exodused 'em out and restored Israel. The army enslavement looked like the demisin' of the King. But Elvis rose forth from his slavery tomb and got delivered 'cross the ocean to the Promised Land.

"Moses was born Hebrew, but Egyptians raised him. Now Parker pretended to be American, calling hisself Colonel, acting the very model of the modern minor Colonel. But he was born in Holland. Now they put baby Moses in a pitch-covered basket and set it floatin' in the river. The Egyptians found Moses and accepted him as their own. So Parker, Andreas Cornelius van Kuijk, his real name sounds like a Telly Savalas TV show, stowed away on a ship that pitched on the sea. He floated 'cross the ocean to grow up in a foreign land where Americans accepted him as one a' their own."

"But did not Moses kill an Egyptian? Colonel Parker did not do that," I proposed.

"Well a' course not, but he made millions," Marie responded, "a killin' on Elvis. And when the Israelites went out from Egypt they saw manna coverin' the ground like hoarfrost. When Elvis returned from Germany, landin' in New York, snow covered the ground like hoarfrost. Waitin' for Elvis, with a stogie, stood Colonel Snow—Parker's nickname. I ain't sure what hoarfrost is. Next time I'm in Vegas I'll find out. I'll ask one a' them ladies. Now there's one more connection of Moses to Elvis. Now you tell me, who was the father-in-law of Moses?"

Several biblical names went through my mind. Afraid to sound foolish, I answered, "I have no idea."

"Jethro," she answered. Thank goodness I had not guessed Jehoshaphat. She continued, "Elvis for a time was friends with, Max Baer. They played golf. But I 'spose Elvis weren't no good at golf: a sport more difficult than shootin' crows in a sproutin' corn field. I can just imagine the King out there swingin' away with his mashie and niblick; slicin' air, slicin' sand more than the ball. 'Cause no man's born a golfer."

I grew impatient. "What has this to do with Moses?" But as the question left my mouth the answer entered my mind. "I see. Max Baer played Jethro Bodine on **The Beverly Hillbillies**."

"Bingo!" Marie responded. "You's readin' the signs. Sometimes Minnie Pearl played on that show; she'd come visit the Clampett mansion. Elvis' grandma, Minnie Mae Presley, came to live at Graceland. Also, some say she looked like Granny. But the connection don't end. **The Beverly Hillbillies** copied the comic strip, Lil' Abner: Jethro as Lil' Abner, Ellie Mae as Daisy Mae, Granny as Mammie Yokum. They made Jed an uncle so he weren't exactly Pappy Yokum, so they couldn't get sued."

"What has this to do with Elvis?" My foolish mouth again revealed itself.

"Max Baer played the Lil' Abner role and befriended Elvis. In the Bible, David had a general named Abner. Max Baer ties Elvis back to the Bible 'cause in a moment I'll 'xplain how David symbolizes Elvis. Not only that, Donna Douglas—Ellie Mae, played Frankie in the Elvis movie, **Frankie and Johnny**."

"Bizarre," I mumbled. She broke her record for twisted logic.

"There's more to the Egyptian slavery of Elvis," she plodded on. "The army gave Elvis serial number: 533-1076-1. For Elvis the number three represents holiness and bein' the chosen one. Eight places make up the serial number, startin' with 5. If ya subtract 2 from the first place and add it to the fourth, ya get 333-3076-1. Next take 3 from 7 in the sixth place and add it to the fifth place. Ya have 333-3346-1."

I pointed to her order book. Understanding instantly, she handed me the book and pencil, then repeated the altered serial number so I could write in down.

"How do you get rid of the 4?" I foolishly asked.

She answered, "His serial number ends with a dash, then 1. This means minus 1. So ya subtract 1 from 4 and ya get 333-3336-1. Now since the 1 on the end is a message number it can be dropped, but ya still have to fill place number eight with a number and ya get that number by dividin' the 6 by 2 and the serial number becomes 333-3333-3. One last thing, remember the holy number 3 times itself is 9. 9 becomes triply significant.

"How does that connect? The serial number has eight places." I tried to sort out the mess.

Marie snapped again, "You've forgotten already. You'll never be able to read the signs! The end of Elvis's serial number as I said is minus 1. That applies here. Ya take 1 from 9 to get eight places.

There ya have it—3 in eight places which equals 24, which divided by 2 gives ya 12 ,and that's the 12 tribes a' Israel and 12 apostles. Need I explain more?"

"No, it is quite clear," I whistled in amazement: another record broken. "I know the Bible well enough to remember the Israelites leaving Egypt by crossing the Red Sea. Is that a sign for Elvis crossing the Atlantic?" I asked with veiled sarcasm.

"Don't be silly, some signs is symbols. For Elvis to be in the army special arrangements was made. To film **King Creole** Elvis got his induction delayed. They also let him live off base. This involved lots of bura'cratic mumbo jumbo. The Red Sea crossin' symbolizes that army red tape."

"Bizarre, incredibly bizarre," I mumbled again.

"What's that?" Marie asked, "Butter?" She pulled a bowl of butter pats stuck between paper squares from the refrigerator and placed it on the counter while explaining, "As those Israelites left Egypt they ate a meal a' lamb, bitter herbs, yeastless bread. Elvis had his Passover meal of burnt hamburgers with banana and peanut butter sandwiches to celebrate his release. He always remembered his army days: tanks for the memories.

"Luckily, Elvis had a peaceful tour a' duty, no one let slip the hogs a' war. By spring of 1960 Elvis returned to the Promised Land. He came home!"

I looked around expecting either the ghost of Elvis or Rod Serling to walk through the diner door.

CHAPTER 7

ELVIS

THE KING

Marie watched as I ate. She grabbed a small vase of flowers and set it in front of me. I supposed she hoped to brighten the atmosphere. The flowers had more than a day's wilt.

"Zinnias," she defended. "What the hell'd you expect? The calla lilies ain't in bloom again! All I needed was the rain but they dried out." Point made, she resumed her discourse: "Freed from his wrongful captivity in Egypt—the army—Elvis returned to Graceland. Now you sir, tell me, what did Elvis become? Answer me in one word!"

"What do you mean?" I asked. "He was a singer, a star, some would say a philanthropist."

"How dare you call him that! Elvis had no strange diseases! He had no problems with his whizzin'!"

"A philanthropist gives money to charity!" I explained.

"That's Elvis!" Marie seemed relieved. "A more generous man you'll never find. Strangers've always relied on the kindness of Elvis. And so I guess a 'pissed philanthro' he be."

I shook my head in dismay. Oblivious, Marie did not pause for an instant, "Yet we must accolade Elvis with one more distinction, the most important hardy, the most important title."

"Celebrity?" I guessed. Where would this answer take me?

"No. King! Elvis reigned as THE KING—royalty in a democracy. Elvis, too famous to live long! America ne'er lost a king of such worth. Virtue he had, deservin' to romance; his brandished guitar, his arms spread wider than eagle's wings, his sparklin' eyes more dazzlin' than midday sun. What more can I say? His deeds exceed speech."

"To love him is a liberal education," I interjected.

"Why yes, hun'," she responded, "you could put it that way. Clearly, liberals need more Elvis. Now Elvis, he reigned as King—like Saul, like David, and like Solomon—three great kings a' the Bible that all represent Elvis. Saul, David, Solomon, with the initials S.D.S. But that don't mean 'Students for a Democratic Society,' with 'Weathermen' blowin' up buildin's.

"We must examine the very symbol a' kingship in the Bible. They didn't swear in a king with his hand on the Good Book like we do presidents. No, they anointed the king's head with oil. Havin' no fear of 'greasy kid's stuff,' and not believin' 'a little dab'll do ya', they poured on the olive oil with a touch a' perfume. 'Course I don't know if they used virgin olive oil—although I cain't figger what sex has to do with oil. By anointin' they coronated their kings. Elvis became the King when he doused his head with hair oil and proclaimed, 'Give me my robe, put on my crown, I have immoral longin's in me.'

"That's his anointin'! Now Bible folk called their kings 'messiahs.' Elvis as the anointed one became Messiah and King. Elvis annointed hisself King, just like that Napolean crowned hisself. 'A course I mean the French emperor, not Napolean Solo.

"In the Bible Saul ranks as the first great king. Admittedly, he don't come off too well. But near as I reckon, the ones who wrote 'bout Saul were hired by the next king, David. These scribes sucked up to David by makin' him look good, by makin' Saul look bad. Saul got the tabloid treatment. Anyways, the great Saul established the kingdom of Israel. Saul—'head and shoulders' 'bove the rest—had problems controllin' both his dandruff and the Philistines.

"The Philistines, an ancient sea people, lived along the coast a' Israel in cities like Ashdod, Ashkelon, Gath and named their boys

Phil. These fierce warriors ached to crush the newborn Kingdom of Israel. This all points to Elvis. Today a 'philistine' ain't no fightin' mariner, but someone who don't know art: someone who cain't tell a Jackson Pollock from a painter's dropcloth. A philistine cain't see the point a' runnin' a clothesline with colored bed sheets all 'cross California. A philistine ignores the smile and instead scopes the cleavage of Mona Lisa." The words "scopes the cleavage" sent a wave of self-conscious embarrassment through my being. Had she noticed my failure to avert my glance when she leaned over the counter? Was she letting me know that she knew? But if she had a point to make she would have lingered. Instead she pressed on:

"Throughout his life Elvis fought philistines, blind to the beauty of his artistry: music critics. In the end the Philistines defeated Saul, although he saved the final touch for hisself a' bellyfloppin' onto his own sword. But Elvis refused to pitch his sweet melodic pearls to those mucilagical swines, music critics. No, Elvis offered his music to common folk, those who gazed upon and contemplated beauty. They proclaimed Elvis as King. Elvis— of the people, by the people, for the people.

"Elvis imitated Saul in many ways: two whales in a pod. Saul, a moody man, had spells of melancholy. Melancholy's a fancy word for the blues. And Elvis knew the blues. He sang all those blue songs: 'Blue Christmas,' 'Milk Cow Blues,' 'Mean Woman Blues,' 'Moody Blue.' In later years Elvis had weeklong fits a' melancholy. He wouldn't talk to no one. He'd stay in bed day and night, night and day; gettin' up only for the john and to go to the icebox to wolf down a box a' Nutty-Buddy ice cream bars.

"Moody old Saul'd get depressed and flash with furious anger. He'd pick up the nearest object and heave it at someone. Elvis, also a melancholy man, raged just the same and became 'Fire Eyes.' His hard-favored rage disguised his fair nature. We all knows 'bout it now. Without warnin' Elvis'd grab a pistol, blast the TV, or shoot the chandelier. They say Robert Goulet was like a spark to a chicken processin' plant fryer when it came to gettin' Elvis to flash and shoot out a TV. But I tell ya, 'Give me that man that ain't passion's slave.'

"I knew a man, Lester, an old boyfriend who desperately wanted to be Elvis. Lester played Elvis records eighteen hours a day. He dressed and acted just like Elvis. Eventually, he crossed over the line, over the great divide 'tween reality and fantasy. Now the logical thing for him would've been to get a job writin' political campaign speeches. Instead he holed up in his room watchin' TV, believin' hisself the King. One day after watchin' Leonard Nimoy search for Hidden Valley Ranch, Lester saw Robert Goulet on TV. Lester, dead sure he was Elvis, took out the 38 from under his pillow and blasted his Sony big screen high dissolution set. But he hadn't figgered on his wife Juanita's ten-thousand dollar, pure breed, award winnin', Angora cat sleepin' in the warm spot behind the set. I shall avoid the bloody details, but what a horrible mess!"

My eyes drifted toward the bottles on the counter: ketchup and chili peppers floating in fluid. Memories of high school biology lab flooded my mind: blood, entrails, pungent formaldehyde. My stomach convulsed. My throat tightened in gag expectation. After years of serving day-old chili, Marie could spot the flushing face of someone about to upchuck. She stared at me, mumbling to herself, "There's matter in these sighs, these profound heaves." Then she leaped:

"Hey, hey, hey, your breakfast, you is bringin' it back. Don't reverse-quaff on me. Ya misunderstand! That bullet only nicked the cat. The blood came from Lester. His wife came home and beat the hell out a' him." Knowing it was only human blood settled my mind and stomach. Marie sensibly returned to Elvis:

"One Saul story fits Elvis exactly. Saul flew into a rage, grabbed hold of a javelin, brandished it right and left, then heaved it, hopin' to pin David to the wall. But nimble David stepped aside—Saul missed. One evening Elvis had a party at his Hollywood home. He was playin' pool with Sonny West when a girl asked Sonny to move his car so she could leave in her car. Elvis, not wantin' the game stopped, wouldn't let Sonny move the car. First the girl pleaded, then she got pissed, and spoke ill-chosen words. Elvis flashed! He hurled his cue stick with deadly accuracy right at her heart. It hit the left side a' her chest. Right in the boob! Had that cue been sharper, she'd 'a died! One more case where the life of Elvis paralleled the Good Book. That woman drove an American Motors Javelin.

"Many people complain, 'How could Elvis act in so barbarian a manner?' But I tells ya, it's the right divine a' kings to govern wrong! Now I 'spose that Elvis didn't like flyin' off like that. He probably tried to control his ragin' by decidin' in his mind never to do it again, but such rules don't stick; for the heart and the brain may devise laws for the blood, but a hot temper leapfrogs over a cold decree. One who saw first-hand the Elvis rages tried to blame it on drugs by sayin', 'Though this be a madman yet there is a methadone in it.'

"Saul foreshadowed Elvis in other ways. As years went by Saul became convinced people wanted to do him in. He became what ya call para . . . paranormal . . . no, that ain't it."

"Paranoid?" I suggested.

"Yes, Saul became paranoid. 'Though I ain't sure you is paranoid if people's really out to get you. Elvis also went paranoid. As years passed Elvis feared more and more that people was using him to get jobs, cars, women, or racquetball court financin'. Some cronies even spied on Elvis to the Colonel.

"Elvis lived as King like Saul. Even more David, the greatest king, prototyped Elvis. As Elvis aged many thought he'd lost his balance. Three Elvis cronies, who got fired when Vernon tried to balance the budget, wrote a book describing Elvis trying to climb the walls when he wanted Mike Stone killed."

I interrupted, "It is so strange a story you tell. Elvis wanted a 'Mike Stone' killed?" My limited knowledge of Elvis trivia had been exhausted.

Marie patiently explained, "Priscilla Presley, when still the wife of Elvis, had a fling with Mike Stone."

"That explains why Elvis wanted the man killed. But why would Elvis climb the walls?" Her answer would be a whopper.

Marie explained, "Elvis imitated the very crafty King David. A young freebootin' David once hid out with the enemy Philistines." She quickly retrieved her Bible which had drifted down the counter and found the correct loose page highlighted with a red magic marker. The rough edge on the binding side indicated this page had not fallen out. Rather, Marie had torn it and other Elvis-appropriate pages and moved them to the front of her Bible for access. I suppose she assumed, "In the beginning was Elvis." She read, "David was 'sore afraid of Achish the king of Gath. And he changed his behavior before them, and feigned himself mad in their hands, and scrabbled on the doors of the gate, and let his spittle fall down upon his beard.' (I Samuel 18:10-11, 19:10) Elvis scrabbled on the walls pretendin' to be bonkers. Cronies told of an unshaven Elvis sittin', droolin', pie-eyed—like he was stoned. But life ain't all beer and spittle. Elvis hadn't flipped; he just used the David routine to throw 'em off by acting crazy man, crazy.

"David as king had a large harem. Elvis as King married once but had his own kind a' harem. He used charm, humor, extravagant gifts a' jewels and cars to entice many women to lay with him. Many an angry and crestfallen young man found his own queen stole by the King. I recall seein' one anguished young man in 1974 as he watched his beloved lady ushered through the Graceland gates. He tore his shirt in despair, spat through the wrought iron, lamentin', 'With witchcraft of his wit, with traitorous gifts—O wicked wit and gifts, that have the power so to seduce!—won to his shameful lust the will of my most seemin'-virtuous queen.' For hours that man stood in the early mornin' rain.

"Now another David story foreshadowed Elvis: the story of David, Bathsheba, and her husband Uriah. But this story fits Elvis backwards. There were other kings besides Elvis. One man claimed to be 'King a' the Hill, Top a' the Heap, A-number one.' I speak a' course a' Frank Sinatra. Ya know I once took the train to New York. I walked down Broadway, givin' my regards, yellin' 'Look out Broadway!' and singin', 'New York, New York,' 'bout 'little town blues meltin' away.' Two toughs knocked me down in the alley and stole my purse. That song probably only works for Sinatra. And a' course ya never get mugged in little towns so I don't feel those blues anymore.

"In the Bathsheba story and only in this particular story, King David represents Sinatra and not Elvis. Bathsheba represents Juliet Prowse in whom Elvis developed an interest while workin' on the movie, **G.I. Blues**. The story goes that Frank considered Juliet his girl. So one evenin' Frank and a pair a polemical bodyguards went backstage to explain to Elvis the health benefits a' extricatin' hisself from Juliet's life—the gist bein' 'leave my woman alone.'

"Elvis, one to take the high road, backed away from Juliet. He escaped the discomforts that befell the biblical Uriah—who also had the misfortune a' windin' up 'tween a powerful man and a desired woman. Uriah, he wound up a heap. But like I said, that's the only place where Elvis ain't represented by the king. Maybe I read this sign wrong.

"Now I want to explain to ya how the most magnificent King of Israel, Solomon, represents Elvis."

"If I remember correctly," I pointed out, "the reputation of Solomon rested on his wisdom—a divine gift. People do not remember Elvis for his wisdom."

"You is very correct," Marie came back. "Ya know's your Bible, at least a bit. Yes, Solomon asked for wisdom instead a' riches, long life, and havin' his enemies kick off. Well he got wisdom and then got the riches and long life thrown in to boot.

"You correctly surmise that Elvis didn't get the wisdom of the ages like Solomon, to go 'round offerin' to split up infants. Instead Elvis received an angelic voice. Solomon couldn't sing a lick—he sounded like a Hereford in heat. Although some calls 'Song of Songs' in the Bible the 'Song of Solomon', the music talent in that family belonged to David. Why that musically declined Solomon couldn't carry a tune in an earthenware jar.

"Gifted only with his voice, Elvis spent his life in search a' wisdom. 'Course he did it without no Fulton Sheen to help. Elvis spent many hours readin' spiritual tracts. He even had a spiritual adviser, Larry Geller, a guru who could do a perm."

"A perm?" I queried.

"Yes, Larry Geller, spiritual adviser and hair stylist to the King: 'Have blow dryer, will travel,'" Marie stated succinctly as if reading from a business card. She explained more fully, "Geller a good man, with the Cremora of human kindness by the quart in every vein. A man steadfast, loyal, and truly spiritual. Geller explained it all. Supposedly he told Elvis, 'How charmin' is the divine philosophy! Not horseshit and crap as dull fools suppose. But a perpetual feast a' necktied sweets, where no crude surfer reigns.' And each time Geller left, Elvis would ask, 'What time's the next swami?'"

Marie returned to her Bible: "Elvis imitated Solomon." She searched among the loose pages. "The Bible says, 'the king made a great throne of ivory, and overlaid it with pure gold.' (II Chronicle 9:17) Elvis made a kingly throne on ivory piano keys. Piano music backs many of his gold record songs. Some folk misread this, saying its points to the fancy bathroom of Elvis with a gold plated commode.

"The Bible says, 'Solomon had four thousand stalls for horses and chariots, and twelve thousand horsemen; whom he bestowed in the chariot cities.' (II Chronicles 9:25) Although Elvis had horses, this passage counts his cars, pick-up trucks, and moto'cycles. 'Chariot cities,' would be garages. Now Solomon had twelve thousand horsemen. Elvis had nowhere near that many cars. But if ya add up the horsepower of each Harley-Davidson and Cadillac and every vehicle that Elvis ever owned, ya get twelve thousand horsepower. Ya add in the trucks he drove for the electric company and a souped up golf-cart or two.

"Now if ya knew your Bible, you'd know that Solomon had even more wives than David."

I shot back, "You cannot connect Elvis to Solomon, for Elvis had only one wife and she divorced him."

"You is right, but see, Solomon made laws so he could marry as many wives as he could afford and keep from quarrelin'. In the

U.S. the law only allows one wife per husband at a time. Such a law even went against Mormons who considered it a divine command to have several wives—in a country that claims freedom a' religion! Anyhow, Elvis had only one legal wife; but hundreds a' 'wives' outside the law: a coast to coast harem."

"Somehow I knew you would tie it all in," I moaned.

"One other thing," she continued. "The cronies of Elvis, the Memphis Mafia, sometimes shared these women after Elvis finished with 'em. They became 'Brethren of the Common Wife.'"

Marie's paced quickened:

"A wealthy and important queen visited Solomon who impressed her with his wisdom and wealth. Now this could be any number a' starlets that frequented Elvis, but actually it symbolizes the Beatles. The Beatles—royalty from a foreign land—visited Elvis in Hollywood. Elvis made a mighty impression on those rag mop tops.

"II Chronicles 12 describes how Shishak, King of Egypt, invaded and took valuables from the temple in Jerusalem. If this happened today, he'd steal the collection box and speaker system. Anyways, accordin' to Indiana Jones, that's when the Ark a' the Covenant disappeared to Egypt. 'Course that's pure Hollywood. Any similarity 'tween movies and reality is pure accident. 'Cause in truth, nobody knows what happened to the ark. Quite likely it's still in Jerusalem, buried where the temple stood. But no one has the guts to ask those a-rabs to move their domed rock so someone can do some diggin'.

"This Shishak symbolizes a raid by the singer Johnny Rivers durin' a visit to Elvis. Elvis sang a new song, 'Memphis, Tennessee,' which Rivers took, then recorded and sold millions."

At this point one of the refrigerators behind the counter began a loud obnoxious groaning.

"Usually it goes right away. She's a machine quite temperamental," Marie stated. Moments passed. The noise grew louder. Marie stared at the machine, then pounded it with the bottom of her fist. The noise worsened. "Do the clamor bother ya?" she asked.

Finally she pulled back her foot and gave the hardest kick I had ever seen. The machine lurched against the wall, then rocked back into place. The groan squealed into silence—instant, but short-lived, relief. A quiet hissing came from the back of the machine. Marie had broken the freon line.

"It sounds serious," I suggested, trying to be helpful.

"To hell with it! We've more important things to worry 'bout!" she snapped. "I must speak. As long as I have you here, I'm countin' on you to get the message so as to pass it along.

"Great King David got old and couldn't keep warm, so they tossed a beautiful maid, Abishag, in his bed. Abishag—an ugly name for a good looker. Anyrate, David and the woman never had sex. In the last days a beautiful woman, Ginger, joined Elvis in bed. Ginger—someone's daughter fair, like Ann Blyth, buxom and debonair. Many think drugs sapped the potency of Elvis, so he and Ginger didn't have sex. Some believe Elvis degenerated beyond the reach a' the caperberry. 'Parently drugs work like booze in sappin' a man's precious bodily fluids. But that Elvis lost it all, I ain't sure. 'Cause although he had scotch'd the snake, he had not kill'd it.

"One last thing 'bout biblical kings—when a king died they called it 'sleepin' with his father.' That's why Elvis today lies entombed alongside his father, Vernon Presley."

She concluded, "There ya have it: Elvis the King, King of the whole wide world—aye, every inch a King."

The freon hissed out—from desperate appliance relieved—the deceased's desperate groan. The refrigerator died—soon, so would a million ozone molecules. One could feel the freon rise and begin its thirty-mile, atmosphere-destroying journey. For a moment I could feel years-old sunburns reignite on my back. A shudder shot up my spine as I worried about skin cancer, sunspots, and the return of the acne of my youth. My mind silently begged this woman, "Release me, I want to be free!"

CHAPTER 8

ELVIS

THE BABYLONIAN CAPTIVITY

Outside the diner, somewhere in the distance, a train whistle found its way through the fog. Inside, on the edge of reality, I searched for a clock but could see only an old broken Coca-Cola clock above aged and dusty boxes of Nabisco shredded wheat on a stainless-steel rack. Marie noticed. She pulled a gold watch and chain from her pocket and opened it. "It's three-thirty. That's the Illinois Central freight heading south." Without waiting for my reaction to the late hour she continued:

"I understand just how you feel, hun'—tired. But I'm movin' on with explainin' Elvis and you is stayin' until it's time to go. The Good Book tells 'bout the Babylonians swoopin' down and haulin' off the leadin' folks of Jerusalem—generals, politicians, pro ball players—and trucking 'em off to exile in foreign Babylon. That's Iraq today. This is called the 'Babylonian captivity of Israel' and it augurs Elvis. I just ciphered out how Elvis returned to Graceland as King after his slavery. Ya'd think things'd be fine, but no, just as Elvis escaped the whirlpool of Charybdis—near Cairo, Illinois—he ran smack dab into the teeth of the sea Monster, Scylla—downstream at Memphis. No sooner free, and he became a prisoner again."

"Let me guess," I tried to intercept her line of reasoning. "You are talking about the song 'Jailhouse Rock.'"

"Your initiative's sound, but off by a mile—so close, yet so far," she answered sadly. "Not 'Jailhouse Rock'—but Hollywood. Elvis exiled off to the New Age Babylon. Now the Bible calls Babylon 'the great whore.' They'd 'a called it 'the great Mother Fucker', but language hadn't evolved that far. I cain't think a' no better words than 'great whore' to label Hollywood which captured the innocent, pure Elvis and in her evil sinfulness, wasted his talent. There Elvis sighed his Memphis breath in foreign smog, eatin' the bitter bread a' banishment. Oh Hollywood, O thou hast the damnedest irritations, and art indeed able to corrupt a saint.

"One man pimped for Hollywood, leavin' the talent of Elvis go to waste while he pocketed thirty pieces a' silver and golden coins for bringin' Elvis to the great whore. But as a good faith-filled woman, I'll not defame the man directly. Ya see, it all came down to money, honey. That's how the web was wove.

"Exiled in Hollywood, Elvis made movies that kept gettin' worse with each one. Like tryin' to patch a plaster wall: the more trowel swipes, the worse it looks." Marie pulled another loose page from her Bible. "Now Psalm 137 describes all this:

> By the rivers of Babylon, we sat down, yea, we wept, when we remembered Zion.
> We hanged our harps upon the willows in the midst therof.
> For there they that carried us away captive required of us a song;
> They that wasted us required of us mirth, saying, sing us one of the songs of Zion.
> How shall we sing the King's song in a strange land?

"Exiled to the belly a' the great whore, Elvis hung up his harp—his guitar. He ceased all live concerts. Can ya believe it? The greatest Rock and Roll singer stopped doin' concerts! The live Elvis disappeared and without such relievin' rain it became a terrible hot drought of eight years.

"What was his sentence than a songless death, which robbed his tongue from breathin' native breath? 'Cause there ain't nothin' like a song a' true Rock sung by Elvis. But Elvis recorded foolish movie songs. Hollywood, she chased Elvis down a hole, then lit and threw in a Gopher Gasser to suffocate his native breath of original Rock and Roll—the Rock of Ages.

"Although his Hollywood captors wanted Elvis to seem happy in the films, how could he sing the music of Zion—Memphis—in a strange, foreign land? And let's face it, California's 'bout as foreign as ya can get from good old hometown America."

I tried to clarify, "Did he sing any good movie songs?"

"In the movies Elvis sang dross, no better than a hill a' foreskins. He became Mr. Songman of Hollywood. Oh, we fans accepted a few, but they sounded sickly pale compared with his first songs. In Hollywood Elvis wasted time and then time done wasted him. Hollywood drowned his glory in a shallow cup: Elvis sold his Rock and Roll reputation for a handful a' lousy songs."

My tape recorder clicked off. I flipped the cassette and pressed "record." Marie pulled out several Bible pages, laid them out on the counter and continued:

"The Bible describes California: 'They sacrifice upon the tops of the mountains, and burn incense on the hills, under oaks, poplars, and elms, because the shadow therof is good: therefore your daughters shall commit whoredoms, and your spouses shall commit adultery.' (Hosea 4:13) That's Hollywood—immoral people swappin' wives, burnin' incense, smokin' marijuana. Hollywood lured Elvis into smokin' weed, but he moved beyond the reefer."

"Please, help me understand," I broke in. "Why didn't Elvis stop making such movies if the songs were so poor?" Again my curiosity drove me to foolishly continue this conversation.

"Nobody rightly knows. The answer's known only to him. He married the whore of Hollywood and wouldn't get divorced."

"I suppose you can find that in the Bible," I lamented.

"Sure, in the Bible a man Hosea, a prophet, married a whore named Gomer: a strange name. But Hosea symbolizes Elvis in Hollywood, where they made the Gomer Pyle T.V. show. Some

Elvis films was a pile. Gomer Pyle was a small town southern boy strugglin' to make it in the big world, just like Elvis.

"Hosea married this Gomer and she birthed him three babies. Hosea named the first kid Jezreel, for the Good Book says, 'I will break the bow of Israel in the valley of Jezreel.' (Hosea 1:5) Israel is Elvis and Jezreel is Los Angeles, the lonesome valley where they broke Elvis. The Bible locates Jezreel near Mt. Carmel. California has its own Carmel, ask Clint Eastwood.

"Hosea and Gomer had a second kid, Lo-ruhamah, which means 'not pitied.' The movie moguls had no pity for Elvis. They made their lousy movies, they made money, and they nearly destroyed Elvis. But like the Phoenix that rises from its ashbin, Elvis rose from the ashes of his movie career.

"The third kid they named, Lo-ammi, meanin', 'Not my people.' The movies of Elvis embarrassed him, so he disowned them. When he'd watch them—a rare event—he'd ask 'Whose that fast-talkin' hillbilly on the screen?' He saw hisself and said 'that is not me.'"

"Why didn't Elvis stop making these movies?" I asked.

"'Cause when ya gets right down to it, Elvis received a command to make 'em. The Good Book says, 'Take unto thee a wife of whoredoms and children of whoredoms: for the land hath committed great whoredom.' (Hosea 1:2) The whoredoms, that's the bad movies Elvis made in sin-bound Hollywood.

"Elvis wouldn't stand up for hisself. He became a puppet on a string. He couldn't confront people, 'specially the Colonel. Psalm 39 describes this failure of Elvis—it's what ya call his tragic flaw, 'I was dumb with silence, I held my peace, even from good; and my sorrow was stirred.' But when ya get right down to it, I cain't 'xplain the silence of Elvis. It's a riddle wrapped in a mystery inside an enema.

"But I also think the FBI hired the movie moguls to make these bad movies so's to tame the wild Elvis. Old J. Edgar Hoover just finished up what the army started. Now 'cause Hollywood helped so eagerly, they got a reward: the FBI let a over-aged Hollywood man become president—Ronald Reagan."

"I find that impossible to believe," I argued.

Marie calmly responded, "It's unbelievable all right—that anyone with no ability other than makin' speeches could get elected. That's why I is sure the FBI set the whole thing up."

"Please, please, go back to Elvis," I begged.

"Elvis had chances to make good movies. He coulda been in **The Rainmaker** with Burt Lancaster, or **Thunder Road**, or **In Cold Blood**. Barbra Streisand wanted Elvis to be in **A Star is Born**, but the Colonel wouldn't have it. The one person 'sposed to help the career of Elvis did all he could to limit Elvis. Parker wouldn't let Elvis sing at the White House or sing a command performance for Queen Elizabeth 'cause Parker wouldn't get no cut.

"When Elvis started makin' movies, they didn't even give him actin' lessons like the Staniskowalski method. If anythin' shows the magic of Elvis it's that despite everythin' workin' 'gainst him, he survived. Even to make thirty-one mediocre movies is still an accomplishment.

"The Good Book speaks of punishment for Hollywood for wastin' the talent a' Elvis. It will be 'made as a wilderness, and set like a dry land, and slayed with thirst.' (Hosea 2:3) Hollywood had a terrible five-year drought where people couldn't wash cars or water lawns and plants. The Bible foretold, 'And I will destroy her vines and her fig trees.' (Hosea 2:12) The Hollywood ficus trees withered.

"The prophet Amos described the evil women Elvis found in Hollywood: 'Cows of Bashan' that lie on beds with ivory-colored sheets, stretched upon sofa sleepers; they drink California wine in bowls and anoint themselves with suntan oil while watchin' soap operas, but they is not grieved by the affliction of Elvis.

"In the Bible, Daniel suffered trials and tribulations. The Babylonians threw him into a den a' hungry, ferocious, bulimic lions. Just so, Elvis got thrown into the jaws a' the greedy, ferrous-fisted, bloodthirsty lions of Hollywood. I mean in particular the roarin' jaws of MGM.

"The friends a' Daniel refused to bow down in worship of a golden idol. Elvis refused to bow down and worship the golden idol a' Hollywood, the Academy Awards. Elvis didn't receive a single Oscar for over thirty movies, but it weren't he wasn't good 'nough. Elvis rejected that pagan orgy of idolatry. Hollywood gave those indecent naked statues to actors inferior to Elvis: Gregory Peck, Sidney Poitier, Rex Harrison, Rod Steiger.

"As Daniel refused the food served in those Babylon greasy spoons so Elvis refused the food of Hollywood: California wine, grapes, avocados. He rejected the health food craze a' alfalfa sprouts, granola, carrot juice. Elvis ate American food: milk-shakes, well-burned burgers, extra-crispy bacon, peanut butter and banana sandwiches. Elvis prospered and expanded.

"They tell one rather incredible story: 'bout movie producer Hal Walshazzar celebrating the money he made from Elvis films that he used for high-grade films made with other actors. Well the party got up to steam. With no bowl handy, they grabbed a guitar of Elvis, pulled off the strings, and filled it with fruit juice and wine to make the first wine coolers. As they tipped back their glasses a hand appeared—like Thing on **The Addams Family**—and wrote on the wall: MENE, PERES, TEKEL. MENE describes how Hollywood had been cruel and mean to Elvis. PERES predicts the end of Elvis movies. They would perish. Lastly TEKEL refers to shekels. This predicts the end a' Hollywood exploitin' Elvis for money. For they could no longer press down upon the brow of Elvis Hollywood's crown a' thorns, they could no more crucify Elvis upon a cross a' gold!

"The movies of Elvis represent his Babylonian captivity. Darlin', I know you is thinkin', 'a little less conversation,' but we must talk 'bout those movies. You cain't get out a' here by closin' your eyes and tappin' your heels, Babe."

"Hey, do not call me Babe," I growled. "I am not a babe, your babe, or the Babe."

CHAPTER 9

ELVIS

THE ACTS OF ELVIS

In shock, like a storm disaster victim, I let her lead me and guide me through the treacherous debris of this night.

"The time now has come, darlin'," she stated. "I must speak plainly 'bout the Acts of Elvis: his Hollywood movies. They be thirty-one in number. Twenty-eight chapters in the biblical book of Acts plus three for the key letters in the name of Elvis and one gets thirty-one."

Again she leaned down and searched under the counter. She pulled out a roll of stained white paper. It appeared to be shelf-lining paper, the kind that had devoured endless hours of my Saturday chores: cutting, folding, fitting, trying to get it to lay flat. Finally, my mother abandoned the project as entirely useless without telling me why for fear of legitimizing my suspicions that I had been wasting my time.

Marie had fashioned a kind of scroll from the shelf paper. She had duct-taped large wooden spoons on each end: one up, one down. She lay the scroll on the counter and unrolled it right to left. The spoon blade for the right end of the scroll hung over the counter in front of her. It presented no problem. However, the spoon on the left side did not reach the opposite side of the counter and so, when Marie unrolled the scroll, the spoon flip-flopped down the counter. Strange lines, names, dates, and zodiac signs filled the paper—a homemade Talmud, cafe cabala.

My heart sank like a shanked golf ball in a water hazard. Would Marie describe thirty-one movies? Each plot, with her own critique? No, I would not sit still for this! I mumbled, "That is all I can stands and I can't stands no more." I tried to jump and run but my pants snagged on a screw on the chrome side of the revolving stool. I could not free myself before Marie, pointing to the scroll, launched into the first movie:

"In '56 Elvis made **Love Me Tender,** a pleasant but strange film: a Civil War epic rock video. Elvis dances like the 1950s, dressed like the 1870s. I think Steve Allen thunk it up.

"The first ya see Elvis, damn near fifteen minutes into the film, he's playin' Clint and a'plowin' this field. They don't show no mule—only Elvis, the plow, and the reins. Makes ya wonder if a couple a' stagehands—grips or gaffers—weren't pulling the reins out a' sight a' the camera."

"Grips or gaffers? What are they?" I entreated.

"Don't rightly know, they show up in movie credits. After a movie, while everyone fights to get out, I watch the credits. Then I pry my feet off the sticky floor and head out without no crowds. Movie credits list grips and gaffers. They even got somebody called a Best Boy. I figgered he was for immoral foolin' 'round. Then I realized even Hollywood wouldn't advertise it like that. Then I learned Best Boys are go-fers who get coffee, donuts, bagels, and whatnot."

Frustration, anguish, boredom: I had never known such a potpourri of emotions. "Could we get back to Elvis?" I pleaded.

"Oh yes," she drifted back on course. "Elvis did a good job a' actin'. He died at the end of **Love Me Tender:** the most believable dying scene ever. The movie did well at the box office and Elvis had made it in Hollywood. He was in like Flynn.

"In **Love me Tender** Elvis played Clint Reno. You can divide the films a' Elvis into two groups. In group one Elvis played characters with one syllable names: Clint, Deke, Vince, Glenn, Chad, Ross, Mike—three times, Josh, Rick, Ted, Guy, Scott, Joe, Steve, Greg, Jess, and John. And in group two Elvis played characters with two syllable names: Danny, Tulsa, Pacer, Toby, Walter—two times, Jodie, Lucky, Charlie, Rusty, Lonnie, and Johnny—two times." The detailed lists on her scroll impressed and exhausted me simultaneously. She had other lists to recite:

"The only stranger set a' names tryin' to sound normal is the astronauts," she explained. "Ever notice how their names are usually English words or near words. Ya got your Shepard, Glenn, Carpenter, Cooper." She pointed to handwritten notes on her scroll, "I got this here list. Ya see, I've been searchin' astronaut names for signs relatin' to Elvis and great cosmic events. Let's see, after Cooper ya got Young, White, Scott, Armstrong, Bean, Duke, Carr, Brand, Truly, Hartsfield, Peterson, Ride, Bluford, Gardner, Hart, Coats, Walker, McBride, Scully-Power, Lucid, England, Lounge, Fisher, Covey, Furrer, Spring, Cleave, Shepherd, Springer, Adamson, Brown, Baker, Low, Cabana, Akers, Meade, Godwin and Apt. I gave up years ago when I saw there weren't a Kowalski in the bunch. According to films every outfit in WWII had a Kowalski."

"Please, please get back to Elvis," I begged, terrified she would expound on the names of Russian Cosmonauts.

"Oh yes Elvis. In his second movie, **Loving You**, Elvis played a rock singer on his way up: Deke Rivers. The movie starts with the manager usin' Deke. In the end everythin' gets resolved and management treats Deke fair—a carin' family. Fans got the impression that Elvis was treated fair. But it weren't so."

Marie moved down the scroll. She had listed each movie by year. Pasted alongside each title I could make out teen magazine clippings on each movie and pairs of theater ticket stubs. She found the spot on the scroll for the next movie.

"For his third movie Elvis made **Jailhouse Rock**. The Bible predicted this. In the book of Acts, Peter and Paul—without Mary and without candy bars—wind up in jail. That's why Elvis made this prison movie. Elvis was chose 'to open blind eyes, to bring out prisoners from prison, and them that sit in darkness out a' the prison house.' (Isaiah 42:7) We's all imprisoned by emptiness but Elvis freed us. Paul escaped when an earthquake shook his prison and so the rumble a' Elvis fans shook the earth. It ain't called Rock and Roll for nothin'. Lastly, Elvis wore a prison uniform so by his stripes we was healed of loneliness.

"They delayed the army induction of Elvis so he could make his next movie, **King Creole**. Elvis thought this his best film—number four out a' thirty-one. How could he peak so early if it weren't for that bunglin', greedy Hollywood? In **King Creole** Elvis tries to steer clear of Morticia from the Addams family who played Ronnie and one half a' the original odd couple.

"King Creole was the last black and white movie of Elvis. I've heard talk 'bout Hollywood wantin' to colorize these movies. But I cain't figger the point. Why make Elvis colored? Would he then have a white sound? A black man singin' like Tony Bennett? An African-American Mel Torment?

"In **King Creole** Elvis played a troubled young Danny Fisher, all mixed up inside—like the real Elvis. His beauty caught the eye of Ronnie. She fell for Danny's way a' waftin' his eyes to the contrary and fallin' a lip a' much contempt. By playin' Danny Fisher, Elvis became the King Fisher—the Fisher King." On her scroll, next to the title **King Creole**, twenty theater tickets had been pasted. I would have asked about the quantity but that would only prolong the ordeal. I let her speak.

"After **King Creole** Elvis went into slavery and changed forever. His wild fire got smothered. Elvis's fifth movie, **G.I. Blues**, proves this, for ya see a tamed, sideburn-stripped, goody-two-shoes Elvis. A strange scene shows the unfoldin' disaster. Elvis, playin' a G.I. named Tulsa, stands in a German bar singin' a sappy ballad—somethin' 'bout givin' his heart—like an organ donor. Another G.I. wants to quash the singin' of Tulsa so he coins up the JukeBox selectin' 'Blue Suede Shoes' by Elvis Presley.' Someone tells the G.I. to turn it off, but the G.I. says 'I want to hear the original.' A fight breaks out and Tulsa starts walin' away at this man until the M.P.s arrive. There it played out, big as life: a man yearnin' for the original Elvis bein' beaten to a pulp by an ajaxed, spiced, spanned, sanitized Elvis. I swear they must a' hypnotized or brainwashed Elvis.

"Odd 'nough, the man Elvis beat up in **G.I. Blues** looks 'xactly like the punk Elvis beat up in the Buckhorn Tavern in **Loving You**. The German bar owner, he looked a lot like Colonel Parker. Also, Elvis as Tulsa sang 'Frankfurt Special' 'bout the train the soldiers took to Frankfurt, Germany. This song has no symbolic meanin'. I say this 'cause a friend swore it referred to Little Elvis, but I assure ya, it ain't so.

"In the end Elvis gets the girl, Lili—played by Juliet Prowse. They's 'bout to kiss, and Elvis looks up with a sneer and asks, 'Didja ever?' That's the whole question. Did ya ever see such willful, shameless destruction a' true Rock and Roll?

"After that, Hollywood did what she pleased. For movie six, **Flaming Star**, she tanned up Elvis as the half Indian: Pacer Burton, a part originally intended for Marlin Brando. At least Elvis'd read his lines and not make up his own. I watched that movie on my VCR, it sounded like an echo chamber. Barbara Eden played the love interest for Elvis. Later she played Jeannie on **I Dream of Jeannie**. That was 'fore Larry Hagman quit NASA and went back to his family's ranch outside a' Dallas.

"In one scene Dolores Del Rio, playin' the mother, stumbles out a' her house durin' a storm so she can die in the cornfield. 'Parently she'd seen her 'flamin' star' tellin' her she was a goner. She hunts a decent keelin'-over spot, the wind and dust blow fierce, yet the trees hardly move. Such is Hollywood.

"Dolores Del Rio is a double sing cause she's mentioned in the play **Bye Bye Birdie**. Red West, one a' the Memphis Mafia, does a bit part as an Indian fightin' 'gainst Elvis. Thus began a long career for Red as 'Elvis Enemy Number One.'"

"What does that mean?" I asked skeptically.

"Just that Red West shows up in restaurants and bars takin' pokes, fightin', and tryin' to assassinate Elvis in these movies. After **Flaming Star** Elvis next made **Wild in the Country** in '61 with Red West as his mean brother. Figger this movie out if ya can. At the end of **Wild in the Country** Elvis has the choice a' three knockout babes: Tuesday Weld, Hope Lange, Millie Perkins, and what's his choice? College! Can ya believe it? College: 'bout the last place you'd expect to see Elvis.

"They made two endin's for this film. My friend Marcie had gone to California to get away from her mean brother who had put a frog down her back at the Carroll County Picture Show. She got tickets for the test audience 'cause the producers didn't know which endin' to use. The audience voted for the happy endin' of Hope Lange as Irene Sperry livin' after tryin' to off herself, and Elvis on the college steps. Marcie, she voted for death by givin' the thumbs down. She lost.

"Once Hollywood had broke Elvis, she could train him as she chose. Elvis got shipped off to make an hour and a half commercial for Hawaii with scenic vistas and blowin' conch shells. I speak a' course of movie eight: **Blue Hawaii**. Elvis plays Chad Gates who comes out of the service and winds up tour-guiding three over-age actresses playin' seventeen-year-olds.

"This movie paints a picture far different from reality. First Elvis as Chad Gates knows what he's doin'. He makes his own decisions, has business sense, wants to be independent, stands up to people, and refuses to run his old man's pineapple operation. 'Parently, unlike the Bible, Chad didn't want to be 'bout his father's business. Then Chad runs teenage girls out a' his bedroom. These things weren't the real Elvis.

"They had a food fight in **Blue Hawaii** but it lacked the cinematic excellence of a Three Stooges food fight. Floyd the barber from **The Andy Griffith Show** turns up. And early in the film Elvis takes his girlfriend for a picnic. That's 'sposed to symbolize some famous French paintin' called, Lunchin' on the Grass. That's what my friend Bernie told me.

"After **Blue Hawaii**, came **Follow That Dream** in 1962. Elvis played Toby Kwimper, a slow thinker who outwits everyone: mobsters, thugs, social workers, and judges. In one scene everyone thinks Toby is robbin' the bank. If ya look close at the bank customers ya can see Alfred the butler of Batman fixin' his glasses. Red West plays a bank guard tryin' to arrest Toby. Floyd the barber shows up as a bank officer.

"Still in 1962 Elvis made **Kid Galahad** with Charles Bronson 'fore Bronson made a movie career shootin' scum low-lifes. Bronson gets beat up by a mobster who looks like opera singer Placebo Domingo. This movie starts with Elvis again comin' out a' the service. It also begins the Elvis film tradition of unresolved plots. All kinds a' details is left hangin', unanswered. We fans had to fill the blanks while the producers made money by savin' film. All through Kid Galahad they's hintin' the trainin' camp could be turned into a resort yet it never says what happens. At the end the mobsters get arrested and just disappear. We'll see more disappearin' mobsters in a bit.

"One last thing, in **Kid Galahad** we learned that Elvis as Walter Gulick had been baptized Roman Catholic. Who would a' thunk it? But stranger things have happened. Who would a thunk the Singin' Nun would wind up in a lesbian double-suicide?

"For the last 1963 movie Elvis made **Girls!, Girls!, Girls!**. Why didn't they label this movie usin' shortcut math: callin' it **Girls!** with a little '3' after it in the air.

"Early in the film, Elvis throws a drunk out of a nightclub and ya figger 'here comes the fight scene' cause the drunk looks like the man Elvis beat up in **Loving You** and **G.I. Blues**. But there ain't no fight. Elvis saves his punchin' for his boss, Wesley Johnson. Now that drunk, if I ain't mistaken, looks like Monroe, the old boyfriend a' Lou Ann before she met Gomer Pyle.

"In **Girls!, Girls!, Girls!**, Elvis, playin' Ross Carpenter, lives by tuna fishin'. That's a' course a symbol for Elvis fishin' for girls. My second husband told me 'fish' is Shakespeare talk for 'girl'—somethin' to do with a fishmonger, Balonius. Anyways, Ross sells tuna to the BumbleBee Tuna Company—another sign. In **Bye Bye Birdie** the manager's Ma winds up in a trashcan with BumbleBee Tuna cans.

"The films ends in an out-a'-the-way paradise cove. But girls show up from a half-dozen countries. Where'd they come from other than a Hollywood castin' office? The movie ends with Ross and Laurel: a Juliet Prowse look-a-like. He gives her the option a' marryin' him or livin' in sin. She asks for both so ya don't know if they marry. And ya don't find out what happens to Ross's old girl, Robin. Again we fans is just 'sposed to know.

"Next in '63 Elvis played Mike Edwards in **It Happened at the World's Fair**—a hour and a half commercial for the Seattle World's Fair. After it, ya asks yourself, 'what was the "it" that happened?' Nothin' happened more than Elvis beatin' up Red West at a card game and Elvis gettin' the girl. Elvis did nothing at the world's fair but walk 'round and scope babes. There's lots a' songs, but Elvis sings four a' them to a little girl. In one song, at a trailer park called Century 21 Estates, Elvis is backed by the singing Mello Men. You may think I is stretchin' the connections here, but my friend Marcie after seein' this film got a yellow jacket and started sellin' real estate.

"Elvis next made **Fun in Acapulco** with the buxom Ursula Andress. To me, her name's a joke of sublime nature. 'Cause I think guys hear that name and think 'Arsula Undress.' I heard she started in movies in a film, **East of Mark Eden. Fun in Acapulco** leaves ya hangin' again. Does Elvis marry Marguerita Dauphin? Does the Mexican diver marry the lady Bullfighter?

"One other thing, in this movie Elvis had a Mexican boy manager who got a 50% cut. It's funny in the film, but in real life it weren't no joke with Parker gettin' a 50% cut. We fans joked 'bout it, but ignored reality. And a' course Floyd the barber shows up, this time as a doctor. Now that's a sign cause the red on barber poles comes from when barbers did doctor work."

Another fly caught my attention, then vanished. It reappeared, circled Marie's head, then was gone again—a large fly. There, it showed itself, swooping down in front of Marie's face. She casually brushed it away. In a swirl of turbulence it flew into my face and I saw not a fly, but a honeybee. It flew toward the ceiling. Pausing at the apogee of its climb, it fell backwards rolling into a dive. It strafed the counter then rose toward Marie's head, circled her hair and disappeared through a curl into the cavernous bouffant of teased, shellac-sprayed hair.

Unaware, Marie continued her discourse: "The first Elvis movie released in 1964 was **Kissin' Cousins** where Elvis plays Josh Morgan and Jodie Tatum. I already explained how **The Beverly Hillbillies** took off on 'Lil Abner. In **Kissin' Cousins** Elvis did the same. Now every time they do a movie 'bout the hills they show beautiful backwoods girls. Well it ain't so, with hill people gettin' no dental care, no vaccinations, no doctors for stomach problems, and no hot water for washin'.

"The film starts with Elvis as Josh Morgan back in the service: the Air Force. Fanciful made-up stuff takes place. Elvis sings 'bout huntin' grizzly bears. Ain't no grizzlies in the Smokey's where the film takes place. There's a dance scene where a couple trip over each other. They didn't reshoot the scene! Was our Elvis not worth fifty extra feet a' film?

"Finally there's Ronald Reagan's daughter, Maureen Reagan, playin' Lorraine, leader a' the Kittyhawks: a bunch a' wild women lookin' for men. Never was such a thing in the hills. Just like a Reagan to be actin' and believin' somethin' that ain't real."

I attempted to break her rhythm. "How do you know so much about the hills? I thought you were from Memphis."

"I was born in my father's house in North Carolina while he was overseas. Ya see he served in the infantry, WWII, the big one, with a Good Conduct Medal. 'Course he said ya had to really screw up not to get that medal. He met my Ma at a dance hall in Raleigh in the fall a' 1940. He'd been drafted, had finished boot camp, and was on leave. Glenn Miller was playin' and my Ma had too many Rum and Coca-Colas. Ma was eager to get married so's the neighbors would forget about that mess that happened when a colored boy busted up a chifforobe for her.

"Anyways, Pa promised my Ma a bright future. She fell for it: hook, line, sinker, and stink bait. I was conceived during the second verse of 'Chattanooga Choo Choo' in the back of a '36 Buick.

When next on leave they got married. Four months later I was born. Pa, he shipped out to the Aleutians, then North Africa, and then France. He spent four years searchin' foxholes looking for an atheist. All he found was Ernie Pyle.

"Ma didn't see him till '45. He came home, but with none a' the nylons and chocolate bars he promised in his letters. He went back to minin' coal in a small town 'bout fifty miles from Mayberry. But he didn't treat my Ma right. He were a different man after years a' soldierin' and fightin' and seein' Pariee.

"He stayed with Ma for a while, long 'nough for her to birth three more babies. One day he up and left. We felt blessed, though we found ourselves poor. Ma didn't know what do to. But she had a cousin: a beautician in Memphis. We took the Greyhound—the grey dog—headin' for Memphis. Ma learned hair dressin' and did well. 'Fore long she had started her own shop. She saved up and bought a house on the southside a' Memphis, high up on a ridge, just a half mile from the Mississippi bridge. But my life ain't nearly the import a' the life of Elvis.

"Elvis next made **Viva Las Vegas** with Ann-Margret. She's a double sign. She starred in the movie version a' **Bye Bye Birdie**. Elvis had many nicknames for Ann: Bunny, Thumper, Scoobie, Rusty Ammo. Her real name was Ann-Margret Olsson. Some claim she's the long lost daughter of Mrs. Olsson from the coffee commercials. But actually, I see Ann-Margret as Bunny—a spring fertility symbol—a love goddess like Aphrodite. They released **Viva Las Vegas** in '64 but they filmed it in the summer of '63.

"My younger sister, Judy, worked summers in Vegas as a lifeguard. In May she'd drive Route 66, trying to get her kicks. Once she was poolside at the Sahara Hotel. She looked up and saw Elvis, his body gleamin' in the early evenin' sunset, standin' on the balcony of the Presidential Suite, in boxer shorts. It was a moment that takes your breath away, like flyin' a kite on a crisp autumn day, a brilliant sunrise, or bronchial asthma.

"Actually Elvis weren't on the balcony but stood behind the glass door—I guess for security reasons. Judy, she stood up on her lifeguard stand. She saw Elvis starin' at her body. Then she grabbed the bullhorn hangin' from the chair," Marie read from lines written on a Las Vegas restaurant paper placemat taped onto the scroll, "and Judy called out to him:

> But soft! What white boy through yonder slidin' door breaks?
> It is the east, and Elvis is the sun.
> Arise, fair Elvis, shoot the envious Kentucky moon,
> Who is already sickly and grievin' with blues,
> That you are made far more fair than she:
> Her best liver and onions is but sick and green
> And none but fools rush in to eat of it.
> It is my Elvis, O, it is my love!
> O, that he knew he were!
> He speaks, yet he says nothin': what of that?
> His eyes sing; I will answer them.
> But I's too bold, it ain't to me he sings:
> Two of the flaming stars in all the heaven,
> Havin' some tinklin' to do, ask the eyes a' Elvis
> To twinkle in their place till they return.
> The firmness of his cheeks shame all movie stars.
> See how he leans his cheek upon his hand!
> O, that I were a baseball glove upon that hand,
> That I might be spat upon by that cheek!
> O Elvis, Elvis! Where the hell are you Elvis?
> Deny Vernon and refuse his name;
> Or, if thou wilt not, be but sworn my love,
> And I'll no longer wear a chantilly lace chaplet.

"I don't know that Elvis knew Judy's name, 'cause he stood behind the slidin' glass door poundin' in anguish, screamin', 'Elaine! Elaine!' Then men pulled Elvis away and Judy watched as they taped tin foil over the window. Elvis stayed in Vegas only long 'nough to finish the movie where Red West bilocates."

"He bilocates? Two places at once?" My mouth fell open.

Marie's patience oscillated and at this moment she calmly explained, "In one scene in **Viva Las Vegas,** Elvis as Lucky goes in the Swingers Casino full a' rowdy Texans. As Lucky enters, out comes Red West carryin' off this girl. But next thing ya know, Red West's inside with the Texans. He bilocates.

"One last thing. This is the first Elvis 'fix the machine by race time' movie. He fixes his sports car in the nick a' time to drive in the Las Vegas Grand Prix. Course 'Prix', that's a French word. Even I knows ya don't say 'Grand Pricks.'

"About this time my Ma moved out of Memphis to the town of Harper Valley with my sister. But few things seem to work out for Ma. She left town after some trouble with the local PTA."

She unrolled the scroll. The left spoon smacked repeatedly on the counter. "Listen," I said, "this scroll thing would work better if you had used a straight stick instead of a spoon." She looked at the scroll, then at me, "I was just tryin' to remember how we made Bible scrolls as kids in VBS."

"VBS? What's that?" I sorted through my memory files of Vietnam War era acronyms.

"Vacation Bible School," she said. "I didn't have no straight stick. But you is right." She grabbed the left end of the scroll. With a forceful snap she broke the wooden spoon off the wooden handle. "Here, darlin'," handing the broken spoon blade to me, "keep this as proof a' what happened here."

The tape recorder clicked off again. I inserted another cassette. This pause freed my mind to finally pay attention to my long-ignored bladder. I stood up. "I need the Men's Room." Marie pointed left. I walked down the counter and entered the door marked "RESTROOM." Unfortunately I found my experience of relief tempered by the acoustics of the restroom, a tiled echo chamber. Surely she could hear me. I redirected my efforts to minimize the noise. I washed my hands and self-consciously left the restroom. Before I could regain my stool, Marie, as if our conversation had never been interrupted, went on:

"In '64 Elvis made **Roustabout** with Barbara Stanwyck from that TV show **The Big Valley**. 'Course she never found no peace in the valley what with a daughter too impetuous to play it safe, a hot-tempered Nick, and Heath, a outsider fightin' for recognition. Barbara Stanwyck played Maggie Morgan who worked with Joe Lean played by Leif Erickson. Joe Lean, who don't look like no Vikin', runs Elvis and his moto'cycle off the road into a fence. Later Elvis as Charlie Rogers gets in a fight with Leif Erickson. You'll be relieved, Floyd the barber don't show up, but Mr. Haney from **Green Acres** does.

"In the first Elvis film a' '65, **Girl Happy**, Elvis played Rusty Wells who sings in a band with Bing Crosby's son on guitar. The band plays in these nightclubs and ya keep wonderin' when the fight'll break out. Elvis always fights in restaurants and nightclubs. Finally, at the end comes the fight. Seems ya cain't get through a Elvis movie without a fight. Why if Elvis'd played Gandhi he still would a' punched somebody! In **Girl Happy** Elvis played 'long side Shelley Fabares for the first time.

"For his second 1965 movie Elvis played Lonnie Beale in **Tickle Me**, though there ain't much ticklin'. Hollywood combined Elvis with Mr. Ed and **Gilligan's Island**. Lonnie befriends one Stanley Potter, a land-locked Gilligan with Brussels sprouts 'round his neck. Durin' the song 'Dirty, Dirty Feeling' a horse starts talkin'. More strange things happen. Elvis answers the thoughts a' Stanley. Then at the pool shows up one Mr. Dabney who looks and sounds like he's the father a' Gomer Pyle. Here's another film where the bad guys just disappear. A' course Red West fights Elvis in a restaurant.

"Elvis lived in Hollywood and Memphis. Now he had a sleepwalkin' problem. He'd get up all hours a' the day or night. Someone always spent the night watchin' so's he wouldn't jump out the window or somethin'. They'd say to Elvis, 'We's here if you talk in your sleep or get up.' Once they saw Elvis get up, grab his police flashlight off the nightstand, stumble into the john, and start washin' his hands. Elvis yelled, 'Out, damned spot!' They 'sposed he dreamed 'bout some dog, but Elvis said, 'All the perfumes of Arabia will not sweeten this little hand. Oh, oh, oh!' This happened while filming **Harum Scarum**.

"In **Harum Scarum** Elvis played Johnny Tyronne, a movie star trapped in a lost kingdom—an Arab Shangri-la. Elvis joined a band a' thieves and musicians with Billy Barty from the old Spike Jones T.V. show. Red West got promoted to 'Assassin.' In a black tunic he wandered 'round tryin' kill Elvis. In **Paradise, Hawaiian Style**, Red went back to jumpin' Elvis in restaurants.

"They couldn't have Elvis leave the Service again. We fans weren't stupid. So Elvis wore a uniform and left an airline. In **Paradise, Hawaiian Style** Elvis started a helicopter business and flies around the fella who looks like Gomer Pyle's old man playin' Mr. Cubberson, an alligator shoe salesman. Elvis felt the doldrums of the islands and tired of Hawaii films.

"Wait a minute, I mixed these up." So involved in describing the films, Marie had not followed her scroll. Staring at her sacred shelf-paper she found her error. "After **Harum Scarum** Elvis didn't make **Paradise, Hawaiian Style**, no he made **Frankie and Johnny**, the film that brought **The Beverly Hillbillies** full circle. Donna Douglas, Elly Mae on the **Hillbillies**, played Frankie. And Colonel Potter from **M.A.S.H.** played the piano. He never shows this on **M.A.S.H.**; didn't want to show up Fr. Mulcahey. Did you know that after the war Potter got him a job in the Los Angeles Police Department?

"They cut a scene where the southern beauty Frankie wants to fix a special dinner for Johnny, so she starts afishin' off the back a' the showboat. Elvis as Johnny asks a deckhand why she's fishin' in her fancy dress. He answers, 'Never asks to know for whom the belle trolls, she trolls for thee.'

"Now my friend Marcie, she got to go to Hollywood a second time. She went on a studio tour and saw Elvis drive out." Marie pointed to postcards taped on the scroll. "Marcie sent me these:

> The limo he sat in, like a varnish'd throne,
> Burn'd rubber on the pavement. The hood was beaten gold;

> Purple the curtains, and so perfumed with Brut that
> The winds were love-sick; the silvery Mag wheels,
> Which to the tune a' the eight-track kept beat, and made
> The pavement on which they rolled move faster,
> As amorous of their smoke.
> On each side a' him,
> Sat pretty heavy, dimpled bodyguards, like smilin' Cupids.
> As for his own person,
> It panhandled all description.

That's how she put it.

"Elvis made **Spinout** in 1966. It could a' been called **Spin Off**. I's sure those movie moguls cut a deal with the fashion moguls to make this film: a commercial for 1960s mod clothes. It's also another film with Elvis surrounded by dozens a' bikini-clad dolls. This time at a pool. In other films it's at the beach. Know what this reminds me of?"

"Frankie Avalon movies?" I speculated.

"Frankie Avalon? Hell no. Elvis is a beach master."

"A beach master?" I gasped in ignorance.

"Yea, a beach master. Don't ya watch no educational TV? Ya see, if ya watch'd nature shows, like Jacques Cousteau, you'd know 'bout beach masters. A beach master's a male sea elephant. In matin' season he comes up out a' the ocean and drags his carcass onto the beach to stake out his territory. If other males enter his turf he runs 'em off. Soon the females arrive. Each male claims all the females in his territory. That's a beach master—just like Elvis and his guitar.

"Oh, one last thing. They had a car race in this movie and a' course Elvis struggled to get his machine ready by race time. And speakin' of Frankie Avalon, I heard some time ago he wanted to do socially relevant movies. So he planned a film, **Beach Blanket Bosnia**. That's what I heard.

"Next for Elvis came **Easy Come, Easy Go**. How Elvis suffered through this, singin' 'bout yoga and watchin' spaghetti artwork, I don't know. Hollywood desperate for a movie beginning put Elvis back in the service: the navy. In this film Elvis had his only underwater fight scene, like Mike Nelson in **Sea Hunt**.

"Besides movies, Elvis did recordin'. In '67 Elvis released 'How Great Thou Art.' Later, after 'In The Ghetto' became such a hit, Elvis thought about doing a album of Ghetto religious songs called 'How Bad You Is.' Nothin' came of it.

"Before the year was out Elvis did **Double Trouble** and **Clambake**. **Double Trouble**'s another fashion commercial for mod clothes. Except for Elvis. In short jackets, he looks like a waiter. The movie try's to cross the Beatle's **HELP** with **The Pink Panther**. Ya wonder if plots in Elvis movies weren't just excuses to string a bunch a' songs together.

"Typical Elvis movie stuff happens. Elvis as Guy sings on a truck tailgate, like in **Kid Galahad**. Elvis visits a European festival with a kraut Shirley Temple, flamingo dancers, and Arab dancers in costumes left from **Harum Scarum**. Our beloved Elvis walked through a swirlin' screen a' foolishness. A man falls down the oldest well in Antwerp and its got corrugated steel sides! At the end a parrot on a sinkin' boat squawks, 'This is another fine mess you got me into, Matie.' It ain't talkin' to the man in the boat, the parrot's talkin' to the producer.

"In **Clambake** Elvis made another 'fix up the machine by race time' movie. This time it's a boat. The bizarre thing in this film is that Shelley Fabares as Dianne Carter tries to decide 'tween Bill Bixby as James Jamison and Elvis as Scott Hayward. It takes her all movie to finally pick Elvis over Eddie's father. Can ya believe it? Oh and Flipper the dolphin shows up and Red West sells ice cream: a' course maybe he was practicin' disguises as 'Elvis Enemy Number One.'

"Hollywood released **Stay Away, Joe** in 1968. It should a' been called Stay Awake, Joe—a movie so tedious ya squirm. They tries to spice it up by addin' tush shots like some sorta' cheesecake special. It don't help. They got Elvis playin' Joe, a half Indian who rides a Triumph moto'cycle. You'd think he'd own a Indian moto'cycle. Burgess Meredith plays Joe's Indian father, but I liked him better as the Penguin. Joan Blondell runs Callahan's grocery store and tavern, practicin' to run the saloon on **Here Come the Brides**. At Joe's house they throw wild parties that sound like the Tijuana Brass is in the background.

"Late in the movie Elvis, playin' Joe, bets a half-dozen rodeo men they cain't ride his bull. So they all take turns tryin'. Each time the bull comes out its horns is different: sometimes up, sometimes down, one time missin'. The movie ends with a comic fight with sound effects put in. But it couldn't match the quality of a Three Stooges fight scene.

"Elvis fights in most a' his movies 'cause it sold tickets. Hollywood figgered he shall fight on the beaches, he shall fight in the restaurants, he shall fight in the fields and in the streets, he shall fight in the hills; he will never surrender.

"The most unusual thing 'bout **Stay Away, Joe**—Elvis don't wind up with any girl. And we fans had no clue as to which girl he should a' got. Also, instead a' gettin' his car ready for a race, Elvis finds his car bein' tore to pieces.

"'At this point Elvis figgered his movie career a bust. He thought he shoulda gone into plastics like the man told Ben in **The Graduate**. Hollywood decided to go back to 'fix the machine by race time' and 'Elvis gets the main girl' formulas for **Speedway**. They got Nancy Sinatra, with her boots made for walkin', singin' 'bout her groovy self. Ya can guess the endin'.

"**Live a Little, Love a Little** is movie twenty-eight. Michele Carey plays Bernice, an obsessed dingbat out to get Elvis. Ya know in the end Elvis will fall in love with her, but ya don't want him too. I don't believe it's right for a man to strike a woman, but in this film I'd make an exception. Ya keep wantin' Elvis to slap Bernice 'round, and throw her out the door.

"They got a dream scene of Elvis dancin' in blue lamé pajamas. Elvis never goes into a bar or restaurant so there's no chance for a regular Elvis fight scene. They just have Red West and a workman try to beat him up in a newspaper pressroom. Ya watch this movie and understand why Elvis'd get sick before startin' a movie. The only sensible part a' this film is that Bernice gets straightened out emotionally by sleepin' with Elvis.

"**Live a Little, Love a Little** is another fashion show. Michele Carey looks like a mannequin, with a new outfit for every scene. They only put four lousy songs in the film which weren't 'nough to give it socially redeemin' value. As ya see, these movies kept gettin' worse."

If Marie expected sympathy she deceived herself. The effort required to suffer through this discourse left no energy for pity for anyone but myself. Marie finished movie twenty-eight—only three more to go. A distant, but finite end existed.

Marie sighed, "We had thought Elvis lost. The King a' Rock and Roll dead and buried under a monstrous pile a' Hollywood horseshit. But then, when we least expected it, he came back, like one raised from the dead. Just as Isis picked up the pieces of her dead husband, Osiris, and brought him back to life, so the dead pieces of the career of Elvis was picked up by one Steve Binder and new life breathed into Elvis.

"I speak a' the 1968 Comeback Special of Elvis. Dread and anticipation filled us the weeks before the show. We fear'd they turn Elvis into Andy Williams. But with the first moment we saw the Elvis we once knew—alive! The Elvis a' real Rock and Roll! There stood Lazarus askin' us, 'If you're lookin' for trouble,' and a' course we was. We sat stunned. I wrote this psalm." From the scroll Marie pulled a folded and crease-torn Mod Squad poster with writing on the margins.

> When they brought back Elvis the captive of Hollywood,
> We was like men and women dreamin',
> Then our mouth was filled with laughter and our tongue
>   with rejoicin'.
> Then they said among the nations,
> "The King has done great things."
> "The King had done great things for us;"
> We is glad indeed.

> Restore your fortunes, O King, like the torrents in the southern desert.
> Those that sow in tears shall reap rejoicin'.
> Although they go forth weepin', carryin' the seed to be sown,
> They shall come back rejoicin' carryin' sheaves of new releases.
> For we can dream, we can dream

"Elvis ended the show in white, a preacher man talkin' 'bout peace and understandin'. He sang 'If I Can Dream'—Elvis the King grasping the torch and the message of Martin Luther King!

"The show ended: an event so wondrous it left us speechless. Our old RCA went black. We sat in silence on foldin' chairs behind collapsible TV tables each with a six-ounce Coke bottle and a bag a' Frito's. After thirty minutes, Bernie—she always said the right thing—spoke." Marie read a torn page of TV Guide where Bernie's words had been scrawled next to an ad for a nostril hair trimming tool. "'Let us therefore brace ourselves to our duties, and so bear ourselves that, if the memory of Elvis last for a thousand years, men will still say: "This was his finest hour!"' After that we had dessert of vanilla ice cream covered with Creme de Menthe liquor. We loved that treat—'til they came out with green mouthwash. After that Creme de Menthe looked like Scope on your ice cream.

"Back to Elvis. Like the last spasms of a dyin' hog shot before slaughter, Hollywood jerked three last movies out a' Elvis and squeezed a few more drops a his blood: **Charro!**, **The Trouble With Girls**, and **Change of Habit**. In **Charro!** Elvis did not sing. He just acted in his version of a Clint Eastwood western. But you see, Clint Eastwood could just stand there, doing nothin', and look dangerous, but Elvis standin' and doing nothin' looks stupid. Elvis had to be movin'.

"Next came **The Trouble with Girls**. This is one bizarre film with Elvis wearin' costumes from the wrong era. The movie jumps 'round so much ya think the editors was on drugs. The full title is **The Trouble with Girls and How To Get Into It**. But Elvis only had one girl and gave no advice to lonely men seekin' entanglements. Somebody could sue for false advertisin'.

"Lastly Elvis made **Change of Habit** as Dr. John Carpenter. It starts with the only nun strip scene in film history. Even Doctor Elvis gets into a fight, beatin' up mobsters who just disappear. A' course the movie leaves ya hangin'. Does Mary Tyler Moore as Sister Michelle choose Elvis or God? Does she stay a nun or marry Elvis? Does she choose the King or the King?

"The movie ends with Elvis singin' at a Catholic mass. My Catholic friend Marcie, said it weren't real, 'cause Elvis sang all the verses. Catholics never do that." My mind sorted its file of Roman Catholic memories and except for the Litany of the Saints could find no record of singing more than two verses.

Marie continued, "The camera zoomed back, with' Elvis singin' in the chapel—the last movie scene for Elvis. His film career ended. Thirty-one films—even if they weren't the greatest and didn't make that French Canned Film Festival, or the Sundance Kid Festival—that's quite a 'complishment. Despite the quality of those movies, Elvis shines through. Ya often walk away from an Elvis movie thinkin' it weren't no good. But ya never think Elvis weren't no good. He saved those movies. He's the reason they made money. He's the reason people still watch those films.

"A' course that's the tragedy—Hollywood never figgered out how to use Elvis. The best movies match the life a' Elvis. He had to supply the main film ideas. Hollywood wasted the talent and beauty of Elvis. No one can match the beauty of Elvis.

"Elvis imitators match the hair, sideburns, voice, clothes, gestures, even the singin' of Elvis. But they cain't match his beauty. The face a' Elvis was unique. It filled the screen—the dark eyes set under jet black hair, that half-cocky, confident and friendly sneerin' smile drawin' ya near, makin' ya want to be his closest friend. Nobody can duplicate that.

"Hollywood, not knowing what to do with Elvis, squandered him: too much greed and too much monkey business." Marie finished her cinematic review. Her speed in describing thirty-one movies impressed me. As she ticked off the films I had been summoning up courage to insist on my exit. I said, "Listen, it is very late. I have to go. I am sorry, but I have to go!"

Marie stared. "Mister, bein' sorry means never havin' to say you're in love. Now if ya have no love for life, for Elvis, or for your fated duty, you may go and leave behind the burden chosen for you. You have no fear a' your fate. But for me, 'twas fate that taught my soul to fear. If ya go, I'll pray the force by with you. I knows ya want to go, ya think you've got a lot of livin' to do. But as long as I have you hope remains that my message'll be heard. If ya leave, my voice shall be silent and what should be shouted from the condo tops will not be heard.

"But I plead with you, don't leave me now. I'll not repeat what I say—once is enough. I ain't askin' one more day, just a couple a' hours. I am doin' the best I can to not take too long. Sit there and take it like a man! The 'gentleman' doth protest too damn much methinks!" Her steely eyes stared—shaking in intensity. Ever face muscle taut, holding back an expression of great disappointment—that if I left I would crush her, her last hope and her only reason for living—I would have failed her, myself, and every living being on earth. I could not move.

The empty coffeepot had ceased steaming. Acrid burnt-coffee odor curled upward. A dull crunch preceded a four part cracking as the glass pot disintegrated on the burner. The handle and ring fell into a sink of standing water. An intense sizzle came up from the dead soapy water. Marie hardly noticed.

My resolve to flee cracked and fizzled into nothing.

CHAPTER 10

ELVIS

A WEDDING OUTSIDE OF CANA

Marie rolled up her scroll and took an oratorical break to clear the dirty pots. She pried the lid off one, then pulled hard on the ladle inside. With the slurp of a swamp-mired boot the utensil dislodged, splattering muddy paste on the refrigerator. Marie stared into the pot, sniffed it, then jerked back in revulsion. "Whew! Three day old chili! Usually we reheat this stuff. But I'm gonna pitch this batch. I've seen too many a man eat this chili; sit there on his stool as gas built up in his gullet and then, bam! He'd hoist himself with his own petard! That's one way to inherit the wind." She laughed.

I had no idea what this babbling meant, but I smiled. Assuming I comprehend, Marie spoke again of Elvis:

"Smack dab in the midst a' makin' movies—human cartoons—Elvis took to hisself a bride: Priscilla Ann Beaulieu. It broke my heart that he'd chosen another, hurtin' far worse than that scorchin' July day they sent my blue ribbon 4H calf to market after I tended, raised, and lavished love on it for a year. I lamented bitterly, 'Elvis, my Elvis, why has you forsaken me?' But in truth, lordy, I was not worthy to receive Elvis.

"The pain turned numb, I yearned for a new Camelot: Elvis as King Arthur takin' his beloved Guinevere. Lee Harvey Oswald, a fourth cousin on my Ma's side, ended an earlier Camelot."

"You were related to Oswald?" Stunned, I tried to separate truth from fantasy in this bizarre conversation.

"Yes darlin', Oswalds was distant kin, we never saw 'em much. As ya probably heard, Lee Harvey Oswald assassinated President Kennedy endin' Camelot," Marie tried to enlighten me.

"I heard someone mention it." I lapsed into the sarcasm of despair.

Marie retied her apron, a certain sign of an impending tangent: "A word 'bout Kennedy. My close friend, Marcie—Marcella—worked here. She grew up papist, ya know Roman Catholic—plaid school uniforms, doilies on the head in church—the whole bit. She told me the Kennedy election in 1960 excited Catholics, 'cause back in 1928, one Hal Smith ran for president and lost cause a' his bein' Catholic. Anyways, Kennedy gave Catholics so much pride; they started hangin' his picture in Catholic schools and churches, right next to Washington and Lincoln. 'Tween John the Baptist and St. Aloysius you'd find Kennedy. A story made the rounds 'bout Kennedy bein' a 'holy Joe'. Marcie's Ma told her Kennedy for many an evenin' prayer said three Hail Mary's, a papist prayer, and sang 'Ave Maria' before bed. Was this story true or was it just P.R.? If true, did JFK say three Hail Mary's the nights he jumped in bed with Marilyn Monroe? Must a' been the quickest prayers in history."

"Elvis sang 'Ave Maria' in his 1970 Vegas show in a medley with 'I Got a Woman.' Many people remember clearly the day Kennedy died. But I asks ya, how many remember the day Colonel Sanders died? 'Cause for most folk, the Colonel had more effect on their lives than JFK."

The juxtaposition of Kennedy and Catholicism brought forth my memory of the moment in November 1963 when I learned of Kennedy's assassination. I sat alone in the cafeteria, staring at a Melmac tray of canned ravioli and dried looking green peas, commanded by the lunch attendant to stay until I finished. When she turned away, ravioli and peas went into my empty milk carton. I took the seemingly empty tray to the dish counter, past the attendant's inspecting eyes, and threw the carton into the trash. I headed not out to recess but upstairs to my classroom where due to the heavy rain and dark clouds—darkness descended when Jesus died—my classmates sat restless and noisy. As I reached the landing on the stairs I saw through the wrought iron rail on the floor above me—one person in shock spoke to another, who spoke to another, and as they passed their grief along I put together the pieces. President Kennedy had been assassinated. It took a moment to comprehend that "assassination" meant Kennedy had been shot. Dismay and fear of the unknown gripped me, but it could not overcome the guilt I felt over the peas and ravioli—denied to starving pagan babies in Borneo—that lay at the bottom of a galvanized trash can reeking of sour milk.

I shook my head to fight these distracting thoughts and painful memories. I looked straight into Marie's eyes. "Elvis!" I pleaded. "Stay with Elvis! You asked me to listen to you. You have convinced me there is so much Elvis world to see. Please, get back to Elvis," I growled.

"You is right, hun', I've drifted onto politics. Stay on Elvis I must. The Bible book a' Acts describes Priscilla the wife of Aquila. 'Aquila' means eagle in Latin. Priscilla of the Bible married the eagle. Priscilla Beaulieu married a soarin' eagle, with a olive branch a' the love ballad in one claw and arrows a' Rock and Roll in another: the Las Vegas, jumpsuited Elvis, blazoned like a glorious peacock in magnificent plumage. The eagle signs Elvis. When Elvis began his career he often sang at the Eagle's Nest in Memphis. Oh, one more sign: they made that play 'bout Elvis goin' in the army, **Bye Bye Birdie**.

"Priscilla can be found in the Bible's Song of Songs." Marie found the loose page. "The woman says this:

> Draw me, we will run after thee: the King brought me into his chambers: we will be glad and rejoice in thee, we will remember thy love more than wine. (Song of Solomon 1:4)

"Priscilla didn't want no artist's renderin' done a' her, like in court. She wanted to chase after the King. Elvis as King and Priscilla as Queen used special royal language. Each said 'we' instead of 'I' or 'me.' Pretty highfalutin, but they did it.

"The man in Song a' Songs went to eloquatin' on Priscilla:

> Behold, thou art fair, my love; behold, thou art fair;
> Thou hast doves' eyes within thy locks:
> Thy hair is as a flock of goats, that appear from mount Gilead.
> Thy teeth are like a flock of sheep that are even shorn, which came up from washin';
> Whereof every one bears twins, and none is barren among them.
> Thy lips are like a thread of scarlet, and thy speech is comely:
> Thy cheeks are like a half of pomegranate within thy locks.
> Thy neck is like the tower of David builded for an armoury,
> Whereon there hang a thousand bucklers,
> All shields of mighty men. (Song of Solomon, 4:1-4)

"Priscilla exactly! Her long black hair, when it weren't in a beehive, looked like a flock a' jet black goats shimmerin' as they ran down a hillside. The bucklers 'round the tower—that baubles and jewels 'round the neck a' Priscilla.

"In 1962 Elvis brought underaged Priscilla from Germany to Graceland. How this scandal escaped the press I don't rightly know. Elvis shaped Priscilla, telling her how to do her makeup and hair, what to wear. He molded his woman in his image, just like in Hogmalion. She attended the Catholic nun-run Immaculate Conception Cathedral High School for girls. Elvis said, 'Get thee to a nunnery!' and she wound up on 'Virginity Row.'

"Now 'bout the hair a' Priscilla. People lookin' at old pictures snicker at her beehive. It looks stupid, but it didn't look ridiculous then. Her towerin' coiffure scaled the heights a' fashion. I know it looks like a bear skin hat worn by British guards, ya know, a busby. If you put horns on her hair she'd look like Fred Flintstone at the

Royal Order a' Waterbuffalo. In the 1960s, Priscilla had respectably cool hair."

I sat baffled. How could Marie joke about Priscilla's hair and not feel self-conscious about her own hair? Hair, which I now attempted to estimate the height of, comparing it to the white ceramic wall tiles. Marie's hair stood four and five tiles in height depending on where the top of her head actually lay. At four inches per tile her coiffure figured in the 16 to 20 inch range. Marie remained oblivious to my head movements as I lined up her hair with the tiles. On she spoke:

"The big worry with that hairstyle was high winds. Why if ya wore high heels and a sudden gust come up, if ya didn't get off the sidewalk and dig them heels into the dirt, you'd be prone, right quick. Here's a picture of Priscilla and her beehive standin' next to the red Corvair Elvis gave her." She pulled a picture from her apron. "I always wondered how she fit into that low roof car. Today she could buy a Toyota with a sunroof and stick her hair out the roof. But I wonder if Marge Simpson's livin' out some Priscilla Presley fantasy.

"After years of Priscilla runnin' 'bout the house, Elvis married her. Some say Elvis didn't want marriage 'cause he enjoyed playin' the field so much he coulda' been awarded the 'Gold Glove of Philanderin'.' Others think Elvis wanted a long trial period, believing the old sayin', 'The unexamined wife is not worth livin' with.' Elvis often said, 'The lady loves me.'"

"But Elvis did marry," I interrupted. "Are you going to use as a symbol the gospel wedding at Cana?" A rookie chess player versus a grand master, I attempted to anticipate her move.

Marie nodded patronizingly at my feeble attempt. "No, ya see Cana and Canaan stand for Memphis. Elvis married in Las Vegas, a weddin' outside a' Cana. No, we must look at Genesis, chapter 29, where crafty Laban tricked Jacob into marryin' both his daughters when Jacob only wanted the better looker."

The flaw of my strategy apparent: I had assumed a logical move on Marie's part. She resumed:

"Just like Laban tricked Jacob into a marriage Jacob didn't want, so Parker tricked Elvis into a unwanted marriage. Fate cut Laban and Parker from the same mold. Both was fast-talkin', cigar-smokin', wheeler-dealers. Parker hawked stage flesh, Laban hawked camel flesh. Laban, he ran a used camelot.

"The Colonel arranged the marriage, setting up the whole event: the date, location, weddin' ceremony, reception, and guest list—all on the cheap with secrecy, no taste, no class. Recall, Parker showed up at the funeral of Elvis in a Hawaiian bowlin' shirt! What did an old carnival man know 'bout weddin's? He probably wanted a parade of elephants, monkeys, and the Elvis Midget Fan Club with hisself in a red coat and top hat as the ringmaster, like it's carnival time. Parker didn't invite the close friends a' Elvis! He brushed 'em off to show his control over Elvis. One a' the Memphis Mafia, thinkin' Elvis made the decision, cursed: 'Shall I be flouted by a dunghill groom?'

"Right after they got hitched, Elvis and Priscilla held a press conference. It never came out 'bout her bein' live-in jailbait at Graceland. Here's a tune describing the press conference." Marie broke into song:

> Whiles a wedlock-hymn we sing,
> Feed yourselves with questioning,
> That reason wonder may diminish,
> How thus they met, and these things finish.

"We knew Elvis'd take good care of her. Nine months later she gave birth to Lisa Marie. Marcie was surprised Priscilla got pregnant so soon what with all Elvis knew 'bout rhythm.

"With Elvis no longer single and available, I decided to get hitched—while I still looked young and beautiful. Other girls threatened to kill theirselves or join convents. Not me. Ya see, I'd met this man, a brown-eyed handsome man: Bubba. A man with Ben Casey hairy arms, who had moved to Memphis after livin' in Canada with those Canucks. He'd gone there to play pro hockey—

to seek fame and fortune. In high school he'd been voted 'Most Likely to Loose Teeth in an Altercation.' But he weren't no good. When it came his turn to leave the bench and get on the ice, he'd actually use the door. Before hockey he played football for some Tom Laundry, or was it Vince Lumbago? I can't recall. Bubba came to Memphis where I met him. He claimed to be from a well-established Biloxi family, the Buxtehude's."

"Bubba Buxtehude of Biloxi?" I gasped in disbelief.

Marie looked surprised, "Oh, so you've heard a' him."

"Buxtehude was a Baroque music composer!" I tried to explain.

"That's the man," she responded, "Bubba—a penniless, mandolin playin', bluegrass, Gordon Lightfoot style, songwriter, who failed at professional sports. Despite his braggin' 'bout his bloodline, I suspect he was of scalawag pedigree. 'Course maybe his family had connections—he never got drafted. I met Bubba when we took courses at the community college. I first saw him in the cafeteria, sittin', readin', and strugglin' to understand some biology textbook. With the other tables full up, I sat down with him. After scratchin' his head at his readin', he looked at me and asked if I knew what 'Homo Erectus' meant? At first I thought he must be a deviant. Then I figgered 'Homo Erectus' meant frozen 2% milk. So I said so. Bubba accepted the answer.

"You could call it love at first sight. But more accurately I'd call it lust at first sight. Passion and cravin' whelmed over our better senses. Me—heartbroke that Elvis had married—thought this mere man could fill my empty soul. I let myself believe I truly loved him. But love is for lovers not fools. He weren't all that handsome, but a' course the more desperate one is, the better lookin' someone else becomes.

"I wanted Ma to let him live at our house, to rent a room. But she had a rule 'gainst renters: repel boarders. Bubba found an apartment, I moved in with him. We hung up a 'Home Sweet Home' sign. Without datin', we found a willin' padre and got hitched. Just like Elvis and Priscilla we dropped 'obey' from our vows. I hoped for a happy marriage—such are young dreams. But his birthday fell in the wrong zodiac sign. How could I 'a thought he coulda' equaled Elvis. 'Fool' I called myself.

"How could our marriage last: a woman reboundin' from Elvis's marriage and a moron husband? It weren't no paradise, Hawaiian style. Blinded by what I thought was burnin' love, I'd married the stupidest man in Memphis. Actually, he didn't have brains enough to rank as stupid. Bubba made Eb Dawson, Clem Kadiddlehopper, and Hank Kimball look like a couple a' geniuses.

"Bubba made Forest Gump look like Albert Einstein. Ya' know, when I saw **Forest Gump** I kept thinkin', 'Ain't I seen this before?' Then it hit like a ton of charcoal briquettes. Forest Gump weren't nothin' but a thinkin' man's Gomer Pyle.

"Now that Bubba, a man who wore Calvin Coolidge jeans and ate Bama Pies by the sackful, once bought a air conditioner. Then he took it back to Sears complainin' it didn't work 'cause when he turned it on, no tinsel came from the vents.

"Bubba worked for United Van Lines. He got fired after two weeks 'cause rather than totin' furniture he sat in the cab listenin' to the radio and eating tacos, lettin' the other men do all the work. I guess his boss had no use for an unmoved mover.

"Bubba couldn't decide what to do with his life, never got his shit together. Talk 'bout needin' emotional Kaopectate. I knew I was in trouble when I found books hidden in his dresser: **How to Have an Affair on a Budget** and **The Joy of Adultery** and somethin' called **Lady Chitterling's Lover**. I ain't surprised that Bubba had interests in other women. 'Cause the bird in the bush looks two times better than the bird in the hand. As they say, 'The ass is keener on the other side of the fence.'

"Anyways, after six months I moved out. My weddin' ring had been inscribed 'I love you, Bubba'. I first thought of puttin' it on a railroad track and after it had been flattened mailin' it to Bubba. Instead I went to the river and threw it into the muddy waters off the Mississippi bridge. Where romance had been, I found only faded love. Ya see hun', love ain't nothin' like the Beatles said it'd be. We got divorced, luckily agreein' on a friendly settlement. I was terrified we'd have a custody fight over my records and black velvet Elvis paintin's.

"There ain't no happy endin'. I got stung. I've struggled to put back together the pieces of my life. As for Bubba, a few years after our divorce he got hisself a job, travelin' the south painting 'ROCK CITY' on barn roofs. This lasted until one hot July day in Alabama. Bubba who painted the letters in reverse order had almost finished a barn roof. He only needed to add the one leg on the 'R' so it didn't look like a 'P'. Well as he moved 'round to finish he stepped on the wet paint of 'C'. His foot slipped and he tumbled down the roof into a loaded manure spreader parked next to the barn. As he fell he tossed up his pail a' white paint. It landed on the roof just left a' the unfinished 'R'. The pail rolled off the roof makin' a nice 'S' curve 'cause of the wire handle. Paint spilled all over. From the nearby interstate the barn roof spelled 'SPOCK CITY'. Within days thousands a' bewildered misled Trekkies descended on the place. Bubba got fired: his boss checked his previous work, discoverin' how many ways one could misspell 'ROCK CITY.'

"Then Bubba had a 'get rich quick' scheme. Ya see he noticed most folk prefer corn on the cob but buy the cheaper canned corn. Bubba designed a Kernel Press that forced canned corn onto reusable fiberglass cobs. Nothin' ever came of it. When that fizzled Bubba wandered from job to job. For a time he sold insurance for Liberty Valance, or some company. Last I heard, he'd been arrested in Hawaii. Seems he'd gone to a luau to watch grass skirt dancers and took with him a weedeater."

Frustrated, I glared at her, "Listen, either you stop wandering off the topic or you let me go. I have no interest in the exploits of second-rate hockey players."

"Neither do I—only I had to learn it the hard way," she said. "But you is right, I must get back to Elvis and Priscilla.

"Priscilla went with Elvis to a prayer breakfast where the Jaycees named him one a' the Ten Outstanding Young Men in America for 1970. I ask you—who the hell were the other nine? 'Cause Elvis alone was truly outstandin' in America.

"But Elvis left Priscilla alone when he went to Hollywood. Unfortunately Elvis fooled 'round with many a starlet and pseudonymph, figurin' 'I bear a charmed life which must not yield to just one darn woman.' He couldn't be faithful to one woman. Playin' 'round was in his blood, like he had fickle cell anemia.

"Many stories tell 'bout Elvis and his womanizin'. Once while foreplayin' a starlet he felt a lump on her chest. Let me tell ya, that ended Elvis's interest then and there. Nothin' spoils a romance so much as a sense of a tumor in a woman.

"Priscilla wanted to stop all this. She went to Elvis in Hollywood, saying 'I will rise now, and go about the city in the streets, and in the broad ways I will seek him whom my soul loveth: I sought him but I found him not.' (Song of Solomon, 3:2) She asked the studio watchmen for Elvis but they turned her away. A' course 'broad ways' refers to those Hollywood women.

"After years a' neglect, Priscilla got involved with Mike Stone, her Karate teacher. This went on and Elvis didn't know." Marie grabbed her green-stamp booklet. "Nostradamus predicted:

> The furious woman through adulterous rage,
> Will conspire in silence to not tell her Prince:
> Without delay the fault will be made known,
> So that seventeen will die in martyrdom. (VI, 59)

"As things developed, Priscilla became a mature, worldly woman. She stopped readin' teen magazines like **Seventeen**; they became martyrs to her new freedom. Elvis found them in the trash. His suspicious mind led to discovery, as Nostradamus had predicted:

> The sudden coming terror will overwhelm,
> Kept secret by the principal one in the affair:
> The charcoaled lady will be hidden from view,
> Bit by bit the great one's fury will grow. (V, 65)

"Well 'the charcoaled lady' is Priscilla with black hair colorin' and mascara. She's the principal one. Elvis, the great one, became furious." Marie flipped past several pages in her green-stamp booklet that actually had stamps.

"This led to divorce, just as Nostradamus predicted:

> Unwilling to agree to divorce,
> Which will later be seen as unworthy:
> By force will the Island King be driven out,
> One without the mark of kingship will rule. (X, 22)

"'Island King' represents Elvis in Hawaiian movies. Priscilla became involved with men lackin' the marks a' kingship. Elvis didn't want divorce, but agreed. Priscilla accepted a financial settlement, then later came back with lawyers claimin' the settlement unworthy. No way they could patch it up. And believe it or not, another prediction described Priscilla:

> The honored Queen will find herself vanquished,
> Yet she will act with abundant manly courage:
> Riding naked on a horse, she will cross the river,
> Followed by the sword of the outraged faithful. (I, 86)

"Priscilla, vanquished by the divorce, acted with great and manly courage in publishin' her book, **Elvis and Me**, tellin' the truth 'bout it bein' near impossible to live with Elvis. For the first time we knew what's she's really like. With that book she passed over the river. Cause ya see river's a symbol, just like Julius Caesar crossin' the Rubicube to become emperor."

I corrected, "'Rubics Cube' is a puzzle. Julius Caesar crossed the river Rubicon."

"Oh, darned if education ain't a handy thing. Any rate, Priscilla crossed this river—she kind a' rode her horse through it—she bared her soul and told the naked truth. She told how life with Elvis weren't no Camelot but the Keystone Cops. But fans a' Elvis didn't want to hear it. They wanted to believe a fairy tale 'tween Elvis and Priscilla. They attacked Priscilla's book—'followed by the sword' symbolizes this. They claimed her book, even though true, outraged their faith in Elvis.

"Since all that Priscilla's been sellin' her perfume, **Moments**. Some years ago she did commercials hintin' at how Elvis kissed her. Then came the slogan 'bout how a single moment can change your life. Ya can say that again! My uncle Nicholas plowed a field one August day when a thunderstorm came up. A thunderbolt shot out a' the heavens and seared his ass. He ain't been able to sit right since. He's one who'll tell 'bout the effects of a single moment changin' your life. His wife also tells 'bout the disappointin' effects a' that single moment.

"The divorce of Elvis has meanin' of great import of iron. Elvis sang many love songs. He seemed an expert on love. But when it came to Elvis lovin' just one woman, he couldn't do it, even though he kept her like a bird in a guilty cage.

"It didn't work 'cause the course a' true love never ran unclogged—even with the heart of Romeo. The jaws a' darkness wolf love down: so quick bright things come to confusion. Ya see Elvis was a poet, a musical poet. He was a lover, oh lordy how he could love, and he was also like a madman. For lovers and madmen have such seethin' brains, like a cornered possum. And the lunatic, the lover, and the poet—their imaginations come from the same trash compactor. One sees more devils in disguise than vast hell can hold. The lover, all frantic, sees Lucy's beauty in the brow of a fourteen-year-old. The poet's eye, in a fine frenzy roustaboutin', doth glance from heaven to earth, from earth to heaven, claimin', 'This is my heaven.'

"Ya see, those a' us searchin' to love and to be loved looked to Elvis as our beacon. The way he sang 'bout love we believed he must know it intimately. But he was no better at love than us, the lowly ones on the pavement."

The bee had not emerged from Marie's hair. Would it stay in

there? Did it live there? Each speculation fueled another. How could the honeybee live there if Marie washed her hair? But did she wash her hair? How did she get it to look like that? How long did it take to build that Babel's Tower of the tonsorial art? What binding, what epoxy, held it together? What hairpin girders gave it strength and shape? Did she sleep with her hair that way? Had she cut a hole in the headboard to make room for it? And about that bee—did other bees live in her hair? Could there be a honeycomb in there? In terror I looked at the bear-shaped plastic squeeze bottle of honey hibernating on the counter next to the stainless steel napkin dispenser. There, inside the honey bear, I could just barely make out a jet-black hair. My stomach turned as I pushed the honey bear far down the counter.

CHAPTER 11

ELVIS

THE SONS OF ELI

In anxious boredom I drummed my fingers on the counter. Then it hit me: Allen Funt. Allen Funt and Durward Kirby must be here somewhere. Behind the outdated calendar on the wall, behind the stack of plates, behind the Heimlich Maneuver poster, somewhere in this diner there must be a Candid Camera.

Then I heard it again: another train whistle. "Illinois Central?" I asked forgetting my search for the hidden camera. "No, that's the Amtrak," she answered. "Cain't ya tell the difference, hun? This whistle has a higher pitch and is shorter in time. And if ya listen carefully for the rumble a' the train it don't last long. But this don't seem the right time for the Amtrak to New Orleans. Anyways let's get back to Elvis. And note, it was you, not me, who got us off the track this time.

"Yet another Bible person symbolizes Elvis: Eli in the book a' I Samuel," Marie continued, relentless as old age. "First, ya find the name 'Eli' buried in the name Elvis. Second, Elvis died just like Eli. But you'll have to wait for that story.

"Now Eli worked the shrine at Shiloh. But he had wicked sons. For Elvis—who lived 'bout a hundred miles from Shiloh—the sons of Eli represent Colonel Parker and the cronies of Elvis, men they called the 'Memphis Mafia,' who got in good with Elvis by helpin' him, tellin' Elvis he's the greatest, sayin' 'You're the boss,' laughin' at his jokes, and givin' him things. Elvis never heard the warnin', 'Beware a' geeks bearin' gifts.'

"The sons of Eli frolicked in mischief. They'd stick this big fork into meat offerin's the people brought to the shrine and keep whatever came up on the fork. That describes the Colonel. He'd arrange deals for Elvis but keep all the cash he could stab into, then celebrate with steak dinner memorials.

"The sons a' Eli seduced female pilgrims at Shiloh. If that ain't a symbol for Elvis, I don't know what is. Many women pilgrimaged to Graceland, the studio, or the Hollywood homes. Some wanted to gaze upon Elvis, others wanted his John Hancock, and many ached, liked she-camels in heat to embrace Elvis in a split-leg scissors hold. They came for Elvis, but on the sidelines—intensely patient—perched those baldin', overweight, girl happy, sex-starved, copathetic vultures: the Memphis Mafia waitin' for any nymph beyond the appetite of Elvis. Like Syro-Phoenician dogs hungry for table scraps, followin' animal instinct, they licked their chops, anticipatin' the fringe benefits of Elvis employ. Like greedy moneychangers these men struck deals: introduction to the King in exchange for the coin a' the realm: sex.

"Now Elvis—a fellow of infinite jest, of excellent fantasy—threw wild orgy parties at his Hollywood homes. Well ya talk about the good times of Elvis—it was the Hollywood years." Again she referred to her green-stamp book. "Nostradamus predicted this:

> Scandalous things in the holy temple will be perpetrated,
> These will be considered as honors worthy of
>   commendation:
> These will be rewarded with engraved gold and silver
>   medals,
> In strange torment will the end come. (VI, 9)

"Elvis figgered he's got a lot a' livin' to do. Scandalous things happened at these parties, but they was considered honors. To commend the immoral exploits a' the ass-kissin' toads 'round him,

Elvis awarded medals a' silver and gold emblems engraved with 'TCB', meanin' 'Takin' Care of Business.' I think it meant 'Take Carnally Broads.' By livin' in a sea of immorality Elvis justified his own philanderin' while the abandoned Priscilla cried herself to sleep in Memphis. And we knows what 'strange torment' ended the life of Elvis when he paid for the good times.

"A Hollywood home of Elvis, on Perugia Way—that's the street—had been owned by the Shah of Iran. Ya know, the guy who pissed off the Ayatollah Khomeini. Nostradamus predicted this house:

> The Perugia Lake will be evidence,
> Within Perugia the conspirators will be imprisoned:
> The sage will be imitated by a fool,
> Killing bouts and a German cut apart. (VIII, 47)

"Ya see, 'round the pool—the Perugia Lake—locked up within the wall 'round the house, one fool of the entourage mocked Larry Geller, the sage; while the others played football—killin' bouts—and ate cut-up German chocolate cake.

"Let me tell ya 'bout those poolside parties a' Bacchus. Elvis and the boys put a two-way shoppin' store mirror in the girls dressin' room so they could peep in. They put another such mirror in a bedroom so they could watch each other in the act with loose women.

"They skinny dipped with harlots... I mean 'starlets.' That just slipped out. Elvis joined the recreation. Although neither healthy nor good for buildin' character, he joined the debauchery, figurin': 'Let me play the fool! With girth and laughter let old wrinkles come, and let my liver rather be stoked up with wine than my heart chill out with mortifyin' groans.' He committed the oldest sins the newest kinds a' ways."

I could take no more. I blurted out, "This all sounds shameless and unethical. Elvis Presley was a blight on the moral conscience of this country!"

Marie looked shocked. "You're so square. Come darlin', you are too severe a moraler. As the time, the place, and the condition a' this country stands, I suspect you heartily wish these activities had befallen you: but, since it is as it is, mind your own goddamn business."

Offended and stunned, I could not respond. Marie resumed: "Elvis did good things too. Once he spotted a young man in a wheelchair that always came to the gates at Graceland. Elvis invited him to join the group just as Nostradamus predicted, 'a crippled one will enter the realm.' (III, 73)

"Nostradamus predicted Elvis's black belt in karate:

> One in black with savage fury will try
> His blood covered hand at sword, fire, and archery:
> His many subjects will find terrible fear,
> They watch the best one hanging by feet and neck. (IV, 47)

"Elvis dazzled and terrified his audiences with on-stage karate. He inspired that Hai Karate cologne, that came with self-defense instructions to fight off all the women who'd be attracted. Although Elvis hisself rarely fought 'em off."

With surprising speed I had regained enough self-composure to participate in this conversation. "Pardon me for interrupting, but how is it that you know all these Nostradamus passages?"

"Well now, that's an intriguin' question requirin' a bit of a story," she answered as I again cursed my curiosity. She explained, "Ya see, many years ago a dirty, unshaven man who smelled a' liquor and his own humanity walked into this diner and sat on the very stool you is usin'. He looked down on his luck, poor, and broken-hearted. He asked for a handout, I gave him breakfast and listened to him tell his woes: his woman that left him, his soybean farm that went bust, his repossessed pick-up, and his dog that died a' heartworms. I listened the best I could and when he finished his sobbin', 'bout this earthly pail a' tears, I could think a' nothin' to say to him 'cept an old prayer, 'Lord grant me a serenade to accept the things I cain't change, wisdom to change the things I can, and courage to make a difference.'

"Well that prayer—after he repeated it several times to get the words straight—gave him somethin' to think 'bout. He thanked me. I'd guessed from the beginnin' he had no cash. But he insisted on payin' somethin' for the food, so he gave me his last three cigarettes—a great sacrifice—and the book he'd been readin': his only possessions other than the ragged clothes on his back. Then he left. Well the book turned out to be the prophecies of Nostradamus which I studied most carefully.

"Some two years later a handsome, well-dressed man drivin' a Porsche showed up, exudin' a elegance rarely seen here. He orders breakfast like anyone else, but after we talked 'bout weather and prices a' barrows and gilts none a' which seemed to interest him, he asked if I knew anythin' 'bout Nostradamus. 'Well sure' said I and pulled out the Nostradamus book and began to cite him chapter and verse 'bout what I'd ciphered out.

"Well he asked if he could buy the book. I said I didn't want to sell. But he opens his wallet and started layin' out hundred dollar bills on the counter. I's so stunned I didn't know what to say. So I just stared into his eyes. And then I saw it: the look I had seen years before in a forlorn, poorly, and woebegone man. 'You is the man who gave the book to me.'

"'Yes,' he answered, 'it is I. Your words and prayer turned my life around. I owe everything to you. After I left here, I took the pledge. I charted a new course. You are responsible for the change that has come over me. I want to show my thanks with these small tokens.' He pointed to the money and said, 'I would like my book back as a memory of that fateful day.'

"'Well sure,' said I, 'you can have the book. Only give me a moment to copy down some things.' I quickly wrote the key passages in this here stamp book. I gave him his Nostradamus book and he disappeared leavin' me with a thousand dollars cash—the only time in my life I held so much money. I never saw him 'gain. Though I did see his picture years later in **Time** or **Newsweek** when I was at the beauty shop. The magazine talked 'bout his bein' a financial wiz, how he made millions on somethin' called 'Junk Bonds.' I don't know how one fares so well bondin' garbage but 'parently he did.

"So that's how I know Nostradamus. This next prophecy is important. Ya see, in the late 60s Elvis got bored and bought the Circle G Ranch in Mississippi from Jack Adams—a Bible sign.

> The empire of the great one will be transferred
> A small location which will start to grow large:
> A humble modest place in a petty country
> Where the royal sceptre will be laid down. (1, 33)

"Elvis laid down his Kingly sceptre, transferrin' his empire to that ranch in the sticks. 'Course there's a typo by Nostradamus who wanted to say, 'pretty county.' A sceptre's a silver stick with a ball at the end, covered with jewels, that represents the power and authority a' the king. Elvis lay down his royal sceptre, his chrome microphone. Ya used to find the ranch by drivin' south and followin' the old Burma Shave signs.

"Why did Elvis shut hisself up with his cronies at the Circle G? Elvis received a divine command. It says in Ezekiel 'Go, shut thyself within thine house.' (3:24) He also received a command to tolerate his boys and their wild goin's on. 'I will make thy tongue cleave to the roof of thy mouth, that thou shalt be dumb, and shalt not be to them a reprover: for they are a rebellious house.' (3:26) The tolerance a' Elvis encouraged the boys. As they say, 'Nothin' bolsters sin so much as mercy.' Elvis didn't criticize them and he damn sure didn't want criticism from them, saying, 'Whoever he be that tells my faults, I hate him mortally.'

"If we'd time I'd describe all the Memphis Mafia. But ya seem in a hurry for some self-important business. Let's just talk 'bout Red West and Larry Geller. Nostradamus made a big deal 'bout Red West callin' him 'The pale red one, the male in the royal court,' (IX, 51) cause Red followed Elvis all durin' his reign.

Nostradamus described the Memphis Mafia led by Red: 'Fourteen conspirators led by intrigues of the wise one of red hair.' (I, 7) When danger threatened Elvis 'the reds march.' (VIII, 19) 'Reds' refers to Red West and his brother Sonny West, bodyguards to Elvis. Sometimes they got rough and Elvis got sued for 'many wrongs done by the great Red One.' (VIII, 80) Vernon Presley fired them, 'only blood of the red one will appease furious anger.' (IX, 2)

"Red pleaded with Vernon, describin' how his family'd be evicted and starve. Vernon listened quietly, starin' straight at him, then said, 'Frankly, Red, I don't give a damn!'

"After that, Red West and Sonny West helped write the book **Elvis—What Happened?**. When Elvis found out he wanted to do 'em in. Nostradamus described the terror a' Red: 'Red opponent will turn ashen with fear.' (III, 1) Red found hisself runnin' scared. But Elvis soon died and Red feared no more. Probably they made money on the book for Nostradamus said, 'two red ones will celebrate joyously.' (V, 22) But maliciousness did not drive them. They wanted to speak what they saw as truth. All in all, Nostradamus cites 'the Red One' a dozen times.

"Nostradamus also talked 'bout Larry Geller, who led Elvis in ways spiritual. The other cronies didn't like him. Parker hated Geller, but waited 'til Elvis tripped in the bathroom and busted up his head. Parker blamed the whole thing on Geller's influence and drove him like a scapegoat out into the wilderness." Again she searched through her stamp book. "Nostradamus predicted:

> The great prophet's writings will be taken,
> The tyrant will gain their possession:
> The king will be deceived by his enterprises,
> But trouble will come from the tyrant's maneuvers. (II, 36)

"Well they seized the spiritual books of Elvis, includin' his favorite by Kahlil Gibran, **The Prophet**. A tyrant—Parker pitched 'em out for burnin' and deceived the King by takin' the spiritual nourishment Elvis needed. Parker yelled 'bout Geller, 'He'll have to go.' These actions brought agony and double trouble for Elvis.

"Ya see, apparently Parker and the cronies viewed Geller as a Rasputin leading Elvis astray. Geller weren't no such type. The original Russian Rasputin believed he could ball hisself into a state of 'holy passionlessness' where once he exhausted hisself he'd have a religious experience. Elvis didn't need no lessons in that or in sinning to obtain forgiveness. And this is a double sign. That play **Bye Bye Birdie** had a girl, Gloria Rasputin.

"Nostradamus explained how Larry Geller'd be banished:

> The innocent one will again go into exile,
> Due to plague, to the boundaries of 'Nonseggle,'
> The answer to the red one will lead him astray,
> The King shall remove himself to Frog and Eagle. (VI, 46)

"Plague refers to Elvis's head gash. Geller tried to explain he'd nothin' to do with it, wrongly believing the others liked him. They packed up Geller's things and got rid a' them. I guess 'Nonseggle' is New Age talk for a wilderness journey. Nostradamus said the King went to the Frog: he met a French girl while wearing his eagle jumpsuit. It was no surprise that Geller left. Gurus don't last. 'After many a summer dies the swami.'"

"Why did Elvis keep all these men around him?" I asked.

Marie answered, "Honestly, darlin', I don't know. It's impossible to know for sure. His reasons is like two kernels a' corn hid in two bushels a' cobs: ya can hunt 'round all day 'fore ya find 'em, and when ya get 'em, they ain't worth the search.

"One important thing: the cronies of Elvis did little to stop his drug takin'. As years went by Elvis took more and more drugs. He kept a drug-filled doctor's bag at his side. I 'spose Elvis figgered he'd preserve life in medicine portable. Elvis'd been playin' with fire and nobody stopped him.

"I said the sons a' Eli symbolize both the Memphis Mafia and Colonel Parker. Now it's time to say more 'bout old Colonel Tom.

Cause an important question must be asked, 'who controlled the life of Elvis?' Most likely, nobody controlled it. Elvis certainly didn't. The Colonel came closest, as described by Nostradamus:

> The one well ahead in the royal court,
> With a red leader close to the monarchy,
> Cruel and harsh, and he will become an object of fear,
> He will take over the holy throne. (VI, 57)

"The Colonel, callin' hisself 'the benevolent con man,' controlled the realm. Parker—a man of pole vaultin' ambition, leapin' over itself. All lived in terror a' him, and by controllin' everythin', although he weren't king, his power made him the successor to the sacred monarchy. They claim Parker said when Elvis died, 'This don't change nothin'.' As Parker saw it, his gravy train was still runnin' at high ball. The red leader, that's a' course Red West.

"It's no secret Elvis let the Colonel run his life. The Colonel controlled the career a' Elvis even 'gainst the best interests a' Elvis. Elvis wouldn't stand up to him." She traded her stamp book for her Bible. "The Bible talks 'bout this:

> Verily, verily, I say unto thee, when thou wast young, thou girdest thyself, and walkedst whither thou wouldest: but when thou shalt be old, thou shalt stretch forth thy hands, and another shall gird thee, and carry thee whither thou wouldest not. (John 21:18)

"Bleatin', a lamb led to slaughter, he lost control a' his destiny. Just like the apostle John, Elvis lost control a' his destiny. Parker kept Elvis trapped in Vegas. Parker signed one a' his first contracts on a Vegas tablecloth. He didn't bother to get paper. Believe it or not, I have a hunk a' that tablecloth." She pulled an old brown envelope from under the counter. She removed a stained and tattered piece of white tablecloth three inches by three inches. "It don't have no words on it. I didn't get that part. Once I spilled lemon juice on this piece and when I held it up to the light, low and behold I saw an image, the face a' Elvis—well only his left eye and cheek. But it didn't look like no photo. It looked more like an old black and white negative. Anyways, I only got this small piece. And it ain't really mine. It belongs to Hortense Turin. Someday I'll have to give it back.

"The Colonel kept Elvis workin' in Vegas. Elvis languished in boredom. A' course Nostradamus had somethin' to say on this.

> In a great theatre the curtain will rise:
> The traps set and the dice cast.
> The first one exhausted himself in the face of death,
> Lying prone due to arches, a long time split. (III, 40)

"With Elvis snared in the Las Vegas showroom, Parker went to the dice tables. At times the feet of Elvis ached. Several times he fell on stage. Once he ripped his outfit durin' a concert and didn't notice. He kept on singin' with his trousers a long time split. That took place on one a' them gruelin' tours, New Years Eve of '75 in Pontiac, Michigan. Some see this was a sign from above: the higher power was tryin' to get in touch with Elvis. But why would the higher power go to such trouble to split the pants a' Elvis when Elvis coulda' been reached on the phone?

"In the last years an exhausted, sickly Elvis worked the small town circuit. Fans looked on, gaspin', 'He's fat, and scant a' breath—a pitiful sight in a mean retchin' wino, but hush my mouth—this is the King!' Elvis could a' made tons a' cash tourin' Europe or Japan. Parker wouldn't have it cause he couldn't get no passport. Parker was an illegal alien, a submarine.

"One last piece a' evidence 'gainst the Colonel. As I mentioned before, Parker rejected Barbra Streisand's offer to make **A Star is Born** with Elvis. Nostradamus saw this with great clarity.

> The bald one shall make a terrible choice,
> Overwhelmed he will not enter the gate:

> Speaking with great raging fury,
> To blood and flames the entire gender consigned. (V, 60)

"'Gate' means how much money you take in. Now Parker, the bald one wanted more money so he kicked up a ruckus, cursin' Streisand 'cause he looked down on all women.

"Perhaps I've drifted to far a'pasture. I must get to the true impo'tance of Elvis."

My heart sank even deeper. Completion of her oratory seemed hours away. Like a sleeper aware of his own nightmare I struggled vainly to wake from this bizarre dream.

CHAPTER 12

ELVIS AND THE APOCALYPSE

"Now all I've said 'bout Hollywood gets to the heart a' what I've to say 'bout Elvis." Onward, onward, Marie pressed. "Ya see, hun', the Bible in the book a' Revelations—or as it should really be called, the Apocalypse—describes the future reign of Elvis.

"I believe Elvis died—his body lies a'molderin' in the grave—smack-dab in Graceland's backyard, the Meditation Gardens. He's at peace now and I don't hurt anymore. I don't believe the scuttlebutt of the hoi polloi claimin' to have seen Elvis. As for such rumormongerin', it's time to nip it, nip it in the bud.

"I know's for sure no aliens abducted Elvis. I got proof. Ya' see when we voted the Elvis stamp we all picked the young 1950s Elvis over the later Elvis. Us ordinary folk with little education knew the young Elvis to be better. There's no way alien bein's of superior intelligence would a' waited to kidnap the old Elvis—they'd a got him in the days of Sputnik. And don't tell me it took aliens twenty years to get an abduction machine up and runnin'.

"Elvis died in 1977. But we've now a new understandin' of his death. 'Cause when you sir, first entered, by a miraculous divine word we deciphered how the name a' Elvis prophesies that after a thousand years Elvis will return. Now I don't 'xactly knows how or when, but the King shall return! Maybe he'll have a descendant in the line of Lisa Marie. Or maybe a thousand years from now they'll clone a new Elvis from a lock a' his hair.

"I hear rumors of a secret FBI lab outside a' Pittsburgh, chock-full a' padlocked deep freezes stuffed with hair samples of famous people. I just cain't help believin' that they got a big hunk a' Elvis hair. Hundreds a' years from now, they'll clone back to life anyone they wants. And they'll mix and match the clonin'.

"They'll clone back the brain of Albert Einstein with the body a' Arnold Schwarzenegger. They'll clone back Phyllis Diller with the body a' Rita Hayworth and the hair a' Farah Fawcett. Why they could even clone Spiro Agnew with the heart a' Billy Graham and the voice of Charlton Heston. Pat Buchanan—they'll clone him back with the mind a' Ted Kennedy. I'll tell you!

"I've drifted a fur piece from the return of Elvis. As I said, the King could come through his bloodline or through a clone, or maybe there'll be wars and rumors a' wars, earthquakes and famines, and there'll be signs in the heavens and then a trumpet blast and from the sky, he'll come forth, one like a son of a gun. Elvis'll descend on a white cloud to once again reign over us!

"Maybe he'll not come from the clouds. The earth might tremble, the granite and bronze slab over his grave crack, a brilliant light will shine and Elvis, his mother, and father will awake and come forth to begin a true new world order. Course I's only speculatin'. But if that happens, it's my dream that I'll be there to see it. That's my desire. A' course I'll be long dead.

"If this expectoration 'bout Elvis has merit I must show how the book a' Revelations—the Apocalypse—prefiggers Elvis. Search we must, the signs! Startin' with the omenous portents 'round the great whore—the great beast a' Hollywood. We must read the signs, for as they say, 'Red sky at night, sailor's delight. Red sky at mornin', sailor been drinkin'.'

"A blastin' horn called the first beast—a huge moker of a monster described in Revelations—more vivid and terrifyin' than the pukin' girl in **The Exorcist**. The beast dragged itself out a' the sea—ten horns, seven heads, screamin' blasphemous names—leopard-spotted, bear-pawed, lion-mouthed. A frightened world fell in worship of its authority. This beast a' Hollywood crawled from the Pacific onto the California coast: the lion mouth of MGM, the paws of Fox, the spotted leopard of United Artists. The beast screamed at Marion Morrison and Bernard Schwartz. In terror they took blasphemous names a' John Wayne, Tony Curtis. Those bumper stickers ought to say, 'God Bless Marion Michael Morrison.'

"With the earth tremblin', came forth a second more horrible creature: a ram speakin' dragon fire." Marie turned to the end of her Bible to intact pages containing arrows, underlinings, question marks, and exclamation points. She read, "This horrid beast:

> Exerciseth all the power of the first beast before him, and causeth the earth and them which dwell therein to worship the first beast, whose deadly wound was healed. And he doeth great wonders, so that he maketh fire come down from heaven on the earth in the sight of men. (Revelations 13:12-13)

"The second beast—Television, breathin' dragon fire of radiation with two horns: NBC and CBS. This beast promoted Hollywood with movie reruns; healin' the deadly wound—the fear that TV would destroy Hollywood. Television, doin' great wonders, bringin' fire—TV signals from heaven while the men of earth looked on.

"Revelations 13:16 warns a' the beast of Television: 'And he causeth all, both small and great, rich and poor, free and bond, to receive a mark in their right hand, or in their foreheads': calluses on the hand from workin' TV remotes and images of sin, violence, and stupidity burned right through the forehead and stamped on the brain. This beast, like a ram, livin' in the home a' the Los Angeles Rams, before they moved to St. Louis. Hollywood and television: the beasts a' the end time, proven by Revelations!"

"But," I asked, "does not the book of Revelations speak of a mark of the beast, the number 666?"

"I believe, deep within, ya know all this truth, sahib. 666 is the number! Elvis hisself wore the mark of the beast! In the dance scene in **Jailhouse Rock** Hollywood gave Elvis prisoner number 6240—a code number for 666. It works like this. First ya ignore the 0 because 0 is nothin'. Now the first number in 624 is 6."

I asked, "The first digit? 624 has three digits. The first digit is 6, the second digit is 2, the last digit is 4."

"It's easy for you, ya got your education. You know this digitalis," she answered. "O.K. Ya call 'em digits. Well the first digit is 6 and that fits the number 666. Now if ya take the second, what'd ya call it? Oh, yea, digit. Take the second digit, 2, and add the 2 to the 4, then ya have 6 for the last digit. If ya take the last 4 and add it to the middle digit, 2, ya get a 6 in the middle also. So if ya knows the code ya decipher 6240 as 666."

"How does 666 represent the beast—Hollywood?" I asked.

"Well," said Marie, "that's quite simple. 666 is a code number that works like this. Ya take the alphabet and ya give each letter a number startin' with A. Now the key number is 60. Ya take 6, the beast number, multiply it by 10. That's 60. Now ya make 'A' 60, 'B' 61, 'C' 62, and so on. Once ya do that, ya take the letters a' Hollywood and get the number for each letter. Now let's see 'H' would be 60, 61, 62," she counted on her fingers, "63, 64, 65, 66, 67. And the 'O' would be, . . . hell, you figger it out. Anyways if ya do that with all the letters a' 'Hollywood' ya get a total of 660. Then lastly, ya add the beast number 6 to it and ya got the whole number 666.

"Now this code also shows Hollywood movie studios as beasts. Elvis made some movies for United Artists. Now if ya start with 'A' as 38 and 'B' as 39 and so on, then add up the letters of 'United Artists' and then add 6 ya gets 666.

"For Metro-Goldwyn-Mayer ya make 'A' 26, 'B' 27, and so on. Then ya add 6. That gets 664. So ya adds an two extra counts for the spaces between words and you get 666!

"It's all here in my chart:

For 'Hollywood' A = 60,
for 'United Artists' A = 38,
for Metro-Goldwyn Mayer, A = 26.

H	67	U	58	M	38
O	74	N	51	E	30
L	71	I	46	T	45
L	71	T	57	R	43
Y	84	E	42	O	40
W	82	D	41	—	1
O	74			G	32
O	74	A	38	O	40
D	63	R	55	L	37
Total	660	T	57	D	29
	6	I	46	W	48
	666	S	56	Y	50
		T	57	N	39
		S	56	—	1
		Total	660	M	38
			6	A	26
			666	Y	50
				E	30
				R	43
				Total	660
					6
					666

"Elvis wore the mark a' the beast a' Hollywood. Now one sign in Revelations had me outright confused: the four horsemen. I racked my brain for months 'fore I saw the meanin'. Ya see, the four Apocalypse horsemen are colored: white, red, black, green. I thought this symbolized the Cartwright family on Bonanza. When the show opened, after the fire burnt a hole in the Nevada map, you'd see four horsemen ridin' over the hill. I figgered the black horseman to be Adam Cartwright who wore black. The horseman had to be Pa Cartwright played by Lorne Greene. I couldn't figger out whether to make Hoss the red or white horseman, and I's also lost 'bout little Joe. Then when Adam left the Bonanza there were only three horsemen. So I needed a new interpretation.

"Still confused, even though Elvis had a stable built at Graceland—then it hit me; like it hits a man whizzin' on a 'lectric fence. The horsemen symbolize not riders but singers. Clearly Elvis in titanium bright jumpsuits must be the white horseman. Well the black horseman could be no one but Johnny Cash, the Man in Black. He only wears black. I'll bet his wife, June Carter Cash, has a hell of a time keepin' lint off a' him.

"Now the green horseman. What grows greener than holly? The green horseman must be Buddy Holly. On the green holly grows the red berry. It all fits—Chuck Berry the red horseman. And so the four horsemen a' the Apocalypse must be: White Horseman—Elvis; Red Horseman—Chuck Berry; Black Horseman—Johnny Cash; Green Horseman—Buddy Holly. Now a' course Chuck Berry was one of the last Rock and Rollers to actually smile on an album cover.

"The book a' Revelations has more to say 'bout Hollywood. In Chapter 14 verse 8 an angel cried out, 'Babylon is fallen, is fallen, that great city, because she made all nations drink of the wine of the wrath of her fornication.' Well a' course the poisoned wine a' fornication symbolizes the immorality and violence of Hollywood movies." She had been waving and gesturing on and off with her Bible. She reopened it and read, "Revelations says:

> And the third angel followed them, saying with a loud voice. If any man worship the beast and his image [television], and receive his mark in his forehead, or in his hand. The same shall drink of the wine of the wrath of the almighty, which is poured out without mixture into the cup of indignation and he shall be tormented with fire and brimstone. (14:9-10)

"Ya see, everyone watched immoral movies, then tried to do it. We had a sexual reevolt. And revoltin' it was. Just 'cause James Bond could screw all those women and get away with it don't mean the ordinary Joe could. We had millions of abortions, unmarried pregnancies, unwanted children, all kinds a' diseases. We still don't see the anger poured forth full industrial strength into the cup. A' course Hollywood seduced the pure Elvis into that California immorality. He joined in and it dissipated his music energy. He didn't keep his essence and thus he received the punishment of his body worn out in middle age.

"Revelations 18 verse 2 says 'Babylon the great is fallen, is fallen, and is become the habitation of devils.' That's those movies **Exorcist**, **Omen**, and **Popeye**. It also says 'bout Hollywood, she is 'the hold of every foul spirit, and a cage of every unclean and disgustin' bird.' As I said before, 'Bird' is Brit for girl. This passage also talks 'bout immoral Hollywood movies.

"It says in Revelations 18 verse 3:

> For all nations have drunk of the wine of the wrath of her fornication, and the kings of the earth have committed fornication with her, and the merchants of the earth are waxed rich through the abundance of her delicacies.

"Well Hollywood wanted to control the world. She wanted her people as rulers. That's why she used all that media magic to get a man incapable of government as head a' this country: Ronald Reagan. And what did Reagan do? He helped the rich get richer. As for poor they was 'sposed to get the leftovers."

"You speak of 'Trickle Down' economics," I pointed out.

"Trickle Down?" she snapped. "That means they got pissed on! The poor got treated like peons. Revelations 18 verse 21 condemns Hollywood, 'and a mighty angel took up a stone like a great millstone, and cast it into the sea.' A great earthquake will come and punish Hollywood for its sins. The angel said, 'Thus with violence shall that great city Babylon be thrown down, and shall be found no more at all.' Violence will precede the earthquake. We saw riotin' in Los Angeles a few years ago. Soon California will fall into the sea! The Babylon of Hollywood will 'be found no more at all!'

"There's more in this chapter. Verses 22-24 reveals the future a' Hollywood: 'And the voice of harpers, and musicians, and of pipers, and trumpeters shall be heard no more at all in thee.' Well ya hardly hear those things now. Most a' the movie music is done on computers. 'And no craftsman, of whatsoever craft he be, shall be found any more in thee; and the sound of a millstone shall be heard no more at all in thee.' Well the movie studios will be gone and the millstones, that's the movie projector reels, will be silent. 'And the light of a candle shall shine no more at all in thee.' A' course that's the movie projector lamps. 'The voice of the bridegroom and of the bride shall be heard no more at all in thee.' They will all go to Las Vegas, and why? 'For thy merchants [of Hollywood] were the great men of the earth; for by thy sorceries were all nations deceived.'

"Lastly it says, 'In her [Hollywood] was found the blood of prophets and of saints and of all that were slain upon the earth,' meaning the 'blood of profits' taken from Elvis, denied a true actin' career. Hollywood: a greater hive of villainy and scum you'll not find elsewhere in the galaxy.

"But one day, as predicted, the great beast a' Hollywood will be punished for its sins 'gainst Elvis and he will return—comin' on the clouds with his Rock and Roll heaven band. There might be trumpets, trombones, an overgrown fluegelhorn, or Dizzy Gillespie with chipmunk cheeks blowin' that horn a' his that sticks up in the air, like a trumpet with a hard on. Elvis, clutchin' the mic'll sing, 'Glory, Glory, Hallelujah!'"

Marie had reached another emotional climax. Whether to heighten the drama or to protect her job I am not sure, but she took a break to continue straightening the cooking area. Marie rummaged through a drawer. She searched for a pancake turner, mumbling, "Where the devil are my flippers." Several utensils jammed in the drawer. She pulled hard on the blades of an eggbeater and sent spatulas, meat forks, and ladles tumbling to the floor. She bent over to pick them up. My moment at last!

Impulse, stupidity, and adrenaline pumped my veins. I jumped from the stool and ran four steps for the door. My right foot grabbed the floormat as I attempted a quick running turn out the door. Marie looked up, yelling, "Hey, hey, hey, stop where you are!" Then horror of horrors, as if she had cast a spell, the dry dust under the mat lubricated the floor and the mat slid sideways as I tumbled to the floor blocking my own exit. Despite pulled muscles in every conceivable place, I lifted my body to open the door when Marie vaulted over the counter with a meat fork in one hand. With hardly a step between the counter and me, she bounded, landing with both legs straddling my chest. I lay pinned to the tile floor. She held the fork to my throat. "How would you like to be buried in Memphis? I need you so the message a' Elvis can be known. Now I gotta know. Is you with me or is you ain't? I's givin' you a free choice to reconsider baby. I suggest you stick with me, 'cause God don't need you, Jack, He's got Elvis."

Her words hardly made sense. Her weight crushed my chest, each breath more difficult than pulling on an undersized boot. My head spun as her voice drowned in a buzzing fog. I began to pass out, struggling, "What now," I can't breathe; "what next," death; "where to," Nirvana or Nada? At least death would mean freedom. For a moment I heard a sweet voice calling.

Marie leaped up. "My God he's turnin' blue." She grabbed a glass of water and threw it in my face. With her weight off of my chest I sucked air fully and quickly grew conscious of the Marie menace standing over me. Heaven or Hell? "What a great awakening," thought I, bleary after my near-death experience.

Marie spoke, "Sorry 'bout the water, I was jus' tryin' to get you to breathe. But sweetheart you done me wrong. I just cain't make it without you. I don't care how the world's treatin' you. A woman's got to do, what a woman's got to do. How do you think I feel havin' to ram this down your throat even though it's for your own good and for the good a' the whole world? I'm all kattywumpus, like a diabetic kid on Halloween, like a cat on a hot tin shithouse.

"Now I knows ya think this is happenstance—your walkin' in my door—and that don't give me the right to hold ya. And I knows ya think tomorrow is a long time away. But stay you must."

She grabbed me by the arm and pulled my body of aches to its feet ordering, "Up, Simba." She led me staggering to the stool where she sat me down. I turned in disgust and growled at the twisted floor mat, "Now, wherefore stoppest thou me?"

CHAPTER 13

ELVIS

THE SUFFERING ONE

By now I had lost all track of how much coffee filled my gullet. And despite the huge breakfast I had eaten, I found myself wanting more. Marie sensed my omnipresent hunger.

"Ya hungry still? Want more?" She asked or stated, I was not quite sure.

"Well yes, I am hungry, but I do not want more breakfast."

"Course not, I have what ya wants, hun'." She walked to the far end of the counter and turned a pie case around. From the top shelf she took a pie pan with one last piece. I must have looked skeptical for she said, "Pie! Pie! Unknit that threatenin' unfriendly brow and poke not scornful glances from those eyes."

She put the pie on a plate, then took my long empty breakfast plate and set the pie before me. Although day-old, it glistened: the thickest, most luscious piece of apple pie I had ever seen.

Marie explained, "This apple pie's right decent, but ya should a' tasted the heavenly meringue pie dear Lucy used to make. The present cook runs the egg whites through a colander and that ruins it, 'cause the quality a' meringue is not strained."

Marie put a fork on the table and more coffee in my cup. "Yes I consider Lucy the best cook we ever had here and my friend Bernie the worst. Bernie claimed she learned culinary from a famous Italian chef, Al Dente. I didn't believe that. She learned cookin' from Sal Manila. Bernie made a layer cake of angel food and devil's food chocolate—applying all techniques into one—called Armageddon cake. When Star Wars came out she made wok-fried cookies called 'wookies.' Bernie hummed when she cooked, something called 'My Dessert Serenade.'

"Bernie, she couldn't cook and couldn't keep house. Once I opened her mobile home fridge—the bakin' soda had mold. One Tupperware had strange growin's: brown, purple, a little bit of green. I told Bernie, 'It's life, but not as we know it.' In the back of the icebox I found six bottles of Milk Mate. Didn't know Bernie was so lonely. When I looked out her trailer window I asked, 'Woman, why don't ya clean up your own back yard?'

"She'd tried to shape up her body by watchin' Jack Lalane. Then she wanted to buy a belt massager. Ya stood in front a' this 'lectric motor with a four-inch leather strap 'round your waist. It was 'sposed to vibrate the fat off ya. Bernie couldn't afford one, so her brother made one using stake-bed-truck fan belts and a rusty Evinrude outboard. The contraption filled her mobile home with two-cycle engine smoke and cut big gashes in her back.

"Bernie loved to make jambalaya and fry fish, though she'd burn it all the time. She invented Cajun Blackfish! She'd serve it with salsa and call it 'el charro.' She thought fish a healthy food; she'd eat it every day. She'd made a fish and oyster meat loaf, flavored with liquid smoke, Cajun Clambake. She'd broil Channel Catfish over a smudge pot. She even had a motto on her apron, 'Carp per diem.' When ya got right down to it, cookin' just weren't her bailiwick. She couldn't roast a hot dog right. Last place she worked was an old folk's home. Wanting to bring back home cookin' memories, she fixed ham steaks with red-eye gravy not knowing the patients was on low salt diets. When the twelfth person got took to the hospital, she got fired. Seems I have an affinity for being 'round people who cain't hold down jobs.

"Despite all these failures a' the cuisin' art, Bernie loved Elvis. She'd been at the 1955 Gatorbowl concert in Jacksonville that turned into a riot. She had a piece a' the shirt that got ripped off Elvis in the rumble. In the '70s Bernie joined the Indian rights movement, some organization to stop slander of Indians: a sort of Indian Defense League called B'nai Hekowi. She quit after her oversized turquoise earrings caught in the mimeo machine. She'd seen **A Man Called Horse** with Richard Harris dangling from the ceiling with skewers in her chest. She didn't see scarred ear lobes as something to brag about."

Ignoring Marie's meanderings, I launched into that glorious piece of pie as Marie launched into more disclosures:

"When ya watch Elvis films ya see a happy, self-assured man. We worshipped him 'cause he extruded a self-confidence beyond ordinary men. Peculiarity haunts this world: Elvis lacked the very confidence he so magnificently displayed. Under the facade lived a man filled with pain and agony; a man accustomed to sorrow, a man a' constant sorrows, a melancholy man. Things is seldom what they seem, white dust masquerades as coffee cream." Marie pondered a packet of coffee creamer.

"Elvis suffered from his youth. In high school, crewcut roughnecks taunted him 'cause a' his hair and clothes." Marie reopened her Bible to an intact chapter. "The book of Isaiah describes this exactly: 'I gave my back to the smiters, and my cheeks to them that plucked off the hair: I hid not my face from shame and spittin'.' (52:14) The plaidshirted bastards plucked the very sideburns on his hallowed cheeks. Isaiah describes how young Elvis suffered with acne, 'his visage was so marred more than any man.' (52:14) 'Visage' that's French for face. This exaggerates, Elvis had acne but it weren't that bad.

"Now Elvis had only high school education 'cause it says in Ecclesiastes, 'For in much wisdom is much grief: and he that increaseth knowledge increaseth sorrow.'" (1:18) Marie explained the importance of this Bible book:

"Ecclesiastes portrays Elvis to the 'E'. Written by a king-philosopher—same as Elvis—the book laments, 'Vanity of vanities, all is vanity.' That describes Elvis." I expected Marie to pull more loose pages from her Bible. Instead she pulled a small envelope from the book of Psalms. She poured out tattered pieces of Bible pages on the counter: passages handled so many times they were falling apart. Marie sorted the fragments. "It says here, 'What profit hath a man of all his labour which he taketh under the sun?' (1:3) Yes, where now lies the wealth a' Elvis? In the hands of others! Yes 'Vanity of vanities, all is vanity.' Now the word 'vanity' means 'futility,' or 'uselessness'; like arguin' with the IRS. I say this 'cause fools read Ecclesiastes and think it's talkin' 'bout bathroom sink cabinets." She lifted another piece.

"Ecclesiastes details how Elvis created Graceland:

> I made me great works; I builded me houses; I planted me vineyards: I made me gardens and orchards, and I planted trees in them of all kind of fruits: I made me pools of water, to water therewith the wood that bringeth forth trees. (2:4-6)

"Stay here in Memphis. Go to Graceland. See for yourself, the swimmin' pool, gardens, trees. But Ecclesiastes says more:

> I got me servants and maidens, and servants born in my house; I had great possessions of great and small cattle. (2:7)

"Elvis had servants and maids. 'Course this passage could refer to maidens of a recreational nature. And as for 'servants born in my house' I doubt anyone ever gave birth at Graceland but it might refer to paternity suits 'gainst Elvis. And a' course Elvis had great and small cattle at the Circle G Ranch.

"I ain't done with this book which could be called Elvisiastes." She pointed out another passage. "For it says, 'I gathered me also silver and gold, and the peculiar treasure of kings and of the provinces.' (2:8) Elvis loved jewelry—spending thousands on silver and gold, even buried some in his backyard. Elvis owned the treasure of kings and jewelry from the states a' Canada. But the more jewelry he had the more weight he gained, for right quick nature falls in revolt when gold becomes her object.

"The book then says, 'I gat me men singers and women singers, and the delights of the sons of men, as musical instruments.' (2:8) Does that describe Elvis or not, with the Stamps and Sweet Inspirations as his back up? There's more: 'So I was great, and increased more than all that were before me in Jerusalem' (2:9) That's Memphis a' course, but it became a kind a' prison for Elvis, although a goodly one, in which there are many concubines, wards, and dungarees; Whitehaven bein' one a' the worst.

"Elvis had whatever he wanted. 'And whatsoever mine eyes desired I kept not from them, I withheld not my heart from any joy; for my heart rejoiced in all my labour.' (2:10) For Elvis, a spiritual man, such things'd never satisfy. Thus the book describes him: 'Then I looked on all the works that my hands had wrought, and on the labour that I had laboured to do: and, behold, all was vanity and vexation of spirit, and there was no profit under the sun.' (2:11) Now one thing needs to be made clear, that 'under the sun' refers to the adulation of his fans." She searched the shards of Bible pages. "Here it is. It says, 'Yea, I hated all my labour which I had taken under the sun: because I should leave it unto the man that shall be after me.' (2:18) You'd think a king with everythin' would be happy but tain't so, for uneasy lies the head that wears a crown.

"Elvis suffered greatly d'spite all he did for music." She returned to her Bible. "Isaiah 49 verse 4 says, 'I have laboured in vain, I have spent my strength for nought, and in vain.' Elvis didn't wanna suffer. He prayed to be delivered from inordinate and sinful infections, from the deceits of the world, the flesh, and the devil. His prayers remained unanswered.

"So what then did Elvis do?" She returned to the Bible scraps. "He did what Ecclesiastes recommended: 'There is nothin' better for a man, than that he should eat and drink, and that he should make his soul enjoy good in his labour.' (2:24) And a' course Elvis did just that. He drank, he ate potato chips and peanut butter/banana sandwiches. This didn't stop the sufferin'.

"Elvis suffered horribly: a modern Job. Job's a funny name. Ya say it 'Joe' with a 'b'. Once in a while some fool says 'job' like 'lube job.' Elvis suffered terrible, painful feelings in heart and mind. Deeply troubled, Elvis moaned, 'O, now, forever farewell the Nyquil mind! Farewell content!'

"Satan tested Job, life tested Elvis. Job lost his wife, family, wealth, and health. This happened to Elvis! Gladys died, Priscilla left him. He was broke near the end, his wealth squandered. Cursed not with boils like Job, Elvis suffered a worse affliction: obesity. That's why when we voted the Elvis stamp we all wanted the young Elvis: the slim handsome man we remembered. For yet we has ever but slenderly known him. His weight problem was the infirmity of his middle age."

I interrupted, "Why didn't Elvis control his eating habits since it so endangered his health and ruined his appearance." Marie pondered, "I knows you're thinkin' the old advice, wrestle and pin your appetites and you've conquered human nature.' I 'spose Elvis resolved rather to die than to famish. Ya see, achin' hunger drove Elvis to eat the way a mosquito sucks blood. That lard-fried southern cookin' didn't help neither. Even you'd get fat on that. For ya cannot change the laws of physiques.

"Elvis had terrible weight problems: the bloat king. It's hard to be proud when you're paunchy. He tried diets, livin' for days in sweatsuits tryin' to burn it off, moanin', 'O, that this too too solid flesh would melt, thaw, and resolve itself into dippity dew!' Elvis ate unhealthy and so he suffered the sappin' and impurification of his precious bodily fluids.

"But for all his sufferin', Elvis never cursed Rock and Roll." She pointed to her Bible which remained open to the book of Isaiah. "He suffered in silence. As Isaiah says:

> He shall not cry, nor lift up, nor cause his voice to be heard in the street. A bruised reed shall he not break, and the smoking flax shall he not quench. (42:2-4)

"The unquenched smokin' flax—that's marijuana. Though I's pretty sure Elvis didn't inhale.

"Some fools argue that Elvis suffered 'cause a' his sins. That the sins a' Elvis worried his mother to an early grave. They quote Isaiah 50:1: 'Behold, for your iniquities have ye sold yourselves, and for your transgressions is your mother put away.' But Gladys died not 'cause a' the sins a' Elvis but for the sins of our nation—the Industrial Military Complex—to which we've sold ourselves. The Industrial Military Complex plucked the innocent Elvis from Memphis, threw him into the army, and broke the heart a' Gladys. 'Course I 'xplained all this earlier.

"Now back to Job. He had three so-called friends: Eliphaz, Zophar, and Bildad. I see ya snicker at those names. They are a bit unusual. As I see it, they's the ancient version a' Tom, Dick, and Harry. These friends come to Job sayin' he's sufferin' 'cause a' his sins. They wanted Job to admit his sins to prove his sufferin' was a just punishment.

"This parallels Elvis exactly. As I said three friends a' Elvis published **Elvis—What Happened?**, telling all the bad things Elvis did with the intention a' gettin' Elvis to confess. They wanted to shock Elvis into seeing that he brought on his own sufferin' by his actions, such as doin' drugs. They didn't realize that Elvis suffered not for his sins, but for our sins. He took them upon hisself! Elvis suffered as a bronze serpent lifted up for our failures. He did this with no complaint, even when he became so fat we turned our eyes from him.

> He is despised and rejected of men; a man of sorrows, and acquainted with grief: and we hid as it were our faces from him; he was despised, and we esteemed him not. Surely he hath borne our griefs, and carried our sorrows: yet we did esteem him stricken, smitten, and afflicted. He was oppressed, and he was afflicted, yet he opened not his mouth: he is brought as a lamb to the slaughter, and as a sheep before her shearers is dumb, so he openeth not his mouth. (Isaiah 53:3-4,7)

"Elvis opened not his mouth to complain 'gainst his fate. His greatness brought him down. For he sought the greatness that overwhelmed him. As Bernie said, 'Yet never in the field of human affliction was so much owed by so many to such a one.'

"Sadly Elvis took drugs 'cause he suffered so much. He went to detox, but lay dreamin', 'When shall I see those Halcion days?' He almost choked to death several times, yet wouldn't quit. Elvis choked, called it fate, and kept on druggin'."

Describing the suffering of Elvis brought great pain to Marie. Her eyes watered, emotion gripped her throat and stifled the words. I had little hope the condition would be more than momentary. So I suffered through a lecture on the woe and hard luck of Elvis. I felt like screaming at this woman, "No more! You gotta stop! This is too much!" But I knew this hard headed woman would not treat me nice and allow me to walk out. Then I noticed a steak knife on the counter. I thought, "Is this a dagger which I see before me, the handle toward my hand?" I shook my head trying to regain my senses. No, threatening her with a knife would be suicide. She probably had a twelve-gauge shotgun hidden in the hamburger buns. The only sensible course seemed surrender.

CHAPTER 14

ELVIS

THE MESSIANIC LIFE

As I sat at the counter the light above began to flicker and buzz. Marie, while putting the Ecclesiastes pieces back into the envelope, looked up at the pair of four-foot neon tubes in a coverless white metal fixture—a later addition to the diner. The light suffered from a bad ballast. Marie shook her head:

"I cain't stand a naked neon bulb anymore than I stand a vulgar remark or a rude action."

Now, tired of this rambling, I ached for freedom. Could I find a flaw in her argument and maneuver her into silence? A gap in her logic flashed before me. I pounced:

"Did not you earlier call Elvis the Messiah?"

"Yes sir, I did indeed," answered Marie.

"But according to the Bible the Messiah worked as a carpenter. Elvis drove delivery trucks. He was no carpenter." I had nailed her at last.

"True," Marie patiently restored her defensive lines, "but the famous Elvis used fake names for business. To insiders he called hisself 'Dr. John Carpenter' a name from the movie **Change of Habit**, a movie that compared Elvis to the Savior."

Foolishly, I tried another attack strategy, "But what about the title 'Dr?' That cannot be a sign."

"A' course," said Marie as she unwrapped a piece of Juicy Fruit and started chewing. "The Good Book quotes a sayin', 'Physician heal thyself.' That's why Elvis wrote his TCB—'Taking Care of Business' oath as a set a' goals for perfection. The oath called for body and mental conditionin', meditation for stillin' and calmin' a' the body and mind. It promised more self-respect and more respect for fellow men. But the tag line read, 'Freedom from constipation.' Ya see, Elvis had a problem. He couldn't take care a' his business. That's why he added this last line. He was one with us in our struggles.

"And so the King spent much time in the can. He enlarged the upstairs john at Graceland so he could sit in a chair, read spiritual books, meditate, and pray. Seeing the remodeled bathroom a' black and gold tiles, gold fixtures, and jet black commode; Elvis exclaimed, 'My privy is dukedom large enough!' Elvis passed many an evenin' in luxury, sittin' on the brass plumbin' hopin' all things would pass." She retrieved her green-stamp book. "A' course, Nostradamus foretold this.

> Seated in the dark in a secret room,
> Resting all alone on a seat of brass:
> A tiny fire is seen in the loneliness,
> Those things not believed in vain will succeed. (I, 1)

"Elvis languished in the can 'cause drugs had fouled his gut. His intestines rebelled, feudin' against the very body that held them. Also, as Elvis grew older, resentment churned within him that his talent had been wasted by the Colonel. This boilin' anger damn near cooked his innards and 'course that's a sign. 'Cause ya say 'Colonel' like ya say corn 'kernel' but ya spell it, C-O-L-O-N-E-L, and thus the word 'colon' sits in 'colonel.' Elvis took his outside problem and swallowed it into his very bowels. And so constipation became his thorn in the flesh.

"Elvis could a' solved his bowel problem by goin' to the Holy Land and visitin' the place where Joshua camped before he fit the battle of Jericho: Shittim. Or he could a' gone up to French Lick, Indiana and got some Pluto Water. 'Cause as they say 'When nature won't, Pluto will!' Sadly, Elvis suffered long hours a' constipation, and brevity's the soul of a good shit. What does I mean by this? Nothin' but to show ya how the King didn't progress though his guts got bigger."

From that moment onward, anytime I thought of the health problems of Elvis, I had an uncontrollable urge to jog five miles, throw out all medicines, and eat high-fiber bran muffins. I attempted to return the conversation to its bizarre mean. "You call Elvis the Messiah. But a Judas betrayed the Messiah. How does that apply to Elvis?" I asked.

She replied, "Yes a Judas existed, but as a Christian woman I shouldn't malign that man no more. But I'll tell ya the sign."

"Oh, God," I moaned.

"Now tell me. How did Judas Iscariot die?" She asked.

"Hmmm, I remember, he committed suicide. He hung himself."

"Don't ya knows English? He 'hanged' hisself." She went on, "And where did they bury Judas."

"I have no idea," I stumbled.

"In the potter's field. That's a sign: 'potter's field.'"

"How can that be?" I asked, still confused.

"Well, the one who betrayed Elvis, his name sounded like the first word in the sign, and part a' his name had a meanin' like the second word." She smiled. "So now ya knows the truth." Again she had dumbfounded me.

"In the Good Book, Judas betrayed for silver: thirty pieces to be exact," Marie continued. "The modern Judas betrayed Elvis into bad movies with dull songs for silver, gold, and green. He led Elvis from Rock and Roll into a smear a' middle-class pap.

"The Bible Messiah passed 'round wine sayin' 'this ye do, in remembrance of me.' Elvis drank little alcohol but is remembered in a glass of Always Elvis Wine. He is recognized in the drinkin' of this wine. I ain't sure it's great wine, when I drank it my heart burned within me.

"Elvis lived the life a' the Messiah: he had followers, his Memphis Mafia, 'bout a dozen in number called, 'the twelve.' The gospels tell of James and John the sons of Zebedee, hotheads wanting special favors. Among the mafia some wanted to sit at the right hand a' Elvis, next to the King in importance. The others resented this. Rivalry defined 'the twelve' of Elvis.

"Now there's a story of Elvis as Messiah. My friend, Hortense, read of Parsifal and his search for the holy grail: the Messiah's holy cup. Inspired, she sought the cup of Elvis. She hoped to get his drinkin' glass or buttermilk mug. She wrote to Elvis. She tried to bribe the guard at the Graceland gates. But no luck.

"Desperate, she offered to sleep with the trashmen who had the Graceland pickup. But they was righteous men who read the Bible durin' coffee breaks. They offered to help for free, as an act of charity. They discerned that if they didn't help she'd seek out other, less-righteous trashmen. And they hoped they'd save her soul. That's why Hortense received several Bible tracts the men claimed came from the trash of Elvis. With their help she quested on for the grail of Elvis, the cup! And can ya believe it? She found it—Elvis's athletic supporter! The holy cup! Just as Parsifal believed the holy grail had magical powers, so did Hortense. She makes her husband wear that jockstrap every time before they get, well ...

"Intimate," I suggested.

"That's it, intimate." She nodded. "I asked Hortense if I could a' borrowed the cup for my last husband, but she didn't trust I'd ever give it back. Such is life. I doubt if it could a' saved that marriage. I 'spose I should put the blame on me.

"That was years ago. Last I talked with Hortense on the phone she told what she's been up to. Seems for the longest time she's wanted to go on a' daytime TV freak show—ya now, like Jenny, Oprah, or Sally. That's where they comb the country lookin' for sufferin' fools willin' to bear their souls and shamelessly talk 'bout the most private things. It's like talkin' to a shrink with ten million peepin' at the keyhole.

"Hortense wanted in the worst way to get on one a' these shows, not in the audience, but up on stage. But bein' a basically healthy person, she had the problem a' not havin' any problems. Everyone in her life had treated her decently. Try as she might, she couldn't get on. Well after bein' rejected several times she got depressed and lost all desire to live. Luckily, she found this support group of other people that felt the same despair at not bein' messed up 'nough to go on national TV. After attendin' these group meetin's Hortense is back to her old self. Not only that, her group might get on Sally after all. Accordin' to Hortense they might go on explaining how they suffer from 'Lack of Syndrome, Syndrome.' Hortense also found a 12-Step group for those who can't program a VCR."

I stood up in desperate anger. How many hours had I wasted listening to this crazy woman? I knew she would not let me walk out the front door, maybe there was another door. And if I had to leave my tape recorder behind, so be it.

"I need to use the restroom again," I got up.

"Not surprisin', considerin' how much coffee you've had. Ya know where it be, hun'."

I walked to the restroom. Scanning the end of the diner I found no door marked EXIT. Only a door marked RESTROOM and a door marked EMPLOYEES ONLY. I went into the restroom to relieve myself again doing all I could to minimize the sound echoing in the room. When complete, I washed my hands with a minimum of quiet water and silently opened the restroom door. Marie, busy at the stove, had her back to me. Quietly I stepped out of the restroom, closed the door behind me, opened the EMPLOYEES ONLY door, quickly stepped in, and shut the door.

Expecting to be in the back kitchen with a rear exit door, I found myself in total darkness. I slid my foot out to find which way to step only to kick a box. "Shit!" I whispered emphatically, "Now what?" I grabbed the wall to find a light switch. No luck, then I swung my right arm out into the blackness hoping to and then finding the ceiling light string. I pulled the string and braced my now darkness-adjusted eyes for the shock of a bare 150-watt bulb in a porcelain fixture. Not bright light, but soft garish red and green filled the room—or closet. I had walked into an eight by eight-foot closet with no exit doors and no windows. At my feet sat a cardboard case of toilet paper and a case of old green plastic bottles of Janitor in a Drum. The other supplies had been removed to make this closet into . . . well no other word seemed appropriate . . . a shrine. Yes, I had stumbled into Marie's shrine to Elvis.

Posters from two dozen Elvis movies covered the wall. An old Poodle Skirt on a wooden hanger dangled from the metal conduit running to the ceiling light. An unplugged lava lamp sat before four black velvet Elvis images. A strange odor filled the room, bringing back memories of hot summer lawn mowing. In the corner sat the smell's source: a Hefty trash bag filled with rotting handfuls of Graceland grass. On a small shelf sat Marie's cameras: an old Brownie, a Polaroid Swinger. A stack of record albums and forty-fives nearly three-feet tall sat next to a primitive pastel-blue record player on a roll-around metal cart, with speakers covered with gold-threaded fabric. It took but a moment to absorb the entire scene. I had to sneak out of the closet and back into the diner before my delay aroused Marie's suspicion. My great escape had failed! I turned off the light. And to this day I do not know why—perhaps Roman Catholicism still gripped my subconscious—but as I grabbed the doorknob I genuflected. I cautiously opened the door.

Marie's back was still turned. I quickly stepped out and over to appear as if walking from the restroom.

Marie looked at me. "Ya took quite awhile in there. Everythin' workin' all right, Gunga Din?"

Afraid that a discussion of my tarrying might uncover my blunder, and unsure whether she asked about the diner's plumbing or my own, I pulled her back to the Elvis lecture. "You were explaining about the Messiah." Ignoring her desire to follow her suspicions, she resumed her discourse:

"Oh, yes. I call Elvis the messiah 'cause he came and spoke to us, the poor and lowly. Born like us, he understood and cared for us. I must be clear 'bout this. Had Elvis not come in the middle fifties and showed us at the bottom a' society that we was cared for, terrible things would a' happened. There'd have been a great revolt of the poor 'gainst the rich: startin' amongst southern sharecroppers, spreadin' to southern cities, then to northern ghettos. There'd have been strikes, riots, and armed bandits. The United States would've crumbled into a desolate land of warrin' lords. Elvis prevented all this. The 1950s looked like a golden age of peace and prosperity—but only on the surface. Beneath that gildin', American society groaned for deliverance. Elvis averted the catastrophe. His Rock and Roll vented the steam of the sufferin' masses and saved America.

"But when Elvis started makin' movies he stopped singin' Rock and Roll. And what happened? Society upheaved itself. In the late sixties when Elvis made his worst movies the cities rioted and neighborhoods went up in flames as frustrated folks screamed 'burn baby burn.' Protestin' swept the land: everyone went wild in the country. Society crumbled cause the lower class had been forgot. America tottered on the brink a' collapse.

"But then, with a blindin' flash, came Elvis, like a second comin': the 1968 television comeback special. Months later he told us poor and lowly we'd not been forgotten by singing 'In the Ghetto.' It took a year or so for the message a' Elvis to get through. But things quieted down. Riotin' and burnin' stopped, 'cause Elvis came again to be with his people.

"A year after Elvis did his comeback special I got saved. Depressed as hell 'bout being divorced, I couldn't see the point of it all. I'd been through one husband, two Studebakers, one Buick, and two mobile homes. And I started drinkin' too much Southern Comfort—not that I listened to Janis Joplin or anythin'. But one night, miserable and heart-broke, I stumbled into a church, the Two-by-Four-Square, Dyed in the Wool, Bible-Believing, Six and Seven-Eighth Day Adventist, Refried, Mid-Millennial, Predestined, Limb-Davidian, Baptist Church. One a' them non-denominational denominations. A fiery old preacher named Reverend Decrease Mather worked the podium and claimed his family'd been preaching since the Pilgrims. So aged, they said he studied at

Brigham Old University. He wore cheap suits. Behind his back they called him, 'Polyester Mather.'

"He'd fish for an 'Amen' like the best. Although he could fire brimstone and describe the pains a' hell, we knew him to be a generous man with a heart big as Marie Osmond's teeth. We knew that 'cause of all the healin's he'd done. He told how one boy he healed of a speech pediment grew up to be Howard Cosell. He prayed for a teenage girl not developin' properly—she grew up as Dolly Parton. He wanted to go and pray for healin' of Dizzy Gillespie's cheeks and Karl Malden's nose.

"Reverend Mather's church always sang 'Give Me That Ol' Time Religion.' Then I learned 'bout ancient Canaanite religion with prostitutes right in them temples. Maybe that's why old Reverend Mather enjoyed that song. He wanted to go way back.

"One time he preached 'bout God working in mysterious ways and some fool in back yelled, 'I didn't know God had a job.' Reverend Mather claimed he once gave a marriage retreat for Henny Youngman. Most a' the time he'd rail at the Catholics over the hill at Our Lady of Terrazzo Church. He so inspired me that I wanted to do missionary work in India. I thought 'bout goin' to Calcutta to repair Water Picks. It never panned out.

"Once the old reverend invited a travelin' preacher who got into a long-winded, confusin' sermon on whether at the last judgment the long dead or the recent dead would be judged first. Us new converts didn't much care just so's we made the cut. Anyways, the preacher got into somethin' 'bout LIFO and FIFO. We couldn't figger out what in blazes he meant.

"This visitin' preacher was none other than Brother Genuine hisself. Surely you've heard a' him."

"No, I have never heard of Brother Genuine," I responded.

"That's a shame. He had much to say of an inspirational nature. And a' course he's a man a' honesty and integrity. Ya have to believe Brother Genuine cause his name is in the Good Book, right on the front cover. It says 'Genuine,' his first name; 'Leather,' his last name; Brother Genuine Leather."

I sat in disbelief as Marie rambled on: "After Brother Genuine's visit Reverend Mather saw the Reverend Schuller's Crystal Cathedral. Ol' Decrease wouldn't let hisself be outdone. He hired a architect to design a 400-foot tall Plexiglas Palace. The state beautification commission condemned the project as an eyesore 'cause it wouldn't cover up any of our town. And Reverend Mather's fund raising scheme was a bust. He wanted to sell a miracle cure drink of Evian, ginseng, and Lourdes Holy Water. And so they say about the 'best laid plans of mice and men.' Or like Elvis after a Hollywood starlet turned him down cold, he complained 'bout 'the best planned lays of men and mice.'

"A' course those were my religious days. I've done my share a' backslidin' since. And as the Frenchies say, 'C'est la Vie Die.' But that old Rev. Mather. That's someone you never forget as long as ya live. Even after I get Alzheimer's, I'll still be droolin' and mumblin' 'bout him.

"I see I've wandered again. I'd been talkin' 'bout the disasters a' the late 60s. Twenty years've passed since Elvis died. Still the world groans for his presence. I fear for what might happen next." A wave of terror flashed over Marie's face. Fighting for calm she began to whistle, then hum, and finally as peaceful resignation eased onto her face her humming became song:

> What the world needs now is Elvis, sweet Elvis.
> It's the only thing that there's just too little of.
> What the world needs now is Elvis, sweet Elvis.
> It's the only thing that there's just too little of.
> Lord we don't need another politician,
> There's Republicans and Democrats 'nough to blame.
> Lord we don't need another ska band,
> There's Red Hot Chili Peppers enough to scream.
> What the world needs now is Elvis, sweet Elvis.
> It's the only thing that there's just too little of.

"One last thing: the trickiest part. I believe in Elvis as the messiah, yet I believe him dead. We wait for him to come again. Yet many believe he's still alive, hauntin' the aisles a' some Wal-Mart. They even claim that just like in the gospels, the tomb a' Elvis remains empty. I've said what I believe and I don't agree with them. All I know's, the answer won't be found speculatin', but only by backhoein'."

CHAPTER 15

ELVIS

LIGHT TO ALL NATIONS

As the hours ticked by, I began to fear that tomorrow never comes. Marie pressed her spine against the refrigerator corner.

"Thank God," she said, "they put hinges on this corner. It's a great place to scratch my back. It feels so right." She shifted her position. "Ay, there's the rub."

She babbled relentlessly, "Hun', I've shown you biblical signs for Elvis more numerous than June bugs on a summer night. But there's signs for Elvis all over the world—even in heathen lands—for Elvis dwelt among us as a 'Light to All Nations.' Ya find symbols for Elvis even among the Indians of Oregon and Washington. Ya know, the ones who carved them totem poles".

"Well actually I do." I jumped in, "I have read much on the Native Americans of the Northwest Coast: the Tlingit, Bella Colla, Kwaki . . ." Before I could complete the word "Kwakiutl" Marie had wrestled control of the conversation from me and began expounding on topics of which I had infinitely more knowledge:

"Elvis loved givin': jewelry, moto'cycles, Cadillacs. Armchair shrinks call Elvis insecure: he was buyin' friends. Let the truth be known! Elvis as a great chief performed the Potlatch, a sacred important ceremony of the Indians of the . . . where'd ya say? . . . oh yea, Northwest Coast. At a Potlatch, the leader a' the pack—the chief—generously gave to his followers to prove his authority. Those that accepts the gifts, accepts the chief's authority. And so with the gifts of Elvis.

"At Potlatches, chiefs'd display their wealth, by showin' off 'coppers.' Now by 'coppers' I don't mean no James Cagney word for 'police.' No, the chiefs have these trash can-lid-sized slabs a' copper hammered and painted. At the Potlatch they flaunt these before their peons to clarify who's boss. Elvis did the same, but not with inferior copper. Only gold could match the radiance, dignity, and magnificence a' Elvis. With glistenin' fingers, Elvis flashed gold from every appendage.

"At rare, glorious moments he'd throw gold jewelry from the Las Vegas stage to reward his faithful fawnin' fans. Now evil-minded cynics claim Elvis did this when his show was floppin'. But in truth Elvis acted the great chief a' the Potlatch.

"In old days the great chiefs'd gave skins, like beaver or caribou. Elvis didn't cotton to slaughterin' wildlife just so's he could toss hides to fans. No Elvis, gave away scarves. He'd pull them 'round his neck, impregnate them with the unction of his sweat— the very essence of Elvis—and toss them to the screamin' multitude. He'd pitch that scarf like a highborn princess droppin' her kerchief signalin' knights to battle for her favor. No sooner would the fingers a' Elvis open, then a fight'd break out as fans jousted, jostled, and altercated 'mongst themselves. And in the scarf-fed fracas many a pocketbook became a leather-bound mace.

"Sometimes at Potlatches chiefs'd smash coppers to show their wealth: that even valuable coppers meant little to them. A' course Elvis did this. He'd shoot televisions, fire at chandeliers, or smash his Rolodex watch—to show his great wealth. Blind fools claim these to be acts of a spoiled and undisciplined child. In truth Elvis performed deeply religious acts. Only he knew their true meanin'."

With my elbows on the table, my hands tore my hair in despair at the futility of years of study of Northwest Coast Native Americans. Marie sensed my anguish and consoled, "Vanity of vanities. All is vanity." Deftly she snatched my cup from the counter as she guessed my inner urge to heave it at her.

"I fear I've lost you on this," she tried to calm me. "Just 'cause ya didn't learn this ain't no reason ya cain't relax and take it all in." Sensing her predicament she vectored again:

"I must explain to ya more 'bout gold, the only metal worthy of Elvis. For Elvis not only had gold records, he not only wore gold, Elvis in some mystic way metamorphasized into gold. Now what does I mean? Well I must tell ya 'bout the Indians 'round Mexico and south a' Mexico, ya know, that skinny strip a' land with the Panama Canal cut 'cross it."

"You mean Central America?" I guessed.

"Yea, that's it. Well anyways, the Indians down yonder worshipped gold 'cause it didn't rust. Since gold never changed, it is immortal. So Elvis the Gold King has become in a mystic way immortal. Not only that, those Indians worshipped gold 'cause they said it symbolized the gold in the sky."

"Gold in the sky?" I foolishly asked.

"For a educated man ya seem ignorant of a good many things. I mean the sun! Those people in Central America worshipped it. But they weren't the only ones. I read in **National Geographic** 'bout the Egyptians. At one time they worshipped many gods until an upstart pharaoh forced them to worship only the sun god.

"I suppose you are referring to the attempt of the Pharaoh Akhenaton to establish monotheism in Egypt," I proposed.

"Well for once ya got some a' this right. Yea, that's the one, Akhenatty. Instead of all those statues a' baboons and jackals, he wanted the people to worship the sun called 'Aton.' Before this, they called it Amana-ray."

"Amon-re," I corrected.

"I think ya is right, it is 'Amon-re.' Amana-ray? How'd I come up with that? 'Amana-ray' sounds like those flat fish things ya don't want to step on at the beach. Also sounds like those waves in your microwave." Marie rambled:

"Yes Aton, alias Amon-re. Egyptians worshipped the sun god Aton, a golden disk, like a gold record. So Elvis must be the divine sun, the sun god! He made his first record at Sun Records, with a label of a bright red crowin' rooster on a post greeting the yellow risin' sun. Elvis, the risin' sun-King."

Sensing I might have at last found a hole in her argument, I objected, "You connect the gold records of Elvis to his being the sun god. But Elvis also had platinum records."

Her instant reply signaled my defeat:

"God a' the moon, Elvis was! Yes the moon that fills the night sky—that simonizes and newtons monthly—reminds us each night of Elvis. My friend Hortense had a record by a band named the Moody Blues. 'Course that's a sign 'cause Elvis had his song 'Moody Blue.' This Moody Blues band sang a song called 'Knights in White Satin,' a code for Elvis as the moon roamin' the night sky. Some say it means that Elvis played the knight in his white satin and leather jumpsuits. Others say it means the satin voice a' Elvis singin' as the White Knight of black rhythm and blues.

"I decipher the White Satin song as describin' a searchin' and lost Elvis. The song says he's gazin' at folks, holding hands. Just what he's goin' through, they cain't understands. That's the life of Elvis. The young Elvis said he was all mixed up. No one really understood the man. He had trouble understandin' hisself. The song goes on to say he loves us, yes he loves us. There 'gain ya have Elvis. For although confused and misunderstood he continued to love. For it had been granted that he might never seek so much to be understood as to understand, to be loved as to love with all his soul.

"The song has a speech 'bout a cold-hearted orb ruling the night. That's Elvis as the moon, livin' his backward life a' sleepin' through the day and roamin' all night: the blue moon god of Kentucky, Tennessee, and the world. Now when I describe Elvis like this I ain't thinkin' 'bout the White Knight of Ajax laundry soap who in armor, rode a bleached steed down suburban streets, and with a flash, lanced dirty-clothed folk into cleanliness. And I ain't thinkin' 'bout no White Tornado.

"Well now, let's get back to those pharaohs. After Akhenaton came Tutankhamen the boy King, the golden king—yet another

Elvis sign. And the great accomplishment of Tutankhamen was that he died. For they buried King Tut in gold in a tomb not found 'til the 1920s. So lived Elvis, surrounded by gold records, gold jewelry, a gold Cadillac. Now some take this too far in wantin' to call the womanizin' Elvis, King Tit.

"Believe it or not, the ancient Egyptians had a city named Memphis, built on the river Nile just like Memphis sits on the Mississippi. Outside the ancient Memphis sat pyramids and the great Sphinx. Now the Sphinx has puzzled many people 'cause it's half-animal, half-human. But if ya stare directly at that face, free your mind from ignorance, you will see, with its mane a' swept back hair, the very face a' Elvis. I swear to God!"

She pulled a tattered **National Geographic** from under the counter. It opened to a well-traveled page picturing the Sphinx.

"The Sphinx, it's a portrait of my love, Elvis. People have wondered what kind a' animal sits behind that face." Marie spoke with a steady marathon runner's pacing. "Some say a sheep, or a lion, but I knows it must be a hound dog."

"Oh come on now, that is ridiculous," I fought back.

"Yea," Marie answered, "I thought that too. But ya see fate proved the Sphinx has the face of Elvis. Elvis shaved. He didn't sport no mustache nor beard. For the Sphinx to be Elvis it couldn't have no beard neither. But when the Egyptians chiseled out that sucker, it had a beard. That's what the **Geographic** says. Now the British stole the beard in the 1800s. That's fate, kismet, guidin' the British so a hundred years later the true identity of the Sphinx could be revealed.

"Now this article 'xplains a lot a' history. Those ancient Egyptians used their Memphis to unite their Upper Kingdom with their Lower Kingdom. Elvis in Memphis united the northern states with the southern states through his music. And didn't need no mournfully fiddled 'Ashcan Farewell' to do it.

"Elvis healed the wounds a' the War Between the States. He did this with 'American Trilogy.' It united the South in the song 'Dixie' with the North in the song 'Battle Hymn of the Republic.'

Elvis spliced the two with 'All My Trials' as glue. We is joined—North and South—by his sufferin'. 'All My Trials' says 'Hush little baby, don't ya cry. Ya know your Daddy's bound to die.' That was for Lisa Marie. Elvis sacrificed himself in death to join together a nation torn asunder.

"Ancient Memphis had a great Temple to the god Ptah spelled P-T-A-H. I ain't exactly sure how to pronounce that—sounds like something ya say after bitin' into a green persimmon. Anyways, modern Memphis has its own great columned temple: Graceland.

"You can find Elvis symbols in ancient Egypt and among the old Greeks. Once I saw a Hercules movie. The more I thought about it, the more I was sure Hercules symbolized Elvis. Since the movie came from Hollywood I had to check the facts, so I went to a liberry for the truth. Accordin' to which, Hercules had twelve jobs or labors. I knew then and there the story represented Elvis—if ya interpreted it right. Though Hercules got his chores done, Elvis didn't. Elvis let a couple go right down the tubes.

"Hercules did twelve labors to make up for his mad rampages. Elvis rampaged, so he did twelve labors too." From under the counter Marie pulled a torn fragment of a **National Enquirer** with a headline about aliens in Racine, Wisconsin. She had listed twelve labors in the margins. Pointing to the list she explained, "The first job called for Hercules to kill and fillet this Nemean lion born of the moon goddess."

"What has that got to do with Elvis?" I taunted.

"Well what's the most strikin' thing 'bout a male lion?"

"Uhm, his mane I suppose," I offered fodder to her folly.

"Exactly, the first labor called for Elvis to fix his hair. He combed it ceaselessly. It looked the mane of a lion. Now the lion a' Hercules descended from the moon goddess. One best sees the moon 'gainst a black sky. So Elvis dyed his naturally blond hair. You can see a blond Elvis in **Kissin' Cousins**. A' course that's a blond wig over his dyed-black hair. Elvis painted his hair coal black so the moon goddess would shine bright. Elvis dyed his hair cause he didn't believe 'Blondes have more fun.' Nor did he walk the Mississippi banks ponderin', 'If I've only one life to live, let me live it as a blond.'"

"What about the second labor?" Curiosity again overwhelmed my better judgment.

"For his second job old Herc killed the Hydra of Lerna, a monster with heads that grew back after being cut off. This monster for Elvis must be the Hollywood starlets who lusted after him like she-camels in heat, coursin' back and forth over the deserts a' California. Elvis would no sooner hump and dump one, then seven more would take her place.

"Hercules captured this old boar of Mount Erymanthus for his third job. Ed Sullivan—that's the old boar. For his third labor Elvis performed on the Sullivan show.

"For his fourth job Hercules caught a hind, a kind a' fawn. He caught the deer, then let it go. For Elvis this labor meant marryin' Priscilla, his little dear. Then letting her go—Fate!

"Next Hercules drove away this obnoxious flock a' noisy birds— probably grackles—from a place called Stymphalus. Well as I said before, 'bird' means girl. Elvis labored to drive away the noisy girls from 'round his homes, especially the house on Audubon Drive— Nymphalus. Hercules drove the birds away with a bronze rattle; the gold records of Elvis only drew more birds.

"For his sixth job Hercules cleaned out stables, knee deep in manure. Kind a' like a political convention. Hercules dammed up a crick and flooded the place clean. Now this refers to the gang hangin' around and bullshittin' Elvis. He couldn't get rid a' them, though he tried floodin' them with gifts, which only made 'em stay longer. If Elvis asked a question, they'd give the answer he wanted cause they feared bein' osterized."

"I believe the word is 'ostracized,'" I suggested.

"Oh yes, ostracized. 'Cause those people 'round Elvis were what ya call syncopations," she stated. I accepted a tie in the battle for correct verbiage.

Marie moved down the list, "Next Hercules tied up an ornery bull. The biggest source a' bull 'round Elvis was Parker. That man could lay it on. Elvis couldn't tether this bull, nor ride it like in **Stay Away, Joe**. The eighth chore found Hercules capturin' horses. Elvis captured then gave away horsepower: Cadillacs, Harley-Davidson's, and pick-up trucks.

"For his ninth chore, a rather peculiar task, Hercules stole the Playtex girdles from Amazon women. This could mean the girdle Elvis wore under his outfits when he got large. 'Could also refer to Elvis battlin' amazons tryin' to get to him. A third meanin' might be the wide metal wrestlin' belt Elvis wore with his jumpsuits. Decide this one yourself.

"Hercules then stole cattle from a three-headed man. Elvis labored to become the best leadin' man in the westerns against the three heads of Gary Cooper, John Wayne, and Clint Eastwood. Hollywood sabotaged this labor by beaching Elvis. He became a lonesome cowboy, singin' to bikinied babes instead a' doggies.

"In chore eleven Hercules stole this three-headed dog from Hades the land a' the dead. For Elvis this meant he would somehow cheat death. Elvis died a' course—he's dead and buried. But many fans don't believe it. Elvis cheated death by gettin' so many to believe he's alive, even though he's really dead.

"Finally, for his twelfth chore Hercules stole golden apples from Hera, the wife a' Zeus. Hercules didn't eat them. Elvis failed in this his most impo'tant labor. Although he obtained drugs he weren't 'sposed to use them! But Elvis did and we all know the tragic results.

"After I got done readin' 'bout Hercules I started readin' 'bout other Greek heroes, like a guy called Brometheus. No, that ain't right. Sounds like somethin' ya take after a Cajun barbecue. No, it's Prometheus, that's it. Prometheus stole fire from the gods just as Elvis stole the fire a' Rock and Roll from the heavens. He took the sound a' thunder and harnessed it to 4/4 time. The gods punished Prometheus, chainin' him to a rock. Elvis on the other hand broke the chains and freed Rock and Roll.

"Now earlier the gods punished Prometheus by sendin' a beautiful woman, Pandora, with a cookie jar chock-full of evils. When the jar flew open, evil filled the world. Elvis had his Pandora's box—a doctor's handbag filled with countless prescription drugs. And poor Elvis lacked the wisdom to keep that bag shut. The evil a' Pandora began with Elvis takin' wake-up pills in the army and led to his death. The gods punished Elvis for bringin' so much joy to us mortals.

"So there ya have it—how the life of Elvis represented the chores of Hercules and the adventures of Prometheus. 'Cause every part a' the life of Elvis signs something."

"Every part of his life?" I asked.

"Yes darlin', every part of his life has meanin'."

Searching my limited knowledge of Elvis trivia I sought the tiniest, insignificant tidbit to test her theory. "What about Elvis's song 'Teddy Bear?' There is no great meaning to that."

"If you is out to stump me, you'd better try somethin' harder. 'Cause that's such an easy question. The song 'Teddy Bear' represents Elvis in the stars. Teddy Bear's an astronomical sign. Bear in Latin is 'Ursa' and in the sky ya can see the great bear, 'Ursa major.' A' course most people only know it as the Big Dipper. So just as we had the Big Bopper; so too we had Elvis, the Big Dipper."

"Why the Big Dipper and not the Little Dipper?" I asked.

Marie apparently considered this insulting question unworthy of answer. She simply moved on to her next point:

"And although Elvis has left this earth I still see him every night," Marie stated matter-of-factly.

"What?" Incredible though it may seem, she astounded me once more. "You see a dead man every night?"

"Yes, I see him in the sky."

"Oh, you have returned to astronomy." I searched for a handle on truth. "Perhaps you have seen a nine-hundred-foot tall Elvis, just like Oral Roberts had his vision some years ago."

"Don't mock me," she snapped. "I see Elvis nightly in the sky . . . weather permittin', in the stars and cancellations."

"'Cancellations?' Do you mean 'constellations'? You see Elvis in the constellations of the stars?" a bewildered me asked.

"Well yes, I do. Now them, whad-ja-ma-callits . . ."

"Constellations," I answered.

"Yes. Well them constellations got named by ancient Greeks for gods and supermen. But if ya look up there in the sky ya can see Elvis. First look at the stars they call El Toro, the Bull. I don't know why they named 'em after a lawnmower, but they did."

It seemed pointless to correct her. I let it pass.

Marie continued, "Well that set a' stars, shaped like a 'V', represents the open shirt of the Elvis jumpsuits."

"Hell, that's the stupidest thing I ever heard. You can't do better than that?" My anger stunned us both.

She tried to calm me. "Now just be settled. Look at the stars that make Orion the Hunter. Three stars make up the belt of Elvis. Other stars look like a sword hangin' from the belt. That's the fringe on the belt of Elvis. Where Orion held a shield in front a' him, that's Elvis's guitar. And the sword Orion holds over his head would be Elvis swingin' a scarf. 'Course this is a double sign 'cause ya see, after Elvis died, some said that he faked his death and still did shows as a masked singer named Orion. We knows now it weren't true. Elvis lay six feet under. The singer Jimmy Ellis was that masked man, Orion.

"Now if ya wants to see Elvis doin' karate kicks, just look at the stars they call Hercules. And if ya want a simple one a' Elvis singin' a ballad, you look at Leo the Lion. 'Cause the head a' Leo is the head of Elvis and the back of the lion is the end of his guitar with all the pegs in it."

Afraid to ask, I did anyway. "Are there any more?"

"Well no. That's all," said Marie. I felt relief. But she added, "We could go outside right now and see if we could find more." My heart sank until I recalled my trip there.

"The fog. The fog! We could not see anything."

"Yes, perhaps you is right. Let's forget about the stars."

"I hope your are not going to show how the life of Elvis parallels Homer's **Iliad**," I wondered.

"No, I don't know that song. Was it by Homer and Jethro?"

"Not the bluegrass players. It is an ancient Greek story."

"Nope, never heard of it," she said.

"The Greeks sailed out to rescue Helen from the Trojans. She had the face that launched a thousand ships."

"Boy that must a' hurt! Why didn't they just shove those boats off the dock or use a big pry bar?" she added.

I was relieved there would not be an "Elvissey and Eliad."

Marie shifted again, "Now I ain't finished with all these foreign places. Among the Mohammedans, they have . . ."

"Mohammedans?" I forced an entry, "You mean Muslims?"

She explained, "Yea 'Muslims'—they used to call 'em 'Musselmans,' but not 'cause they pumped iron. I's talkin' the followers of Muhammad and I don't mean Cassius Clay. Now the Mohammedans have five duties, what they call pillars. A true Elvis fan has duties or pillars. First I proclaim 'Elvis is the King, there is no other, and music is his voice.' Second, I think of Elvis five times a day. Sometimes, I even get out a carpet square—a sample from down at the Carpet Barn—face it toward Graceland and get down on my knees.

"Third, I diet for one month each year—durin' the 30 day period 'tween Thanksgivin' and Christmas: the month of 'Ram it down,'—when most people stuff their gullets.

"Fourth, I give to the poor the way Elvis gave Cadillacs. Finally, I and every Elvis fan must pilgrimage to Graceland once in a lifetime. There ain't no excuses for poverty or illness. All true Elvis fans get to Graceland and walk the hallowed home where the halls are alive with the sound of Elvis. Ya join the crowd and walk 'round Graceland seven times. Or even better, get an old Thunderbird convertible and cruise 'round it seven times.

"There you are: five duties, the five 'pillars' of Elvis fans."

I began to yearn for five pillows of a Motel 6.

CHAPTER 16

ELVIS

DEATH OF THE KING

"I'll never forget the last time I saw Elvis: August 6, 1977," said Marie. "We stood watch at the Graceland gates. A deep forebodin' whelmed over us. As I told my friends, 'Now is the summer of our discontent.' In fear and tremblin' we sensed a great catastrophe, a great catechism, 'bout to unfold. We felt a disturbance in the force. Didn't know what or how, but we knew.

"For weeks we'd waited but saw nothin', yet we vigiled on. That evenin' I'd dressed with great care. I showered with Neutrogena soap and used Drene shampoo. From a cedar chest in the attic I found the old poodle skirt and violet sweater I wore the night I became one with the King. I fixed my hair like it looked in my high school yearbook. I even found a twenty-year-old, dried out Elvis—Hound Dog Orange Lipstick from which I got just 'nough to cover my lips. Finally grabbin' my old Brownie camera that sat next to an old plaid picnic basket in the basement, I went to stand my watch at the Graceland gates.

"About 11:00 P.M. a long black limousine led a porcelain-white stretch limo as it slithered down the curvin' drive a' Graceland. The white limo rolled through the open flung gates, bounced at the culvert, and pulled out into the street. Then it lurched to a stop! It backed up and came 'long side a' me. The rear window powered down and there, . . . there sat the King, in his chariot, in all his magnificent glory—a tarnished radiance. His sunglassed eyes scanned me up and down, then he smiled as if old memories a' better, less painful times flooded his mind. His relief lasted a moment before agony and sorrow welled up within him. He yanked the sunglasses off. His puffy, red-swoll eyes stared at my tremblin' face. He ordered, 'Get thee to a beanery!' Least that's what I thought he said. In the wondrous moment a' terror, awe, and sweetness I ain't sure what I heard.

"Elvis put back his glasses. He turned and faced forward, groanin', 'My punishment is greater than I can bear. Oh, that this cup would pass from me!' The window shot up, the limo shot away, and I stood there in silence. Elvis had gone out—one a' his last times—to see the city by night.

"I wanted to stay at Graceland, and had I, I'd a' been there ten days later when the King died. And maybe I could a' done somethin'. If only I could a' talked to him. I'd a' told him he's the King. That he had to live up to his callin', to his Kingly duty, and fight the terrible dragon of drugs now set to devour him. If only he'd known how much I loved him, it could a' made a difference. The power of my love could a' saved him.

"As much as I wanted to stay, I had been commanded to go forth. I never saw him live again. Fate! His last words a mission to me—I came here. Oh what a change of habit! Back in '77 Motel Dewey still was busy, but it closed in 1982 'cause a' the Reagan depression. The diner remains, but only 'cause I've not abandoned my post and I 'spose I'll be here 'til God calls me home. This place ain't no smorgasbord but I's doin' the best I can. Now at last I see the meanin' a' the command of Elvis. For I've waited for years for someone to come and learn the signs. You've arrived. I've told and explained all!"

Marie stopped talking. The end had come! I shut off the recorder and grabbed the tapes. But Marie had not finished, she only paused to gather her breath for the final push—for the final ascent. She slammed the "Record" button and moved onward:

"No! It's important I speak upon the manner a' the death of Elvis. I must complete my message. Now is the hour. It's now or never. I knows you're thinkin', 'This is my comfort; when Marie's words is done my woes end likewise with the night's moon.' But listen, you must! It ain't easy for me either. It hurts me to speak a' these woes. All these years and it keeps on a-hurtin. A heavier task could not a' been imposed than to speak my griefs unspeakable. But I'll utter what my sorrows give me leave. Sometimes it causes me to tremble, tremble, tremble.

"And if I've suffered so much to keep alive this message, you can suffer another hour. For our pain ain't nothin' compared to the pain of Elvis. He suffered a long decline—due mostly to drugs." Marie reopened the green-stamp book. "Nostradamus predicted the blindness of Elvis to the evils of apothecary:

> The royal prince will be surprised by illness from above
> Just before he was to be married,
> His aid and credit will vanish,
> Advice and counsel from the bald one will fail. (I, 88)

"Elvis proposed to Ginger Alden and talked marriage plans just 'fore dyin'. But Elvis had run out a' money, and couldn't get credit. And the advice of the bald one, Colonel Parker, become more useless than ever.

"The night 'fore he died Elvis asked to see the movie **Star Wars**. I 'spose he wanted to watch one more time as OB Wan Kanobe gave his life to save his friends 'fore he passed on to Jedi Heaven. But the theater couldn't get hold a' the film for Elvis.

"The next day Elvis played racquetball. Nostradamus described this last game Elvis played 'fore he died.

> A great bolt of thunder was seen,
> At the game of tennis the royal one took injury. (I, 56)

"Elvis foresaw his death. The day he died, as he dressed and splashed on Brut for the final time, he stared long at the bottle and moaned, 'Et tu Brute. Then fall Elvis.' 'Course he might've been worried 'bout trippin' over his dog Brutus. But he mumbled to hisself, 'I is dyin' Memphis, dyin'. I have become death, the destroyer of worlds.' He sighed most heavy—like a man well acquainted with blues—for the millionth and last time.

"Maybe Elvis prayed for the sentence a' death to deliver him from his affliction and take him to the everlastin' home, just like Tobit in some Bibles. Who knows for sure? Elvis went upstairs to bed, saying, 'It's a hell of a better thing that I do, than I's ever done; it's a hell of a better rest I go to than I's ever known.' Those 'round him figgered him tuckered out.

"They say Elvis died in his bathroom, sittin' on the commode. How fittin', the king died on his throne, like Eli in the Bible who 'fell from off the seat backward by the side of the gate, and his neck brake, and he died.' (I Samuel 4:18) Gate means door. Elvis had no broken neck, only a broken body. Elvis crashed to the floor, wheezin' 'Rosebud.' He died for beauty, yet heard no fly buzz when he went. Nor did he look out the window and see a rained-on wheelbarrow with chickens 'round it.

"Rescue vehicle Unit No. 6—there's that number again—driven by one Ulysses, rushed Elvis to the hospital where a Harvey team—that's emergency doctors, not no puka's—pumped his stomach, waled on his chest, forced more drugs into his blood. Nothin' worked: the fell sheriff, Death, is strict in his arrest.

"'Course Nostradamus had his say on the death of Elvis:

> In the night the greatest one lay strangled in bed
> The blond elect had dallied and not arrived.
> Three would come to enslave the Empire,
> Killing it with unread documents and dispatches. (I, 39)

"Elvis, choked to death, strangled by drugs in the bathroom—off the bedroom—durin' the night of Elvis—daytime for us. 'The blond elect'—that's the doctor who couldn't get there in time. The empire put to death with documents and dispatches unread, well that's the finances of Elvis, ruined by the Colonel's dealin's.

Elvis never read contracts. The three who enslaved the Graceland empire: Priscilla, Lisa Marie, Mister X.

"Some blames those who watched Elvis for deliverin' the drugs that killed him. Maybe they'd taken drugs themselves." The green-stamp book never left her hand. "As for Nostradamus:

> A terrible and grievous suffering,
> Three without guilt yet one of which will carry.
> Poison, betrayed by failing guards:
> The executioners, inebriated, deliver the horror. (I, 68)

There ya have it: high as a kite, those who guarded him, without knowin' it, delivered the killer drugs that poisoned Elvis.

"If Elvis had died two days later he'd a' been on tour. But that couldn't be! For it'd been prophesied to him many years before, that he shouldn't die but in Jerusalem, which vainly he 'sposed the Holy Land. But he died, bare in his own chamber, there he lie, in that Jerusalem of Memphis.

"Where in the Bible can ya find a symbol for the death of Elvis? Some think Elvis committed suicide. They argue Elvis foreshadowed suicide in his 1969 movie, **The Trouble With Girls** when he says, 'It's easy, I just go kill myself.' I don't rightly know. But Elvis brought on death by his drug use. He pulled his end down upon hisself just like Samson pulled the temple of Dagon down on hisself. Samson died under the ruins of the temple. Elvis, betrayed by the Delilah, Dilaudid, died in his temple under the ruins a' his career. But a' course Elvis—like Samson—was blind, not physically, but blind to reality. It's impossible to know if Elvis knew what he did. Elvis died from drugs, either from carelessness, or willful intention, or from the evil schemin's of others. Who knows what evils lurk in the hearts a' men. Lamont Cranston couldn't unravel this one!

"When I heard the news on the radio I drove straight to the hospital from the diner. There I learned that Elvis had died. The whole kingdom a' Memphis contracted in one forehead a' woe.

"One coroner hinted that Elvis died a' heart problems caused by the lifestyle of Elvis. I guess the man figgered that excess makes the heart grow fatter. But who shall decide when doctors disagree? That coroner was dead wrong. Drugs killed Elvis! Drugs that caused his overblown colon to pack up tighter than an old chat driveway. Drugs that shut down his body faster than a thunderstorm shuttin' down a Memorial Day picnic.

"I cain't rightly recall the days that followed. I lived them as a zombie. When they laid Elvis in state we went to him. We prepared ointments, perfumes, and spices. We hoped to put them on his body. 'Course we knew they wouldn't let us.

"We stood in line for hours—hours of agony—to see him one last time. We had to make sure it was really him! And as long as we stood in line, we nurtured a hope—too secret to tell one another though each thought it—that when we got to the casket and gazed in, we'd see they had the wrong man and we could search for Elvis among the livin'. But as the line moved, the awful moment came closer—up the drive, up the steps, through the door and there it sat—the casket. The guards kept people movin'. I yearned to run forward and I ached to run away. My feet shuffled but it seemed the casket moved toward me.

"I stood at the foot of the casket, next to the sooties of Elvis. I dared not look at his face. Two people blocked my view. Then the guards moved them; I could look no more forever. I raised my line a' sight to the coffin handles, to the satin linin', across a human arm, up the necktie to the face. Oh God, oh God, the face! It was Elvis! My dear Elvis! My mind exploded, my body shook. Without him there ain't nothin'. No longer more denied. It's over! Our beloved King has died!

"Too quick the guards nudged us along and out a' the house into the sticky, August, hard-breathin', sob-filled air.

"But I must tell of a peculiar thing that happened—of a man who stood in line—a stranger in the crowd. We paid scant attention to him. Only later did we speculate. For he stood behind us yet he seemed unmoved by the tragedy. We talked to him, but he knew little of the life of Elvis—he seemed strangely aloofed. He claimed to work for the Fort Lauderdale Chamber of Commerce, but we didn't believe that for a moment.

"At the coffin I so trembled with grief that I barely noticed him raise his hands to his eyes in great grief. But he seemed not sad at all moments before. From Graceland he walked quickly, almost happily, away. To this day I wonder if he weren't the Judas who took the picture of Elvis in the coffin that wound up in the **National Enquirer.** Seems likely that when he raised his hands in mock grief he held a miniature camera just like Mr. Phelps on the old **Mission Impossible** show.

"Some said Elvis in state didn't look quite right. When I gazed upon him it seemed he looked smaller than life and half as natural. But a' course Nostradamus predicted this:

> Sisters and brothers, exiled in far away lands
> Will come to pass near and gaze at the king:
> Considering his attentive branches,
> Unhappy to see markings on brow, nose, and chin. (II, 20)

"We fans of Elvis, brothers and sisters in adoration, from all over, captive in Memphis heat, filed by the casket, unsettled by the face of the monarch—so unprepared for death. The branches, the Memphis Mafia looked on.

"After we saw Elvis one last time we staggered down the drive at Graceland. As we passed through the gates an old grizzled man stepped out a' the crowd. He carried old wooden pop bottle crates like I hadn't seen for years. He wore the blue greasy pants and shirt of a mechanic with an 'Oscar' name patch.

"He stacked his crates, climbed on top, and started to make a speech. From the way he talked and his chewed-tobacco teeth, ya knew he'd came from a backwoods holler." From the back of her Bible Marie pulled out a yellowish square of folded paper. As she unfolded it I saw oily food stains, "CHEESEBURGER" printed in red ink diagonally, and pencil scrawlings which she read. "Well he starts a' preachin' and this is what he said:

> Friends, Memphanes, Country Folk, y'all listen up:
> I's here to plant Elvis, not to go on 'bout him.
> The evil that men does, hangs 'round after 'em,
> Like the linger a' road-kill skunk,
> The good goes six feet under with dem bones.
> So let it be with Elvis.
> Elvis was my friend, hound dog faithful, plain nice to me.
> Honorable brutes will say he was an ambitious man.
> But the poor wept, Elvis gave them Cadillacs.
> Y'all did love him once, not without cause:
> Now bear with me;
> My ticker is there in the box with Elvis,
> And I must hang 'round till it come back to me.
> If you've any tears, let the crick flow.

'Poor soul,' his eyes red as fire with weepin' as he bid the last farewell to Elvis. I walked away, far from the saddenin' crowd.

"The funeral followed the next day. We stood by the roadside waitin' for hours. Then slowly came the hearse. I'm with the crowd and we could see the hearse a half-mile away. Like jar-bottom molasses it inched forward. Nearer and nearer. Then as if the gods themselves intervened, the hearse stopped in front a' me. Yes, right in front. Somethin' had halted the police cars in front a' the hearse and for a moment the body of Elvis held before me. I could bear no more! I jumped the striped sawhorse—sort of a saw-zebra—of the police barricade. I jumped it and ran, throwin' myself upon the hearse hood to be near Elvis one more time. I cried and prayed to let all the tears that should bedew his hearse, be drops of balm to sanctify his head. In a flash the policemen jumped me. They pulled me away, my runnin' mascara streakin' the hood. My shoe fell off as they carried me to the sidewalk and dumped me in a heap. The women standin' near tended me while the funeral moved on.

"An hour passed 'fore the crowd broke up. I sat sobbin' as dazed people walked hither and yon. A young man with puffed red eyes came up holdin' my shoe: flattened. He'd gone into the street, after the funeral corsage, and grabbed my shoe crushed by the hearse. He wanted a remembrance, a souvenir, but guilt overwhelmed him. He knew it'd mean more to me. He said, 'Woman, why weepest thou? Whom seekest thou? The sufferin's of Elvis are over and he is gone. Doncha' think it's time you went home. What's gone and what's past help should be past grief.' But I answered, 'I shall not be moved. I have good cause for bawlin', but this heart shall be torn like a hundred-thousand pieces a' dental floss or before I stop weepin', oh, Fool, I shall go mad!'

"And look," she said, "there's the shoe today."

Lo, to my astonishment, next to the "Grade A" sign on the wall behind her, locked within a Seal-a-Meal bag, I saw a crushed, red, high-heeled shoe, darkened by tire and asphalt.

"I keep it there," she explained, "as a good luck charm. As I said before, Parker showed up at the funeral in a Hawaiian shirt, yellin' to Vernon Presley, 'This don't change anythin'.' Parker didn't show much sorrow at the loss of 'the boy':

> Holy ones will come to anoint the great dead King
> Before his spirit has gone:
> One will not be grieved,
> Through beasts and Eagles, the royal crown be sold. (VI, 17)

"Nostradamus again?" I concluded.

Marie nodded, "Ya know the rest. They buried Elvis. Now evil-minded cynics bemoan that Elvis was buried in Christian burial when he willfully sought his own salvation. Will ya have the truth on't? Accordin' to them, if he'd not been Elvis he'd a been buried out a' Christian burial.

"If I recall correctly—those days was such a blur—they buried

Elvis in a suit and tie—strange since Elvis rarely wore ties. It's the custom to bury men this way. But tie styles change so quickly. One is buried with a stylish tie that in months is considered gaudy, unsightly, and in poor taste. So we condemn men to an eternity a' being out a' fashion. For the Fickle Finger a' Fate reigns supreme when it comes to fashion.

"In the weeks after, things didn't go well at the cemetery. Police couldn't control the crowds payin' respect at the grave. They even arrested three grave robbers who conspired with the enemies of Elvis. These thiefs weren't gonna steal the body. As I see it, they planned to make it look like they was stealin' it. Then if Elvis did rise or if the tomb be found empty they'd claim the body had been stole. Do you understands? The attempt to steal the body was a decoy to explain away a empty tomb. I think the conspiracy included high government officials. The Good Book says they gave men hush money with instructions, 'Say, ye, his disciples came by night, and stole him away while we slept. And if this come to the governor's ears, we will persuade him, and secure you.' (Matthew 28, 12-13)

"Finally they moved the body of Elvis to the garden at Graceland. Oh Elvis, my Elvis, your fearful trip is done.

"I've always wondered why they didn't use the words from the gravestone of Deke Rivers in the Elvis movie, **Loving You**: 'He was alone but for his friends who miss him.' That would be a wonderful epi . . . epi . . . now mister, what do ya call it?"

"Epitaph," I answered.

"Yes, epitaph. Though I admit, the more I think 'bout that sayin' the less sense it makes." She began to sing softly:

> And will he not come again?
> And will he not come again?
> No, no, he is dead; Gone to his deathbed;
> He will never come again.
>
> His sideburns were as white as snow;

All flaxen was his pompadour.
He is gone, he is gone, And we cast away and moan.
God have mercy on his soul.

"When Elvis died his hair was turning a flaxen white. Before the funeral of Elvis, Larry Geller used black mascara to dye the white roots of Elvis. Ain't that ironic?

"Now 'bout the man who found my shoe. I saw him later that day at Ponderosa. In our pain and emptiness we embraced. Then without anythin' more we went to his hotel room at the Holiday Inn. Ya see, I didn't want to hold back like Hope Lange did in the movie **Wild in the Country** when she spent the night with Elvis at that motel where Zane Grey stayed. I knew this man would help me make it through the fever night after the funeral of Elvis; he might stem the flow of tears on my pillow.

"After my divorce from Bubba I figgered I'm not the marryin' kind. But two days later I drove to Vegas with this man to get married. The passion a' the moment blinded me. All we are is lust in the wind, ain't we, darlin'? For ya see, reason dies between the sperm and the bride. And we fell into a burnin' ring of fire, goin' down, down, down, while the flames went higher. We got married in a fever, hotter than a pepper sprout.

"We was ill-suited for each other. I'd been born a coal miner's daughter, and he, an egghead intellectual who studied philosophy. He thought if he learnt enough he could win an argument with a Jehovah's Witness. Smart he was. He could make sense a' Paul Simon lyrics and knew the second verse to 'We Shall Overcome.'

"He was named Dominick Dellacroix. Now he loved classical music operas like Dristan and Mazola. He loved both opera and Elvis! Dominick could actually listen to 'Bolero' on the stereo and not think a' Bo Derek. And he was smart. Ya know that depressionist French painter Monet, why Dominick could correctly pronounce the name of his water-lily swamp garden.

"Dominick was a contradiction. He used to tell philosophy

jokes 'How does an existentialist spell relief?' He'd answer 'D-E-A-T-H.' 'What kind a' soap does an existentialist use?' 'Camus Camay.' He'd joke 'bout the ancient Romans inventin' 'cross ventilation' and 'cross trainin'.' I'd laugh to humor him, but I never understood his jokes or his poetry by B. S. Elliot. He'd watch foreign films, like Fellini's 6 and 7/8ths. Why he used to go into the bus station, jump up on a bench and yell, 'What's the matter with Memphis? It's all right!' This bizarre man got hate mail from Leo Buscaglia and Mother Teresa.

"A' course that marriage didn't last neither—hardly twenty nights and twenty days. A fool such as I didn't see it weren't real love, only echoes of love. We stayed together a few weeks. Like two paid-out swimmers we clung together and choked each other's air. Our passion ran out with our money. So we divorced. I 'spose I'll never fall in love again. Last I heard 'bout Dominick he was writin' a movie script where Kevin Costner would play a disillusioned farmer who gives up high-tech air-conditioned wheat combines and computerized cattle feedlots to return to plow-mule farmin', called 'Dances with Livestock.' This weren't his first movie script. In the late 70s he wrote a musical—a Disco life of St. Francis called 'Brother Sun, Sister Sledge.' Now he could never watch Jay Leno, 'cause he couldn't help starin' at Leno's eyebrows and this made Dominick seasick. Finally he went off to Big Sur, California to form some self-help group called The Institute of Self-Manipulation.

"I'm positive I won't marry again. I don't wanna be tied down. I don't want to. But I've learned one thing 'bout husbands: easy come, easy go."

As Marie told of her second failed marriage I understood why Elvis would want drugs to obliterate the reality of the moment—eager to make the world go away.

CHAPTER 17

ELVIS

POST MORTEM

APOLOGIA PRO VITA SUA

For an hour a small stream of black smoke rose from the shattered coffeepot on the hot burner. Marie at last looked at the mess. With a lethargic "Oh, shit" she shut the coffee maker off and ignored it. Then she began again:

"I knows you is tired. But I's almost done. It won't be long now. Your discomfort will last just a tad longer, cause as ya know, darlin', ya feel the worst just 'fore the relievin' belch. I've only a bit more concernin' the portentous events after the death of Elvis. Nostradamus spoke on this. But as ya see, ain't much left to my stamp book. First the Memphis Mafia:

> Those of knowledge who lived in the king's realm
> Will find poverty at the passing of the King:
> Sent to exile without money, without gold,
> With letters and without they will not be in demand. (VI, 8)

"Almost all the Mafia lost their jobs, incomes, very way and meanin' a' life: exiled without pension, severance pay, or gold. With the passin' of the King—death—came poverty. Even those who played varsity sports had trouble findin' work. Which only goes to prove that the geek shall not inherit the earth.

"About Lisa Marie, Nostradamus said:

> A woman alone in the kingdom
> Extinguished by the great one on the honorable bed:
> Grieving, she will weep for seven years,
> Yet with great luck the realm shall live. (VI, 63)

"The death of Elvis left Lisa Marie alone in the kingdom. The fire of the unique one extinguished in the bedroom. Seven years she wept for him. Then with great good fortune people kept comin' to Graceland. The realm lives long and prospers. Who knows what the future holds for Lisa Marie now that she's free from Michael Jackson? One suspects that she'll do what Natalie Cole did: make piggyback records by singin' 'long with her father's old songs."

Marie turned the green-stamp book over to the back cover where she had written her final Nostradamus passage. "Lastly, Nostradamus spoke 'bout Colonel Parker who walked with a cane:

> The crippled man who could not rule Sparta,
> He will conspire with means seductive:
> Before long he will be accused and charged
> Of maneuvering against the Monarch. (VI, 84)

"This refers to the court case brought by the estate of Elvis. They accused Parker a' gettin' wealthy at the expense of Elvis by usin' seductive means. They drove Parker from the Presley empire. But it ain't true what some have said, that Parker wanted to make Graceland into a theme park named 'Spartaland.'"

Marie slackened her pace. She straightened up the counter and wiped down the stove. She cleaned the french fry maker mumbling, "O, comfortable fryer! Where is my Lard?" She pushed aside a bottle of corn oil. In magic marker someone had crossed out "Mazola" and written in "Parmigianino." Marie shined the stainless steel. She polished her blender and uttered, "The world's mine

Oster. It's mine." All this gave her a moment to put perspective on what she had said. Then she spoke again:

"Now I pose the most impo'tant question 'bout Elvis: why? Why did a poor southern boy grow so big and spellbind so many folks? Why did millions need Elvis? Well the fault, dear brother, is not in our stars, but in ourselves. For many look at Elvis to find the man, rather we should look at Elvis to discover ourselves. Ya see the paradox of our lives is that although we mean so much to ourselves, we mean nothin' to the universe.

"Now I must warn ya, I've more questions than answers on this. I search for truth, but don't quite got hold of it. I've doubts and uncertainties. But I know it's almost always true that those most certain they've got the truth, is least likely to actually possess it. To think ya understand Elvis is to make your first mistake. Less the none, I will try to explain him.

"I see Elvis as an icon; not Carl Icahn, but a Greek church paintin'. Elvis represented somethin' special and extraordinary. He imaged a glory. Elvis promised somethin' beyond the ordinary, borin', mediocrity of our lives. 'Cause our real problem ain't bills or cranky bosses or naggin' husbands. No, the problem's that while we live our dull lives we's condemned to always yearn for somethin' more. We ache to be delivered from the very lives we live. And in our yearnin' we have searched for a savior.

"So we turned to Elvis, a man of dash, glamour, and extravagance. In Elvis there was a man, a cavalier, a man of the old South. Look for him only in books, movies, and records, for he is no more than a dream remembered, a civil man gone with the wind. Elvis soared 'bove the ordinariness that binds us to earth. For we's all trapped—by sadness and loneliness. We mourn our lives and ache for deliverance from our unromantic, football-watchin', beer-drinkin' men. All us women dated or married Homer Simpson's of some degree. 'Course deliverance never comes. But as long as Elvis lived, we'd share in his escape from mediocrity—if we could just see him, or touch him. For a instant we'd enter that magic world that'd redeem us from our housework, our jobs, our ungrateful kids. Oh, we'd go back to the same sinks to wash the same dishes, but we'd carry with us a spark, a inner light, a warmed heart that had seen glory.

"Elvis had a kind a' magic: a rough magic, I here assure. He possessed somethin' we didn't have. On stage, in films, he seemed confident, cocksure, in control. We worshipped Elvis 'cause our lives is out 'a control. That's why the truth 'bout the lifestyle and death of Elvis shocked worse than learnin' 'bout Rock Hudson bein' gay. We wanted to believe in one who controlled his destiny. It broke our hearts to see the life of Elvis also out a' control. It hurt to see through the tinsel and glitter to the real facade beneath. 'Cause ya see, hun', we believed the purest treasure—like a winnin' lottery ticket—these immoral times can afford is a spotless reputation. But fate blemished the lamb Elvis. He made a mess a' his life too.

"In horror we learned that tedium and loneliness imprisoned Elvis—only worse for him—he had tasted greatness. Elvis was a man before his time. He should a' lived in the time of computer video games. Why he could a' kept hisself entertained for hours with Donkey Kong, Mario Brothers, and Pac Man and probably never would a' used drugs. But all Elvis had was go-carts and slot cars to occupy his furtive mind and so he suffered. Elvis remained a poor, bored, confused boy from Tupelo—trapped like us, only he couldn't look to hisself for hope.

"At the same time, Elvis oozed vulnerability. Many women longed to be the dotin' Gladys Elvis had lost. They believed they could a' saved the King from dyin'. But Elvis had the law and the prophets, if he hadn't listened to them he wouldn't have listened to the most loyal fan. It's like men fantasizin' they could a' saved Marilyn Monroe. 'Course I think each ordinary Joe figgers Marilyn would have ignored him for bein' plain lookin' and poor. But if only he could've offered his devotion and amateur psychology, Marilyn'd throw herself at him. Why do such men think they can succeed where Joe DiMaggio failed?

"Fans don't understand that their feelin's for an idol ain't felt by him. Fans project fulfillment but cain't give it. A fan desperately wants to see or touch her idol and he just walks past. Fans believed Elvis felt 'bout them, like they felt 'bout Elvis. It weren't so, 'cause idols is lonely and empty. And they cain't deceive themselves that some other person can fill their hearts. Ya see, darlin', us plebes, we's all lookin' at the movie and rock stars, but we's still in the gutter.

"I've explained what Elvis means to adult women. It's time to explain what he meant to 1950s teenage girls. Elvis hit radio and TV unleashin' a outburst, a monstrous wave of sexuality. But why? 'Cause in middle-class, Eisenhower America millions a' girls hit puberty in chorus. In schools and homes nobody talked 'bout sex. Yet simmerin' like pressure cookers, these girls knew somethin' more real than Home Economics churned deep inside their bosoms. Society denied it; Elvis exalted it—on stage, thrustin' his groin at eager bodies. Elvis lived by the motto, 'Speak softly and carry a big stick.' Little Elvis, had it been shorter, the whole aspect a' the world would've been altered.

"Elvis, the whirlin' dervish of sex, answered the burnin' ache inside those girls, while parents, teachers, and preachers condemned from ignorance and became irrelevant. Here was an hombre with no need to get in touch with his feminine side! Elvis displayed somethin' more powerful, more fascinatin', and more alive than anythin' us girls ever knew or ever would know.

"Men, they didn't need Elvis. 'Cause they could watch **Leave it to Beaver** and work out their sexual fantasies." She pointed her finger in my face. I sat stunned. Never would I have expected to hear **Leave it to Beaver** and "sexual fantasies" in the same sentence. But I continued to make the mistake of thinking Marie's sentences had something to do with logical coherence.

"Look at the title, **Leave it to Beaver**. I's too much a lady to say what 'beaver' means. A' course Bernie explained it, saying that June Cleaver represented men's Oedipus Complex Surrogate Mother. I's not sure I understand, but sounds good.

"By the 1950s, ya see, the goal a' marriage for girls had changed from findin' a man who'd provide and not beat you, to findin' a man you'd love with all your heart. But no one could tell these young girls anythin' 'bout love. So they looked to Rock and Roll. But they made the mistake a' thinkin' that if musicians sang so much 'bout love, they must a' known somethin' 'bout it. But what made McCartney, Lennon, and Presley experts on love? Turns out they knew less than we did. They only knew how to stay on key when they sang 'bout it.

"Now while young women went crazy over Elvis things was different with boys. Many boys and men was jealous of Elvis 'cause he had such power over women. Women'd throw their panties at Elvis and if given the chance they'd throw their bodies. So men wanted to be like Elvis, and that's the funny part. Every man wanted to be Elvis, every man that is, 'cept Elvis. Elvis felt so bad 'bout hisself that he quaffed drugs 'til it killed him. Though in truth, he was quite a good fellow—nobody's enemy but his own. But he died at his own hands.

"Now Elvis weren't very old. He had a heart a' gold. Now why did such a Presley have to die? Well ya see, Elvis offered hisself up as sacrifice for all the sins a' the Rock and Roll generation. A scapegoat, he took on our sins by becomin' a great sinner hisself. As a terrible sinner he hoped that on the day a' judgment the wrath of the Almighty would be turned to him and turned away from us lesser sinners. In a way, Elvis ran redemptive interference for us in the heavenly stadium, protectin' us from the angelic tackle. Elvis died to save us from the punishment we so rightly deserved. And so that's why Elvis did more than his share a' sinnin'—if ya count all those women he fornicated with. Though some wants to blame those women and proclaim Elvis innocent: more sinned up against than sinnin'.

"Elvis gave all he could—then he died. He is with us no more. Renown and grace is dead, the beer a' life is gone, and the mere belch is left this malt to brag on. Our loneliness remains, and we ponder how can such emptiness exist if there ain't nothin' to fill it. It seems a great cruel trick a' fate that we've such deep yearnin' that cannot be filled? But maybe the very yearnin' proves that somethin' exists to fulfill it. Our hearts, burnin' within, prove that Elvis still exists somehow, somewhere—in the great beyond. And so our hearts are restless, until they rest in thee, Oh Elvis!

"Elvis died. Yet many cain't accept his death. Elvis'll come 'gain, a thousand years hence. But he did die. We all die. Our days pass swifter than a weavin' shuttle bus. Our lives is short and brutish. Many fans cain't face up to life as so much chasin' after wind. That's why they claim the government or aliens captured Elvis. Folks don't want the reality of dead Elvis. They want magic. And that's why they elected Ronald Reagan."

"Ronald Reagan? What has he to do with Elvis Presley?"

"Ever'thin'," she responded. "Elvis offered a magical deliverance from borin' lives. We cain't really escape, so we want magic. Reagan offered political magic, promisin' to fix things with his spells. Carter told the painful truth: we had to use less oil, conserve energy, behave ourselves around the world—we had to change. He got dumped for a magician! Reagan said if we'd take in less tax money we could pay more bills; the rich could have more and the poor'd be better off; if we got more bombs we'd be safer; if we kept doin' things the same things'd get better; and if we cut down trees there'd be less pollution. If the man had a pointed hat and a cloak with stars and moons on it, we'd at least given him credit for honesty.

"Politics promises magic. H. Ross Perot—a short Texan who looks like Bubba's father—came out a' nowhere and people wanted him to be president, believin' he had new magic. Why don't we look square at problems, quit blamin' others, and fix 'em?

"People say that Elvis proves the American dream: a poor southern boy became a rich and famous-lifestyled millionaire. If Elvis could do it, others could. But every poor southern boy I knew grew up to be a poor southern man. That's why Elvis seems impressive, doing what most men can't. He achieved a greatness the ordinary Joe couldn't get. Elvis don't prove the American dream, he proves the rule we know deep down: poor folk cain't make it big. Elvis proves this rule by bein' its exception.

"Enough a' all this philosophizin'. I must tell ya a story 'bout one a' my friends and Elvis. I was an Elvis fan from the beginnin' 'fore everybody came on board the Elvis bandwagon. On July 7, 1954, when I heard Dewey Phillips play 'That's All Right Mama' I converted then and there. My faith never faltered. But not all my friends joined me in my enthusiasm. It took time. One friend a' mine, Juanita, wrote a letter tellin' how she turned to Elvis in a moment a' crisis. For as ya know, a single moment can change your life. She had this to say:"

Marie reopened her Bible and pulled out a tattered piece of pink stationery with strawberries across the top and read.

"'So was I chattin' and cryin' in the most bitter sorrow in my gut, when lo! I heard from the neighbor's house a voice, a girl or boy, hell I didn't know, chantin' and rechantin', 'Pick it up and listen, pick it up and listen.' Instantly, my mood switched. I began to rack my brain on whether children sang such words, nor could I remember ever havin' heard such a song. So puttin' a levee to my tear ducts, I arose, and interpreted it to be a command to turn on the record player and listen to the first song I should find. From the stack I grabbed a record, put it on the player, let the needle fall to one of the grooves between songs and I heard, 'Are you lonesome tonight?'

"'No further would I listen, nor did I need to: for instantly, that song a light, like a car dealership searchlight, ignited my heart. Darkness and doubt vanished like they were flushed down the commode.'

"The first a' many love letters she wrote 'bout Elvis. After an experience like that the next step is love." Marie folded the letter into her Bible. "Well Juanita had been born in Guadalajara, Mexico. She moved to Memphis as a youngster. I met her in high school where all the boys fell in love with her Spanish Eyes. Now sir, tell me your witness to Elvis."

"Witness? I remain unconverted. I am not pledging my love to Elvis. Call me a heathen, but Elvis does not have my heart."

Marie pondered, "Hmm, no wonder you is not pained at the

loss a' Elvis. How can you lose what you never had? It's a pity, you care not. I feel so bad for you. But as Doris Day said, 'Que Sarah, Que Sarah.'"

She continued: "I must tell the strangest part of all. In 1981 the diner still had a bustlin' business. Six people worked here. Then a truck stop opened up down the road called 'Resort Courteous' where waitresses wore lingerie. Can ya imagine servin' hash or cheesecake with your boobs showin' through a silkie chemise? Fryin' eggs in bikini underwear? One waitress caught her slinky nightie in a blender, damn-near liquified her clothes. And that place don't serve home cookin', they serve yuppie food. Other than a hot dog called the frankfurter special they've nothin' to offer but spuds, broil, beers, and sweets. When that place opened this place nearly died.

"Before that porno palace came on line the waitresses here would take a break 'bout midnight on the parkin' lot to smoke Marlboros and bitch 'bout men. We'd sit on car hoods puffin' away. If we had to relieve ourselves we'd go out there by the lot, knowin' it's nature's way and the grass won't pay no mind. Four a' us was pretty close: Marcella, that's Marcie; Bernadette, that's Bernie; and Hortense. It's hard to make a nickname out a' Hortense without gettin' somethin' worse, so we called her Mitch.

"One night as we sat under a dark moon, a fog came on draft horse hooves, up from the river. A very cold night, the air bit like a shrew, a nippin' and eager air." Marie spoke from recall; so vivid an event needed no memory aids. But I kept expecting Marie to pull out something—words written on divorce decrees, speeding tickets, Kotex wrappers, or golden plates to be deciphered with Urim and Thummim.

"Just shy of one, Marcella went to light up when she jumped with a start. I thought she burned herself, but rather than stickin' her fingers in her mouth to cool 'em, she pointed out into the alfalfa field surrounded by three corn patches.

"We stared off across the field and saw a soft glowin' white thing, like a flamin' star move down the line a' fence wire. It moved closer. Lo and behold we saw Elvis hisself, dressed in the very jumpsuit he last wore in Las Vegas surrounded by dainty little moonbeams. But it turned and moved 'way from us. I yelled, 'Stay illusion! Stay earth angel. If y'all hast any sound, or use of voice, Speak to me!' It stopped, looked straight at me. It recognized me, so I yelled:

> Angels and preachers of graces defend us!
> Is you a spirit of health or goblin damn'd,
> Bringin' airs from heaven or blasts from hell?
> Is your intentions wicked or charitable?
> You comes in such a questionable shape
> That I speak to thee.
> I cry, Oh King, Elvis, royal Memphane: O, answer me!

"It beckoned me to go away with it. My friends tried to warn me, sayin' it might lead me to the top a' the river bluffs where I'd fall into the Mississippi. 'Somethin' is rotten in Memphis' they screamed, 'don't let it come close to you.' But I followed. Each petite vein in my body made as hardy as a lion's nerve.

"'Where will ya lead me? Speak; I beg of you. I'll go no further,' I stated.

"'Mark me. My hour's almost come when I to sulfuric acid and tormenting flames, where I must be rendered like lard.

> I am the King's spirit,
> Doom'd for a certain term to walk the night,
> And for the day confined to fast in fires,
> Till the foul crimes done in my days,
> Is burnt and plunged away.
> For I died in the blossom of my sins,
> With all my horrible imperfections on my head.
> O, horrible! O, horrible! Most horrible!
> It be cruel, It be cruel, It be most cruel.

"'Alas, poor Elvis!' said I.

"'Pity me not,' he said, 'but lend your serious hearin' to what I unfold.'

"'Do you suffer only for your own sins?' I asked.

"'I've carried the punishment for my acts so that the divine anger may be turned toward me and turned away from you. I've become the cosmic fall guy. When I complete the punishment, when a thousand years is passed, then I shall return.'

"With that a rooster crowed and the specter moaned, 'Glow little glowworm, show the morning to be near. Adieu, adieu! Marie, please don't stop loving me! Forget me never, never!'

"Steppin' into the fog—Elvis in the mist—before disappearin', he turned for one last look at me. He sneered up his lips for ol' times sake and scowled, 'Didja, ever?' The fog swallowed him up. In shock, I walked back to my friends.

"Bernie looked at me and asked, 'Baby, what you want me to do 'bout this? Call the **Enquirer**?'

"'No, we must agree to come again to wait for him.'

"Marcella asked, 'When shall we four meet again in thunder, lightnin', or in rain?'

"Hortense answered, 'When the Hurdy-Gurdy man comes singin' songs of love.'

"Bernie added, 'That will be 'fore the rise of sun?'

"'Where the place?' I asked.

"Marcella answered, 'Here, bring vigil food: Heath Bars!'

"Bernie added, 'Come what may, there to wait for Elvis.'

"Hortense got ready to leave, 'I go to make grey milkshakes.' I could hear the spring peepers in the trees.

"Bernie added, 'I go to fry fish, Haddock calls.'

"Considerin' Bernie's cookin', I thought, 'Oh, sure, excellent well, fish mangler. You who leave no skone unburned!' But I held my tongue—not physically a' course—as all together we chanted, 'Fair is foul and foul is fair; a filthy baseball through foggy air.' Then we went back to work.

"We spent many predawns sittin' on the dewy grass waitin', but never saw the specter again. We'd hoped he'd come back every year at the same time, like when the swallows come back to San Juan Cappuccino. But nothin' happened. One by one my friends left this diner. Marcella, she got a Graceland tour guide job, then quit to work for the Memphis Chamber a' Commerce; not that she loved Elvis less but that she loved Memphis more."

Marie put down her washrag, and sat on a stool behind the counter. She too was tired. Yawning, she had yet a bit more to discuss. "Which stamp did ya vote for several years back?"

"Stamp, what stamp?" I asked as I thought, "Finish, good lady, the dark night is done, and we are for the light."

"The Elvis stamp. Did ya vote for young or old Elvis?"

"Oh that stamp," I responded. "I didn't vote."

"No surprise," she patronized, "ya neglected your civic duty. I voted for the old stamp. I lost, but youth's a stuff that'll not endure. Most Elvis fans thought that age cannot wither him, no costume stale his infinite variety.

"I heard of a Missouri man opening a museum to prove Elvis still lives. I 'spose he heard a voice in a cornfield sayin' 'if you build it, he will come.' That part's believable. But that one could confuse Missouri with heaven is another thing yet."

My mind pondered all I had heard that night; so much to take in and process. I stared at my yolk-stained, empty plate. She interrupted my ruminations: "Elvis is gone. At least we have his name—we call on him. What's in a name? And why should that name be sounded more than yours? Write them together, your's is as fair a name. But ya see hun', for us the king's name's a tower of strength. A name always on my mind. I will be true to you Elvis, forever. Oh what a friend we have in Elvis!"

Marie, elbows on the counter, her hands together as in prayer, began humming. I recognized the melody, from the musical **Godspel**. Marie softly sang, "Long live, El—Elvis, Long live, El—El—Elvis, Long live El—Elvis, Long Live the King." She repeated it, each time with ever more volume. A tear came to her eye as the clear notes of her psalm filled the empty diner. I found myself humming, "Prepare, ye the way of the King."

CHAPTER 18

ELVIS

THE STORY ENDS

Marie noticed the other coffeepot, now boiling itself dry. She grabbed it from the burner to make more coffee, but finding an empty can of grounds, she went into the back. Minutes passed. I checked my watch: five A.M.

I drank the last drops of coffee. Nervously debating how long to stay, I ate a cold crust from my plate. A night of coffee took effect. I fidgeted, using my finger to clean out the near empty individual-sized plastic grape jelly container. I even ate the parsley garnish and pushed away my plate.

Marie emerged with a new pot of coffee from the back, but with apron gone and make-up freshened. She set down the pot, then applied something to her lips. She held the tube to her nose remarking, "I love the smell of lip balm in the mornin'. Here's more coffee. My shift's up. It's time for me to go. I'm leavin' and goin' home," Marie stated matter-of-factly.

"Don't you have more to say? Are you finished with Elvis?" My change of mood astounded me.

She paused. "Darlin', one's never finished with Elvis: a inexhaustible mystery. Funny how time slips away, but my shift's over, my mission's completed. I've fought a good fight, you've finished your course, I've kept the faith. This servant may depart in peace. You on the other hand, your mission—should ya decide to accept it—begins. I'm leavin' it up to you, only you. You hold the key that unlocks the meanin' of Elvis.

"This crazy world may little note, nor long remember, what I've said here. It's for you the livin', rather, to be dedicated here to the undone work which I've fought to so nobly advance. It's rather for you to be here dedicated to the great task remainin'—that from this honored dead Elvis you take increased devotion to that cause for which he gave the last full measurin' cup a' devotion—that you here highly resolve that he shall not've died in vain—and the memory of Elvis, of the people, by the people, for the people, shall not perish from the earth."

My debate ended. "Give me a little for the road." She poured a half-cup. How far would I get before desperately yearning for a Rest Stop? She walked to the end of the counter.

"What about a check?" I asked.

"Money?" She laughed. "Who needs money? Ya see, money don't matter when your heart belongs to Elvis."

"Don't you want a tip?" I asked.

"Leave somethin' on the counter. Put a tip down softly as I leave you, if ya want. But I say, oh pis on need! Even beggars outside the ballpark are in the poorest things superfluous. We go separate ways. You have promises to keep. And thou'lt come no more, never, never, never, never, never."

She walked through the swinging counter door trying to fasten her sleeve button, but she had put the button in the wrong hole. She thrust her wrist into my face, "Hey you, undo this button." I obliged, saying, "I can help." She answered, "Thank you sir"—the last words I heard her speak. She walked across the black and white checkerboard asphalt tile toward the door. A ditty rose in the back of my mind and I imagined her saying:

> Farewell, farewell! But this I tell
> To thee, oh Diner guest,
> He prayeth well, who loveth well,
> Man, bird, beast, and Elvis.

She walked out. The screen door slammed. Marie had left the building. The throaty grumble of an old, powerful car came to life. I stared through the neon gilded window to see the taillights of an ancient, rusty, dusty 1956 pink Cadillac scratch out and roar down the road, like wheels on high heels.

Had she left the diner alone? Would the next shift arrive soon? Was someone in the back room? I said "So long!" as loud as I could without seeming to yell, hoping someone would answer. I only heard the buzz of the milk dispenser.

I opened my wallet. The son of depression parents, I am frugal bordering on being a tightwad. Strangely, money now seemed unimportant. I took a twenty from my wallet. "I cannot leave a twenty, that is too much," I thought. "No, it is too little." Why, I'll never know, but I placed a five and a twenty on the counter under my heavy scratched cup. "So long," I said again: no response. Picking up the tape recorder, I walked out to the parking lot, my buttonless shirt still wet. With the stars less bright than hours ago, the predawn night began to lift. Fog hung on the surrounding fields. The highway exit appeared a quarter mile down the road. My headlights found the highway 55 South sign. The wheels caught the exit ramp. I scratched my head, "Such a night!" Next stop—New Orleans.

EPILOGUE

The miles to New Orleans dropped to single-digit numbers. A Cajun radio station filled the cramped VW—packed with my life's possessions in grocery boxes—with a fiddle and accordion two-step. But under the gay rhythm—gay according to the old definition—an erratic syncopated click joined the music. A Zydeco washboard-like scratching sound emerged from the engine. Deep from within the carburetor's throat came the death rattle.

I had learned of death rattles in Catholic elementary school, Our Lady of Complacency, when Fr. Gillespie gave his inspirational message. Rather than explaining the Glorious Mysteries of the Rosary, he held our fifth grade interest by describing the most memorable times he gave Last Rites: the suicide who fired a shotgun in his mouth, the drowned woman—whose near-navy-blue color matched our uniform school pants. He told of death rattles coming from dying throats, which along with icy feet tell the nearness of death. For the next weeks as I lay at night, a sleepless ten-year-old in a lower bunk, every chill at the bottom of my bed and every hick or gurgle in my throat left me lying in anguished fear of not seeing the sunrise.

My Volkswagen was dying. My only reliable friend was abandoning me. But no, my car loyally clung to life a few more minutes until it had completed it mission. Like an aged cancer victim in a hospice, holding on for the last out-of-town child to say good-bye, my beloved VW struggled those last miles before it gave up the gas. It sputtered and shook. It smoked, coughing a bluish phlegm of oil and rust out the exhaust. Like a pathetic alcoholic with the DTs, the VW shivered, shook, rattled, and fumaroled. Yet it kept going, deep into New Orleans.

I exited the highway into a neighborhood long past its peak. As smoke poured from the vents my Inner Parent told me the price of repair in Chicago had been too good to be true. A final seizure convulsed my car and it shuddered into silence. I stepped out of the car into a forming pool of hot oily purple fluid hemorrhaging from the transmission. Knowing I couldn't afford to fix my old VW now, I decided to abandon it.

I took out all my possessions. But at least some luck was with me. Nearby stood an empty shopping cart so I put my vast worldly possessions in it. I said good-bye to my old worn out trusted friend with a gentle caress on the roof and walked away.

Next came my second bit of luck. I had only gone four blocks when I found a UPS office. They gave me boxes for everything I owned—now less one Volkswagen—to be shipped to my parents in Kansas City. I kept my valise, a few clothes, and my tape recorder. I used their phone to call my cousin John. We agreed to meet at a nearby bar. After a few days with him I could take the Grey Dog and head home to Kansas City.

I walked with valise in one hand. With the other hand and my teeth I opened a package I found in the back of my car. Inside was a poem—maybe a psalm—about Elvis, typed with carbons on an old manual typewriter with dirty keys. I guessed that Marie put the package in my car before she drove away. I thought I might rip it up and deny that night in Memphis ever happened. But the packaged contained a small box of candy. As I sampled the nutty and creamy candy my mood tempered and I read a message Marie had written on the back of an old Western Union telegram:

Here's some divinity fudge for you being so patient.
But don't eat too much at one time.
It's very rich and you might get sick.
For as they say—

Our indigestion sometimes serves us well
When our deep paunches do fill, and that should learn us

There's a divinity that shapes our ends,
Rough-hew them how we will.

And as I always say—Life is like a box of chocolates.
Some part of it is sweet.
A good part is bland.
And the rest makes you gag!

May your days be numerous as Rock City billboards!
I'll remember you. I hope you'll remember what I have said. Take my words. Hear them, read, mark, learn and digest them in your innards!

Speak true, right wrong, live pure, follow the King!
Live long and prosper!
Blessed is they who have not seen, yet believe!

17 August 1997,
Marie Ishmael

P.S. Enclosed is a few words that say it all.

```
Though he was almost divine,
He did not deem himself to be divine,
Rather he emptied himself,
Became like us in all things,
     including our obesity,
That at the name of Elvis,
     every knee must bow,
Every tongue proclaim:
Elvis is the King!
```

I found the bar, went in, sat at a small table and ordered a marguerita which I drank in silence. I stared out the front window, into a bar across the street. I tried to discern the shapes moving in the garish purple light and shimmering mirrors. The message of Marie filled my mind. With a flourish of music the lights in the bar across the street went out. In twenty minutes John arrived and greeted me. We ordered drinks and exchanged awkward pleasantries. I tried to converse, but each answer he gave to my questions seemed a tortured extraction. After a long moment of silence he spoke.

"I apologize that I am not more conversational but a rather extraordinary event happened recently and I am at a loss to explain it." A dread swept over me. Had I stumbled into another set of revelations? "Why me Lord? Once is enough!" I thought.

"It will take but a moment to describe," he said. Relief surged through my body. He continued, "I have not told anyone fearing they would doubt my sanity. If they would only believe, but they have such suspicious minds. I must tell someone."

He told his tale: "Last week I took a dawn flight from Peru to New Orleans. As the plane climbed higher through the clouds, I examined the safety precautions card, trying to locate the exits. But I could not find them. The card was for a different plane! I turned to look for the stewardess when a flash of light shot through the window on the other side of the plane. A dazzle of bright color flooded onto the empty seats. I opened my seat belt and jumped across the aisle of the still-climbing plane to the opposing window seat. And lo, to my astonishment, as the plane lifted out of the clouds, a dazzling image stood before my eyes. I saw a man, or an image of a man, shaped by the clouds on the edge of the storm. So high, he or it must have been a thousand foot tall, a huge moker of a man dressed in brilliant white. Pink, blue, and purple of the rising sun shimmered the entire sky. I strained my eyes but clearly the giant cloud image held a guitar. I could not believe it, I saw Elvis Presley! Elvis, the guitar man, riding the rainbow with raiment white as snow, whiter than any bleach on earth can whiten. I stared in utter amazement, spellbound. I heard a thunderous voice: 'Woe, ye mothers!' I thought, 'All in all, in toto, I have a feeling we are not in Kansas anymore.' The plane banked left, the image dropped below the wing. I pressed my face to the window trying desperately to see the vanishing image.

"I jumped up, shouting, 'Did you see that? C'mon everybody. Did you see that?' The few passengers stared like I had gone off the deep end. No one had seen it! They heard nothing! As I stepped toward my seat I slipped, I stumbled, I fell into it. I know I saw what I saw—so real, so vivid, so alive. It was no mirage! You may not believe me, but I no longer care. As God is my witness—as God is my witness—they are not going to defeat me! I am going to live through this, and when it is all over I will never scorn Elvis again—no, nor any of my folks. As God is my witness, today, tomorrow, and forever, starting tonight I will never scorn Elvis again. Let people think me crazy, let me be a lonely man—I saw it!"

I grabbed his gesturing hand, held it firmly, and looked at him, reassuring, "That's all right, I believe." His eyes, gazing heavenward, dropped toward me. His preoccupation vanished.

"What are you doing in New Orleans?" He asked. We both hoped conversation might distract our two minds' mullings.

"It's a long, long story . . ." Then it hit me! The ancient manuscripts John found in Peru! Had fate guided me to make a great cosmic link between the manuscripts and Elvis? Was I joining the critical mass of those who take seriously the coincidental experiences of life? The enigmatic words of Marie jostled and collided in my brain like a jar of angry bees.

"John, tell me about your trip to Peru! Tell me about the ancient Peruvian manuscripts, the massive transformations in human society, the spiritual renaissance in human consciousness! Did you find the final Insights?!"

"Oh that!" He pulled a baggy from his flannel shirt pocket, opened it, and removed a fragment of ancient parchment. "Here, take a look." He moved the small table candle closer so I could see better.

"Tell me what is the secret message for all humanity?" I begged.

"What is the key to the human longing? Did you find the next Insights?"

He answered, "This text says, 'Take two measures of parched barley, mix with one measure of water in a ceramic crock and ferment for twelve risings and settings of the sun.'"

"That is the future of mankind!" I gulped in disbelief. "It must be secret code, a symbolic message! Can you decipher it? What does it say about the Apocalypse, the millennium, the new Age, the new world comin' that's just around the bend?"

"Nothing," said John, "it's an ancient beer recipe. There are no Incan prophecies. These fragments are fakes. The writing is not Incan but Ancient Mesopotamian: Sumerian. This other fragment is from the Epic of Gilgamesh; it says 'eat, drink, and bathe yourself.' I guess that's the message for humanity as it faces the millennium: take a shower, shave, don't forget the third 'S,' then order a pizza and have a beer.

"Look closely at this parchment. At first glance it appears ancient but it's a piece of a souvenir, a manufactured copy of the Declaration of Independence. Look here's where someone scraped off Hancock's signature."

"This is not an ancient Incan prophecy?" I despaired.

"Not at all. I was taken in at first and hiked all over Peru looking for more writings. Then after I returned and sent you that package I learned the Incas didn't have written language. They kept records by tying knots of different sizes and colors to sticks. This works for counting llamas and bundles of coca leaves, but is useless for predicting the future destiny of mankind. People foolishly believe someone found ancient Aramaic manuscripts in Peru. Aramaic was a Mediterranean language spoken at the time of Jesus. There's no way an Aramaic document could wind up in ancient Peru. Only a Mormon would believe such rubbish."

"But let me give my predictions for the new Millennium. You will hear of wars, rumors of wars, earthquakes, famines. In other words, the same old stuff! That's my prediction—another thousand years of the same old stuff. So don't fret it. And if anyone thinks paradise is around the bend I'll be happy to bet it won't. If I lose the bet and a millennial paradise arrives no one will care to collect the winnings."

Well there it was. A thousand-mile journey that provided more riddles than answers. I finished my drink. Then a synapse in my brain found its target. Of course! I saw the connection: the mystery of the universe unraveled. Of course: eat, drink, and take a bath. Enjoy the simple things in life, for no dramatic cosmic events will happen: no Armageddon, just decades more of Republicans and Democrats. In face of the same old stuff we should plant our little flower garden, eat, drink, and take a bath.

It all fits with Elvis. He couldn't enjoy a simple meal and a beer. He stuffed his insatiable gullet and when liquor wouldn't work he turned to an endless diet of drugs. As for baths, well, as Marie had explained, cleanliness was not next to kingliness for Elvis. He avoided showers the way Rush Limbaugh avoids Hillary Clinton. Elvis sought fulfillment, but failed at the things that would bring it. Elvis messed up! Now we must wait a thousand years. Had Elvis skipped drugs and taken a bath he might be alive today and found more peace than by reading Kahlil Gibran while stoned on Quaaludes, reeking of Brute.

I ordered a cup of coffee. We passed the next hour in quiet thought. I spent that night at his apartment. The next day John went to work. Using a Gideon Bible from the shelf I searched for Elvis references and marked them in red. I stole that Bible, unable to find a commandment against coveting thy neighbor's holy book. With Marie I had hoped, "out of sight, out of mind." Not so. I'd grown accustomed to her face.

That night I headed out alone to explore Bourbon Street and see the harbor lights. All the noise and excitement held little attraction. Bourbon Street disappointed me. As a pubescent youth I had heard stories of naked women swinging out over the street, but no such display greeted me. Although bawdy spectacles unfolded at several bars within earshot, it required more courage than I could muster to enter. Lurking deep in my Freudian subconscious loomed the terror that if I entered such a place and watched as a naked dancer snaked toward me, a firm but bony hand would grab my shoulder, and as nails dug into my flesh, I would turn in agony to see the glaring eyes of my third-grade teacher demanding to know why I had entered a strip joint.

My third-grade teacher had died years before, and if alive she would have to explain why she had entered a strip joint! Such logic did little to steel my courage. Instead I entered a quiet bar with a struggling guitarist, plugged into a modest amplifier, connected to an electronic percussion and bass machine, next to a magic marker sign: "Good Rocking Tonight." The next day I rented a car for a one-way trip to Kansas City and home.

I wanted to stop in Memphis at the diner. I had many questions for Marie. I drove the long lonely highway—too fast for the Mississippi State Patrol, which ticketed me for going 75 in a 55 mile zone. The $100 fine seemed unimportant. To my dismay, on the outskirts of Memphis, I could not find the right exit. Twenty more miles, I turned around and came back. I came to a familiar-looking exit but found no trace of the diner. After three hours of searching, I gave up.

Since then I have made three trips back to Memphis. I searched a hundred miles of back road but still the diner eluded me. I talked to locals, describing the restaurant, Marie, and her car. Many recalled such a diner from years past, but no one could remember its precise location, though several suggested it lay just beyond the bend, telling me, "take the dirt road and go east young man." No one knew of Marie. As for her car, one couple, a Claude and Thelma, said they had seen it late at night on a foggy back road.

My searching proved to be so much chasing after wind. I found no diner but a billboard proclaiming, "Prepare to Meet Your God." Beneath it lay a quiet Hereford chewing its cud. I saw a hundred triads of hillside wooden crosses—a white cross between two mustard yellow crosses—and a billboard of eyes peering through glasses advertising Doctor T. J. Eckleburg, Jr. I crossed a river on a small ferry run by a Mortimer Charon. Finally, I returned to Kansas City.

At my parents' house, I felt like a stranger in my own home. I continued to have intense headaches, headaches that began after my encounter with Marie. These came whenever I used my reading glasses, which no longer improved but seemed rather to blur my vision. My optometrist, Dr. Eckleburg IV said my eyes had mysteriously improved. I could see clearly without glasses.

He checked my color vision by showing five circles of dots and asking me to name the number in each. I saw 5, 7, 1, 3 and a Roman numeral V. Marie's bizarre numerology came to mind. I rearranged the circles: 3, 7, V, 1, 5. Then I turned 3 and 7 upside down: E, L, V, I, S. "ELVIS!" I screamed and ran out without even paying my bill.

In November 1997, still uncommitted, I fulfilled the fifth duty and went to Graceland, Graceland, Tennessee. In a borrowed car I drove from Kansas to St. Louis down to Memphis. In the Missouri bootheel I stopped for lunch at Lambert's Restaurant in Sikeston, known for its rolls thrown to customers. I ate amidst midair tosses of intra-cafe biscuit missiles, ICBMs, while sitting next to a large table filled with Graceland pilgrims. Twenty-nine, riding the same bus, they had undertaken a Karaoke contest. Each pilgrim was to sing two Elvis songs on the way to Graceland and two songs on the way back. The best imitator of the King would be treated to an all-expense paid dinner at Bob Evans.

I listened as they introduced themselves: a night watchman, a squirrel hunter, "The Yo-yo Man" who entertained at kids' birthday parties, a female Priority Mail clerk, a monkey trainer, a fryer who worked for Popeye's chicken, a retired merchant marine, a scholar, an Army Sergeant (who might have been AWOL), the manager of a Ben Franklin store, a Sears clothing buyer, a carpenter, a carpet mill worker, a funeral director, a painter of black velvet masterpieces, a short-order cook, a Mississippi River barge captain, a homeopathic pharmacist, the wife of a hot tub salesman, a parson, a John Deere tractor salesman, a referee, a grain elevator operator, a subpoena server, a near-deaf man who kept saying "Pardon?", a mandolin player, and oddly enough, a several nuns with a priest. I left the restaurant long before them. As to who might win the contest, I had no guess.

In Memphis I headed for "Grand Central Elvis." The tours of Graceland begin across the street at a complex of Elvis Presley shops with ubiquitous Elvis songs permeating the air, even in the restroom. I listened to "All I Needed Was the Rain" as I stepped up to the urinal. I had forgotten to remove my 35mm camera from around my neck. There I stood, self-conscious, hoping no one would see me and inwardly accuse me of great braggadocio for standing at the urinal with a heavy-lense camera pointing downward. But the camera had a telephoto lens. This posed even greater threat of embarrassment.

From the restroom I walked outside to inspect the jets of Elvis, two aircraft that symbolize the victory of Elvis. He died as a Rock and Roll singer in his own bedroom and not in a flaming plane crash. He died in pajamas, with his booties on.

I took the bus to the Graceland Mansion across the street. Then at last, I entered Graceland. By long-buried Catholic instinct, as I entered, I absentmindedly reached for the holy water font.

I had seen pictures of the interior. Little in the house surprised me other than its smallness. After the dining room, living room, and music room my tour walked past the stairs that led to the bedroom where Elvis died. I stared upward at the chandelier and mirrors, forbidden to go up into the Holy of Holies despite a fierce urge to break free and dash into the secret upper room to see the torn curtains Marie had described. My tour went down into the basement, then up to the Jungle Room.

In the Jungle Room rumors that Elvis still lived flooded my mind. Could there be any truth to them? I saw a telephone on a table. From deep subconscious roots came a desperate yearning within me. "E. P. phone home. E. P. phone home. E. P. PHONE HOME!" The phone rang! I reached for it, only to nearly lose my balance on the crowd control rope. Matter-of-factly the tour guide reached out with her right hand, caught me in my fall, and with her left hand picked up the receiver to answer a mundane call on the progress of our group.

Our tour went outside, where I realized the inaccuracy of a dream I had. One restless night, after hours of reading about Elvis to verify Marie's account, I dreamt of Graceland's backyard—more a park than a yard—rising in several tiers. But the backyard of Graceland, with its horse pastures, dips down, not up. I ignored my dream as meaningless.

The tour led to the trophy room of Elvis paraphernalia. The jumpsuits of Elvis seemed so lifeless, lacking the fire they once held, fitting awkwardly on faceless mannequins. Although Marie insisted that Elvis died due to his drug abuse, the guides said he died to cardiac arrhythmia—an irregular heartbeat. It was no surprise that his heart marched to the beat of a different drummer, but I believed Marie rather than these guides adhering to the image-correct account of his death, and thereby wasting a valuable opportunity to teach the disastrous effects of drugs.

Finally, our group went poolside to the Meditation Gardens, the final resting spot of the man who consumed the thoughts of Marie and now mine. I stood first at the grave of Gladys, then Vernon. Elbowing my way between two silver-haired Grandmas with canes and large black purses, I stood on the very ground where Elvis now lay. A shudder rose up my spine: my life would never be the same. Then and there I accepted the mission which Marie had pointed out to me. A mission appointed for me from time immemorial. Fate guided me. I stood over the bronze slab, the eternal flame before me: "Your will Elvis, not mine." Great peace flowed through my body, a peace I had never known. The crowd left and I stood alone over the grave of Elvis.

I drove away from Graceland past the Elvis Presley Boulevard Almost-Full Gospel Church with a sign announcing a guest speaker "Ex Junk-Bond Dealer Became Evangelist in Prison." South from Memphis I went to see the remains of Circle G Ranch. The property has changed hands several times with most owners experiencing little success. Had fate cursed the property? I then drove to

Tupelo, Mississippi to see the boyhood home of Elvis, and the Elvis Presley Memorial Chapel. Had the chapel been built by a black man in the hire of German nuns? I wanted to climb the tower to look for "Homer Smith" scrawled on top.

Walking back to my car, I saw for the first time, Elvis Presley Park. An eerie shiver traveled my back as I recognized the image from my dream: a park rising in several levels to a hilltop. I ran toward the hill, a hill shaped like the pile of mash potatoes I had unconsciously sculpted on my plate at Lambert's. I ran the path past the ball field, past the restroom, up the hill to the plateau, a place—according to the placard—where Elvis came to reflect. There I stood and listened. A great clap of thunder broke in the sky and a great wind did pass over me. Several semi-trucks drove by on the street below me. The ground trembled under their weight. An old trash truck backfired. Then the still, small voice of a long-gone Tupelo boy said to me, "Bossa Nova, Baby." I hid my face in my jacket.

And so the story of Marie and her revelations are left only to my memory and a handful of cassettes to explain the life of Elvis. Seeing that many others have undertaken to set forth accounts of the events that took place regarding Elvis—accounts that have been passed down to us by eyewitnesses—I in turn have carefully gone over the whole story, from beginning to end and I have decided to write an account for you, oh lover of Elvis, so that you might know the certainty of what you have learned. And yet more can be said about Elvis. For if everything Elvis did or said were written down, Memphis itself could not contain all the books that would have to be written.

And to this day I chant a ditty that expresses how I felt on that cool dawn when I left the diner, never to return:

> I went like one that hath been stunned,
> And is of a sense forlorn:
> A sadder and a wiser man,
> I rose the morrow morn.

POST EPILOGUE

By early January 1998 the sands of time had passed. Unemployed in Kansas City, I daily scanned the want ads wondering, "Where do I go from here?" One day I spied a strange ad in the personal section. "Oh lover of Elvis, I have gone West! Oregon or bust augmentation! Marie Ishmael." I packed my belongings in an old used car I bought and set out for Oregon.

I complete this chronicle, sitting in a cold truck stop in Montana, waiting for the snowplows to clear the highway. To the best of my ability I have tried to locate and identify Marie's bible quotations using my stolen Gideon bible.

In the tabletop before me a trucker has scratched, "ELVIS LIVES!" I sit, drinking coffee, anxious to resume my journey. I grumble at the waitress, "Coffee, give me more, more, more coffee," as I struggle to finish these sentences.

With these last words I complete my mission. I have finished the book that subverted the author. I pass on to you the strange revelations of Marie, Matron of the Motel Dew Beanery.

It is finished!

Steve Werner
8 January 1998